I0729743

Second edition printing, 2025

Editing by Lily Chrzanowski Editing by Belle Manuel Cover art by Haley Burbine

ISBN: 978-1-7383253-3-7

Under
The
Light

Sadie Sheridan

For ten-year-old Sadie, who would never

believe we wrote a whole book.

I do it all for her.

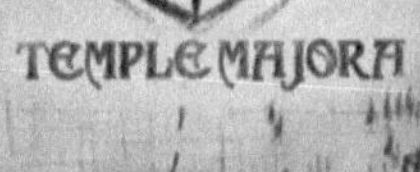

RHEA
FOR THE RULERS PILGRIMAGE
TEMPLE MAJORA

THE SISTERS

N
W
E
S
POLARIS
THE BLESSED RULER SHALL WALK THIS PATH, FOR THE
SISTERS ALONE DECIDE HOW THEY WILL BE KNOWN

1

The Eve Before

I took a large gulp of my drink and came to terms with the whole ballroom watching me vomit tonight. Chunks. All over the elegant marble floor.

How my insides churned made it nearly inevitable, but it couldn't be helped. It was the eve of the most terrifying day of my life, what I had spent twenty-one years preparing for.

After tomorrow, I would be one step closer to becoming the Ruler of Rhea.

The thought made my stomach drop to my feet, and I set my drink down on the large banquet table beside me.

This was the eve of the year that I had been impatiently waiting for, a year filled with traditions and rituals created by The Light to ensure I would be a proper Ruler. It was a year I would much rather have just gotten over with and not thought about. I wanted it to happen swiftly and painlessly.

I did not want to spend this evening in the grand hall, celebrating what I was about to do with people who felt like strangers.

But that was how the evening of my twenty-first birthday was foretold to go. Tonight, a celebration, tomorrow, my blessing ceremony.

My mother, Adella, crossed through the crowd of the hall in front of me, making her way to another councilman or member of the high Polaris society. She looked regal as she moved, her pants, top, and cloak all deep plum with golden beading that complimented her rich brown hair. I was wearing nearly the opposite, all white with my pale blonde hair and fair skin.

Her eyes cut to mine, and she did not have to say a word for me to know what she was thinking.

Fuck.

I was in trouble. I should have been socializing too, wooing our guests with my carefully constructed charm.

The problem was, if I attempted to make conversation with anyone in this room, there was a chance I would empty my stomach all over their shoes. The closer I got to *the* day, the only day that seemed to matter to anyone, the higher the risk of full body failure. Which would not only be embarrassing for me, but the sight of my digested food all over some councilman's finest fabrics would kill my mother. My fingers itched for another sip of that deep amber liquid in my cup and I decided I was best to stay in this small corner for as long as I could.

People took to the dance floor as the music picked up in tempo, bows dancing across the instrument's strings with newfound vigor.

Everyone in the room was dressed in an array of rich colors; emerald greens and cobalt blues. I was the only one in white, and I wondered if that was also because of my mother's planning.

My mother did plan this all very well. I have always loved this grand hall. The room arched high overhead, crisp white marble pillars holding up ceilings made of the same. It was all detailed in gold sculpture. Mostly motifs of sun and fire were displayed with the occasional winged Deity swirling between them. Not all of the palace was this elegant, which made it such a shame that this room was so scarcely used. But, not every event warranted buffet tables full of food and drinks, a full orchestra, and this wide of an invitation list.

If she saw me still standing there, she would not be happy.

Weighing the odds between utter humiliation and my mother's wrath, I scanned the room intently, trying to find someone I could talk to without actually making conversation.

My father was on the other side of the hall, deep in conversation with an old friend. His suit was less formal than what my mother wore, but it matched her choice of deep plum. Shining gold buttons down the center of the jacket replaced the intricate beading. The dark color of the suit made his light hair stand out in contrast.

Like any good Ruler's consort, my father was charming the crowd. Over the dancing figures, I saw his face light up before a laugh burst out. Although I could not hear it over the music and the chatter, I knew exactly what it sounded like.

He was too busy to help me act like I wanted to be here.

I did want to be here. Or rather, I *wanted* to want to be here.

A familiar form came toward me, throwing a side-eye at whomever she had just been talking to.

"You found a perfect little cove to hide in, eh?" Sage gestured to where I hid, between a pillar and the end of a banquet table. Most people likely thought I had not yet arrived.

Sage was my closest friend. We had both grown up within the palace walls, for very different reasons. Sage and her brother were children of two Devoted, those who have dedicated their lives to The Light. As they came from a long, well-respected lineage, they had the honor to serve in the small palace Temple. At least, they had before the fire.

Sage and I had grown close since that day two years ago.

Tonight, she looked stunning, although that was far from unusual. Sage had a dark skin tone with a golden hue that could catch anybody's attention. She had big, deep brown eyes and a small nose with a wide bridge.

If we were to be compared, we were exact opposites. She was petite where I had curves, and she was dark where I was light. Both of us held our own on opposite ends of the spectrum of beauty.

Despite me being two years her senior, she could read me like a book. Being unreadable was a trait I had quite literally been trained in, so her uncanny ability to do so filled me with frustration.

"I am not hiding," I said as my fingers twisted around themselves restlessly.

"Then there must be some councilman or woman hidden with you back here." She peeked her head around the pillar dramatically, braids swinging over her shoulder.

I laughed. "Of course, there is not."

"Are you sure? My evening would be much more interesting if there was." A cat-like smile crept onto her face.

"Can you imagine the scandal?" I gave an empty laugh. "I am just—"

"Trying not to run?"

My hands stilled. My legs shook.

Running would feel very good right about now.

"No, I am thinking."

"You do a lot of that." Sage picked up a square of bread from the table beside us, dipped it into the seasoned oil, and popped it into her mouth.

"I'm not sure that can be helped."

She looked at me, and her joking features softened. Her eyes scanned my face in a way that was so familiar it made me squirm.

"Tomorrow is going to be fine, Adenne," she comforted.

Any mention of tomorrow was little comfort to me. Tomorrow was the day I would be blessed, the first of three steps in order to rule. Just like my mother did, and her father before her and his mother before him.

Upon wider examination, the blessing was the easiest of the three steps. I would walk across the plaza from the palace to the Temple Minora. The whole nation of Rhea would be there to see that walk. They had slowly piled into the city of Polaris over the last week, and their presence created a heightened volume to the whole city. The ground practically shook with the energy they brought with them.

Then, in the Temple Minora, the Deities would come and

bless me.

It was a fact I had known my whole life, yet it made my heart feel like it was made of iron.

The Deities were the closest thing we had to The Light itself. When The Light left all those centuries ago, it created Justus, Manumit, and Hebera to protect and watch over us, which they do well. They bless each new Ruler and bestow guidance on how to rule in a way that The Light would desire.

Tradition states the ceremony is sacred and secret, so my mother has never been able to tell me more about it.

All I know is that tomorrow, I will meet with the three Deities, and they will bless me. My eyes will change from this dark brown to the same molten gold color that my mother has.

For the Ruler will see the vision of The Light and rule with blessed intention.

That was *only* step one.

"You're overthinking again," Sage cautioned.

"Tomorrow will be fine."

I looked at her through slitted eyes. "What if I was not worrying about tomorrow?"

"The pilgrimage, then? That will be fine too. You've been over it a million times. You will leave all blessed and golden and beautiful. You'll mount your horse and travel west along the same route you have mapped out a million times, you'll meet the Sisters and they will give you your title. Now, if you aren't careful, they will call you Adenne the Over-thinker."

"They wouldn't do that."

Sage nodded along with her own ideas. "Or Adenne the Party-Ruiner."

I sighed. "Yeah, they might do that."

Sage smiled. "For real, Adenne, you're more prepared for this than anyone I know." I could see her processing what she had just said. "Not that I know anyone else preparing for what you're doing, but that's not the point. You're ready, you've worked hard, and after these next few months, you will become a fantastic Ruler. I know you will, and I'm so proud of you."

Tears welled in my eyes. Many people saw me putting in the work, but I think Sage was the only one who knew how much work that actually was.

The sweat coating my palms so heavily I had to rub them on my trousers to keep them dry. "That means a lot, thank you."

Sage looked away, ignoring my praise as she rubbed her arms uncomfortably. "If you want to back out now, say the word. Me and you will run away together."

I winced.

"Sorry. Bad choice of words."

It was. Running away always hurt more people than it helped. I picked up my glass and took a big drink of the golden brown liquid.

"Is he here?" I asked.

"Would it matter if he was?" Sage danced around my question, which meant he was.

"I would prefer he was nowhere near here."

Sage sighed. "I believe he is here. Working."

The large drink I took burned when I swallowed. I hadn't seen him when I scanned the rooms, and I knew my eyes would have caught him immediately. That must mean he was lurking in the shadows, waiting for someone to attack me or someone in my family.

"Well, if he has to be here, at least he is out of sight."

Sage stood beside me, scanning the room as I had just been doing.

My mother would not count this as socializing.

"Oh, I'm sure he'll remain out of sight. Leon, on the other hand, may be a different story." Sage's head nodded toward eyes that were right on us.

Leon smiled when I made eye contact, and after saying a few parting words to the crowd he was with, he came my way. His smile grew the closer he got.

I supposed I was socializing now.

"Adenne, I did not know you were here. I figured you were planning on being fashionably late."

Sage suppressed a laugh while I suppressed the urge to jab my elbow into her ribs.

I stepped out from my hiding place. "I have been here. We must have missed each other, but I am happy to see you now, Leon."

It wasn't a lie. Honestly, if I had seen him earlier, I would have approached him. He was one of the few people I could talk to without putting any genuine effort in.

We were friends, at least for the time being. I had known Leon for a long time, growing up in the same circles, attending the same parties. He was always friendly, top of his class, and son of a councilman.

That was likely why my mother had decided he would be a good match for me. Nothing was official, but it was suspected our marriage would take place soon after I returned home. He, and the wedding, are step three. Blessing from the Deities, pilgrimage to the Sisters, marriage to Leon. Three steps over a year and then I would be allowed to rule.

That was why many eyes in the grand hall watched as we conversed, finally noticing I was there, whispering and gossiping about all the things they thought they knew about us.

That we had dated before.

False.

That we were already together.

Also false.

That we hated each other.

False again. We were… friendly.

Sage was always quick to fill me in on the rumors she heard. Once, she heard that some speculated Leon and I were cousins, which was absolutely ridiculous. Beyond the light hair, we looked *nothing* alike.

Despite the rumors, I understood why my mother chose Leon for me. He was a good man and would be a supportive partner while I ruled.

That, and he was handsome. Conventionally so, with long, light, thick hair that parted down the middle and cut off just below a sharp jawline. His eyes were a crisp blue with naturally long lashes that any woman would envy.

He was not my type, historically speaking, but I could see the appeal.

"Are you excited about tomorrow?" He asked.

My heart flipped again, but I smiled through the dizzying feeling. "Yes, very. I am grateful it is finally time."

I swear I heard Sage chuckle lightly. Thankfully, Leon's eyes stayed on me.

"It will be an extraordinary day."

"Thank you, I hope so."

"And your pilgrimage, you must be excited about that."

Leon would need to work on reading people if he was to ever become the Ruler's consort.

I smiled wider. "Yes, of course."

He smirked, "It will be a shame, though, that no one will be able to look at that smile for so long. But tradition is tradition, not to be broken."

No one was to look at me from the end of my blessing to the end of my pilgrimage. That time was for deep introspection and a distracted Ruler was an unsuccessful one.

For a Ruler alone must take the knowledge bestowed from The Light as to not burden their people. To share the weight is to condemn all.

It was a tradition that I wanted to avoid messing with.

Someone called Leon's name from behind him, and I wanted to thank them.

"I suppose I should leave you now." He smiled. "I will see you when you return. Good luck, Adenne." He leaned in and lightly placed a kiss on my cheek.

It was… nice.

I smiled at him, clutching my drink in my hand. "I will see you soon."

Leon was nice. He was thoughtful, kind and truly was a friend, but my heart sank at how little I felt when he looked at me, how little he made me laugh.

He was friendly, intelligent, and attractive, but I did not think I could ever love him.

Love leaves people broken. It takes more than it gives. Love, I thought, was made to be something that kills.

I did not think I wanted to be with someone I loved. I did not want that pain.

When I thought of Leon and the safety he gave me, I felt content and I had decided a long time ago that contentment was not the worst emotion to live with for the rest of my life.

And, if I had to produce an heir with anyone… Well, at least he is handsome.

Not the most handsome I had known, but even still.

Sage and I had talked at length about Leon, and even though I had told her all of this, I could see in those dark brown eyes that she disagreed with my plan to be just content. She asked me once why I was so scared to risk wanting more. I didn't have the heart to explain to her who broke me so profoundly that I changed into… this.

Although, I think she knew. That man had hurt her, too, although in a very different way.

Now that people realized I was here, the dancing had stopped. Instead, they started to circle. I felt like a dead animal, left discarded somewhere for the birds to find and fight over. It was not typical for me to feel this awful at a party. I was generally pleased to be the center of attention, but my heart was beating faster when I realized how many eyes were on me.

A *lot* of eyes were on me.

A councilman I knew came up to me first. A round belly stuck out above his pants, the shirt stretching to make it over the mound. His black hair was graying at the sides, showing his age.

When he smiled, his teeth were yellow. "Adenne," he said with fake affection.

"Councilman Webber, thank you for coming."

From there, the conversation went much like the one with Leon.

Was I excited?

A lie.

This would go well.

I sure fucking hoped so.

Good luck on my pilgrimage.

I hoped I would not need it.

Best wishes.

And off he went.

Then the next one came.

One by one, each person in the room sought me out to have the exact same conversation, and every time, my heart got heavier and my head filled with more fog. Faking excitement was exhausting, but faking calmness was worse.

Calm was not what I was feeling.

My hands clutched my cup to stop their shaking. I let my mind grow numb to the repetitive questions as I wondered how no one in this room could see how little I wanted to be there. Maybe they just didn't care. Their need to see my dark eyes one last time, and to wish me well, went above my need to be left alone to prepare.

I should have done a better job hiding.

Sage stood to my right, diverting as many people away from me as possible. She was bringing attention to herself, the more eyes on her the less on me. Sage was never scared of a show; her arms waved as she said something to an elderly man I vaguely recognized and his wife.

My mother and father stood off to the side, fielding people of their own. Even as they did, both of their eyes strayed toward me. The expression in them could only be described as pride.

It felt great, making them proud. It also made my stomach start to wage a new war inside of me.

They would not be as proud if they knew how I swallowed my own bile while pretending to listen to a councilwoman tell me about what an artist thought the Deities really looked like.

And they kept coming. The forced way my words came out made me feel sick. I was grateful for their good wishes and support, but I wanted to be anywhere else so badly.

I wanted to be alone.

Tears welled up, but I held them in.

More people came.

More conversations.

I held back more tears.

After today, my whole life would be different. It would be dedicated to helping the people as The Light wanted. I was about to give up the rest of my years to that cause, and I was okay with that. It was all I really wanted, all I had ever wanted. I knew in my bones and in my heart that I was supposed to do this.

But, if I were to spend every day serving The Light for the rest of my life, asking for tonight to be for myself did not seem selfish.

And that is what I wanted.

To be alone.

For one last time, to do what *I* wanted to do.

Go where *I* wanted to go.

One night to prepare for what I was about to do, a ceremony that no one else could complete.

To follow in my mother's footsteps and take her place.

My breaths were quick as I nodded along to a man whose mouth was moving, but I could not hear his words.

My ears were ringing.

I pressed my hand to my chest to stop the feeling of my pounding heart.

When did it start pounding?

Leon was watching me to my left. Did he know? Did he know I was falling apart at my own celebration?

I did not want to celebrate.

He raised his glass and smiled at me. He didn't know how my mind whirled, and my head felt light. The chatter in the room mixed with the music, making it harder to hear much else.

I liked the way it silenced everything else.

Sage yelled over the music, her eyebrows gathered in concern.

Maybe I looked as bad as I felt.

And I felt terrible. My stomach twisted over itself. My heart fought to get out of my chest.

Someone was still talking to me.

I smiled and nodded.

And nodded.

My head became lighter.

Then my glass slipped from my grip. I watched it fall in slow motion, the dark liquid splattering down my front, seeping into the light fabric of my trousers.

The glass shattered.

The person I was talking to stopped talking.

Finally. Sage was at my side. Someone was already clearing the mess.

Through my haze, I heard her say something about

Getting changed.

I felt myself nod.

I heard myself apologize.

Sage held my arm as she led me through the crowd.

We passed my parents, and I looked away.

Once we were near the door, Sage let go of me.

"I'll handle this, go." She glanced at the crowd over her shoulder. "*Quickly.*"

Tears burned their way down the back of my throat. I gasped.

"Thank you."

I turned and ran.

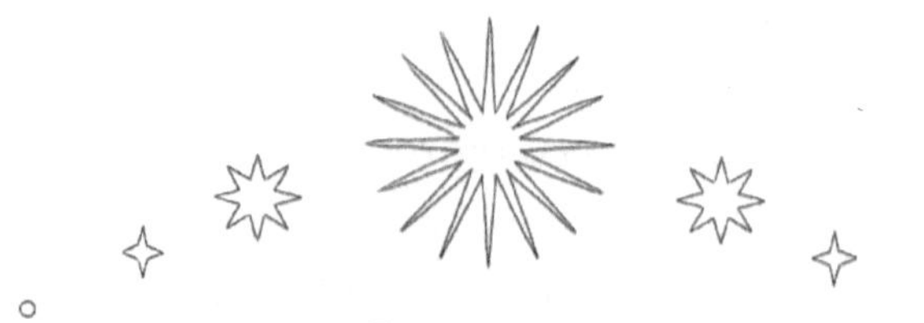

2

Secret Doors

I should have felt guilty for leaving my party early, but as soon as I got out of that noisy room, my shoulders loosened, and I took a deep breath. The blurry crowd of people was behind me, and my vision finally cleared in the empty hallway. Navigating my way through situations like that was something I was trained to do. But tonight, I simply… couldn't.

I wanted to go to the palace Temple. I wanted to lower my knees to my small, padded bench and stay there introspecting until The Light came to me and healed this dull ache in my head.

And when we need it, The Light will fill us, and it will heal.

But that would not do me any good, so that was not where my feet were headed.

My breaths came in and out smoother than before, and I

could almost feel my heart slowing. The calmness that washed over me pulled half of my face into a tilted, twisted smile.

I removed my shoes to stop the echo from the marble floors as I walked in the same direction I had gone a million times before. I would know the way in my sleep.

The deeper I traveled into the palace, the less risk there was of seeing party attendees. There were more rooms than would ever be needed. The ones closest to the main entrance were occupied by offices or meeting places and the rooms near the back of the palace were merely spares that sat empty. Some had furniture that was covered in white sheets and coated with dust. Those rooms felt like they were suspended in the past and gave me an eerie feeling. I avoided them at all costs.

At the end of the main hallway, there was a narrow staircase. It was not often used by the Ruler's family or people higher up in our council. These stairs were used most often by the help and by me.

My hand trailed against the stone walls that led to the lower floors. The cold from the stone made my fingers tingle as I walked down the spiraling steps. My feet silently padded to the bottom.

This is where the workers spent most of their time, running between steaming rooms, shouting at each other as they went. That noise, mixed with the clanging of dishes, was almost deafening. Many were working later than usual to ensure the people at the party were well-fed with both food, liquor and wine. The smell of braised meat lingered in the air. I only saw one person I recognized, Amber, my mother's main lady's maid. She carried a large basket of linens through a crowd of people, her gnarled fingers bent around the handles in a way that made me believe they would never straighten. I wanted to hide my stained clothing from her, but it seemed she was too busy to notice my presence. Most of the workers were.

These people had grown accustomed to seeing me cross through, and if they had questions about why I was here the night before my blessing, they were wise enough not to ask.

As I made my way down the narrow hallway, I heard a shout from a voice I knew.

"I could be mistaken," her voice drifted over the sounds of clanging pans, "but is there not a party in your honor going on upstairs?"

Looking into the small kitchen, I saw my grandmother sitting on the counter, her legs swinging slightly from side to side.

She was dressed in her party attire, her outfit a dark shade of blue and her graying hair pulled back to the nape of her neck. Her aging skin was a shade darker than mine and my mother's.

"I should not be surprised to find you hiding out down here," I shot back.

My grandmother's mouth pulled up at the corner. "I have never been one for parties."

That I did know. Grandmother was never a Ruler herself, that was my Grandfather. She married into this life, as my father had, and was consort to my Grandfather until the day he died. I could never understand how she became part of the Ruler's family, as she never wanted to do the obligatory things the rest of us must, like parties and ceremonies. It was not until I was much older that I saw that there may be more than one reason to marry into this family. I saw how deeply she grieved my Grandfather; she cried and would not leave her bed for days.

Even still she stopped by his portrait every time she walked by. She may not have chosen this life, but her heart had chosen somebody in it.

She grabbed a small pastry from a tray on the counter beside her before hopping off in a way that looked more youthful than she was. Her body may be aging, but she never acted old. She sauntered up to me and clasped my cheek in her spare hand. I wondered if my eyes still looked panicked.

Her mouth pulled tight as she looked at me, and I saw her eyes move back and forth between mine. She nodded like she understood something without me saying a word. Then, she took a deep breath and held it before letting it out. She nodded at me, silently instructing me to follow her lead like I had done so many times before.

We stood like that in the kitchen doorway, breathing together. Eventually, I let go of a tension I did not know my shoulders held. Her hand fell back to her side.

My grandmother smiled, pulling the lines around her mouth tight. "You better go before someone comes looking for you."

"I—" I tried to explain myself, to excuse my running away, but she cut me off.

"It's your last night of freedom, Adenne. Go."

I nodded, having no idea why tears were springing to my eyes.

"Thank you," I whispered as I leaned in and placed my head on her shoulder.

I felt her nod, and she leaned forward to kiss the top of my head. She squeezed me before turning me toward the end of the hallway. When I turned back to look at her, she was already headed toward the party.

At the end of the main hallway was a door, the wood stained so dark it looked black. It must have been the shortest in the palace. If I were any taller, I would have to duck to get through. As a child, I had decided that this must have been the first door they put onto the palace after The Light first came.

And the Deities instructed that a palace shall be built, and the Rulers within it shall be blessed.

I pushed it open, knowing exactly when to stop before it creaked loudly, and finally, my lungs were able to breathe in the outside air.

It was hot, as it often was in Polaris, but this close to the southern coast it was also humid. The heavy air coated my lungs in the most pleasant way, and I knew that it would only get heavier the closer I got to my destination. My grandmother had calmed me down, but this air took the ache away from my temples, and my head stopped pounding.

The stars were so bright that even in the darkness, The Light was shining down on me. The moon was almost full and helped guide my way. So much light in the dark.

The short door I had come through was rarely used as it led to a cliffside with a severe drop. The ledge was just wide enough to stand on. A door at the edge of the world.

A younger me, who had much more time and friends, was once shown the path off to the left. It was the kind of path that one had to be told about to know it existed.

I followed the path, clinging tight to the palace walls until I reached nature's version of a staircase made of huge fallen rocks covered in slick moss. I set my shoes down at the top of the makeshift stairs and headed downward, sometimes turning around and going feet first when the drop was too far. When the moss was slick I ground my feet deep into it to keep from falling. It felt good to be that connected to the earth.

At the bottom, the ground was soft, and I sank deeper than I had in the moss. Mud coated my feet almost to my ankles. The ocean on the other side of the forest ensured that the ground here was always wet. A few large rocks remained here, though, standing up among the trees.

I read in a text that the earth shook years ago, and some of our lands had fallen into the ocean. It was believed to be a Deities' punishment for a Ruler who did not accept their wisdom at their blessing. By The Light's grace, it did not destroy the palace, but the earth around its southernmost side had become a swampy descent toward the ocean.

The event had left behind a maze of tall rocks and swampy ponds, but I knew the path well. There were enough patches of hard ground to walk upon. Feeling the weight dragging behind me, I turned and saw how soiled my white cloak had become. The amount of mud that had accumulated made my gut clench. It was a gift from my father. He said the long train was a length befitting of a Ruler.

I lifted the bottom as I continued, trying to keep it clean. It was not wise of me to come down here without changing first or leaving this cloak on the cliff with my shoes. I may have ruined the shirt and pants when I dropped that glass, but the cloak was still okay. I would have to find time to seek Amber when I returned to have it cleaned before my father saw. The thought of him knowing I had been so careless with his gift tugged at me unpleasantly, but the heavy, damp air still pulled me forward.

I had always felt in a trance with this place. It was where I could breathe without restraint, the only place where I could relax the tightness in my jaw, walk barefoot through the earth and get muddy. There were no expectations or watchful eyes for me here.

As I walked, I let my fingers graze the damp wood of the tall trees around me, feeling the way the grain twisted itself into knots. I savored how the wood felt under my hands and the mud sucked under my feet, the buzzing of the bugs that came out at night and the way the trees created a canopy that left me utterly secluded.

I thought of what my grandmother said about this being my last night of freedom. It wasn't true. I would be back here. It just would not be as frequent. Soon I would have responsibilities that couldn't be put on hold and people who depended on me. I would keep them safe, happy, and fed. I would make sure that the Deities were pleased with the world we lived in. It was an important role, the most crucial role there was. Now it was time to step into what I was raised to do.

All this would happen once I met with the Deities, which was not a big deal, and I was not stressed out about. It was just something only one person in each generation had the honor to do. A ceremony that was forbidden to be written about or recorded, so I had no idea what was coming beyond the fact that the blessing would secure my role as Ruler. The day I had been training for the last twenty-one years. No fucking pressure at all.

The sound of rushing water kept me from spiraling. The air kept me balanced. I was close to my destination; there I could dip my toes in the cold water and let the sound drown out my thoughts, at least for a short while.

The waterfall was around the next bend of rocks, in a clearing that would let the moonlight in. A magical spot where the world ceased to exist. I almost tripped in my excitement to be there.

When I turned the corner, I saw water cascading down over the rock in a heavy, powerful stream. It was my oasis, and I walked toward it until the mist touched my skin. I breathed the damp air, letting that same mist take over my lungs. It smelled so fresh here, like the moss around me seeped its aroma into the air. This place was a blessing in itself.

I knew my peace would be short-lived when I sensed someone behind me.

"Hello?" I called out as I turned around.

I would not be able to catch a single fucking break tonight, it seemed.

Behind me was precisely who I expected and who I least wanted to be here.

Sage's brother hadn't been here in years. In fact, I was fairly certain that Ezrah hadn't returned to what used to be our spot since he changed everything for us and then left Polaris without telling me where he was going or why.

Or saying goodbye.

That was exactly two years and fifty-six days ago. In the two months since his mysterious return, I haven't seen him down here once. I'd barely seen him at all.

That was how I preferred it, to stay away from him. Avoid contact at all costs. He stuck to the shadows, but I always knew when he was around by the way anger settled into my bones. It was like a sixth sense. I could see, taste, smell, touch, hear, and know exactly when someone was around who deserved a swift punch in the jaw.

I would prefer that he was still out wandering the countryside. If it weren't for Sage, I would consider kicking him out of the place he once considered home.

But since he and Sage grew up in the palace Temple, that is where he returned, making Sage exceedingly happy and making me sneak around the hallways for the last month to avoid confrontation, a task which has not been easy.

Ezrah was a very hard person to avoid.

A lot of things changed in our time apart, but there were parts of Ezrah that stayed the same. His skin still held that dark brown tone he had when we were younger, a shade or two lighter than Sage's, but with that distinct golden hint that made it clear they were siblings. It contrasted starkly with my overly fair skin. His hair was still dark with a dense curl to it, although it was cut closer to his head now.

I had not been close enough to him since his return to know if his brow still sat in a heavy line above the wide bridge of his nose or if his bottom lip was still plumper than the top one. I did not get close enough to know. I wanted no proximity to him.

But if I wanted to enjoy my last night of freedom in the place I valued most of all, I would need to get rid of him. That would be challenging at a distance.

I stood and stared at his silhouette, acknowledging he was here without deciding what to do.

"Adenne," he said as he crossed his arms over his broad chest.

I could march up to him now and tell him to leave. The thought thrilled me, how his eyebrows would raise, and his mouth would pull tight. I could picture him being sheepish and ashamed of following me here.

I had made this place my own since he left me. It took a long time to not feel his absence, but I had finally claimed it. It was mine, and I wouldn't let him take that from me by being here. He had no right to return, and I wanted to ensure he knew that.

But, as much as I wanted to make them, my feet would not move forward. They were planted here, slowly sinking into the moss on this rock.

I could walk back, return to the party, or return to bed. Prepare myself for tomorrow. That was likely the wisest thing for me to do. There was no need for confrontation tonight, I had enough going on. It was likely best to focus my mind on tomorrow instead.

The simple thought of tomorrow made my stomach sink.

Before I could decide, he stepped forward. Ezrah always moved nonchalantly, like he was in no rush. It was high on my list of things that irritated me about him.

He looked at me passively, like he did not recognize he was out of place. I saw his head tilt down, looking at the way I grasped my cloak in my hand like a weapon.

Or a lifeline.

He tucked his hands in his pockets as he walked toward me, his brown eyes on the ground. The path here was narrow, to my left was swamp, and to my right, rock. I would have to walk right past him to leave, which would make him way too close.

His gaze stayed down, which filled me with a sense of power. Shame was what must have kept his eyes low. He must have known how badly I didn't want him here, how much he doesn't belong. I hoped he felt how much this place had become *mine*.

My eyes tracked him as he moved toward me. I ignored my quickening heart before it could take over, I spoke up. "You should leave."

Not a request, not a question, a demand.

He looked at me then, his head tilted to the side as he analyzed me, making me want to squirm.

I planted my feet in the moss, refusing to leave.

"I am just doing my job, protecting the Ruler."

I tried not to roll my eyes. Any other Ruler's guard could have followed me here, although they might not know the way. Even if they did, I wouldn't have that amount of protection until I was crowned. Besides, Ezrah was only in training. Sage had whispered to me one night that he enrolled the day after he returned. That had shocked me, not because his being on the guard would involve some unwanted... proximity, but also because the boy I had known was not a fighter.

Although this was not the boy I knew, I could see that clearly across the swampy ground. He had grown up, filled out in a way that surely meant he was strong, but without the distinct definition that some men got when they gained muscle. When we were kids, I was taller than him, larger than him in general.

I could remember telling my mother I didn't like that I was built so big when other girls got to be small. She said, "*You are not built big, you are built sturdy, like a proper Ruler. You are built to be the kind of girl the others can't push around. Someday people will envy that about you. Do not let this world convince you that fragility epitomizes beauty. It is easy to be dainty, it is much harder to be strong.*"

Those words stuck with me, and I saw the envy in people's eyes now that my curves flared from my waist to my hips and breasts. I was still big, but I no longer wanted to be small.

Standing next to Ezrah, though, I felt small. He towered over me now. My fists clenched. The thought made my heart race.

I did not want anyone—any *man*, to make me feel small.

I kept my voice like stone. "I am not Ruler, yet."

He nodded, and I swore I could hear the air escape him in one big breath. "Soon."

For a second, I almost believed he was going to leave me here alone, exactly how I wanted. My stomach pulled at the thought, but he stayed there, our gazes locked on one another like we were suspended in time, neither of us moving.

I wondered what he would do if I walked right up to him and punched him in the gut.

"So you won't leave?"

"No," he said.

"Even if I command it?"

He was close enough now I could see him smirk in the moonlight. "You're not Ruler yet. You can't make commands."

My mouth opened, ready to fight over the double standard he laid at my feet, but he always knew how to irritate me and poke fun until I bit back. I felt ashamed that I ever let him know me so well.

Turning my back to him, I looked at the waterfall one last time. I took a deep breath and tried to remember how the damp air filled my lungs or how the moss felt under my feet, grounding myself here before returning to the life I had planned.

I turned back and saw the man who stole my last night of freedom from me. Not taking my eyes off him, I marched forward.

The path was so thin that I would need to walk precariously close to him to return home. I kept my chin high.

When I was about to cross his path, I angled my body so we would not have to touch. Still, we were close enough that my cloak brushed against his arm. I paused. The waterfall was crashing behind us, but I didn't hear it. The air felt heavier when he looked down at me. For a second, he just stared, looking at me from my feet up, stopping where the cloak was clutched in my hands. His gaze was slow, making my skin itch, but like everything else in his life, Ezrah took his time. He finally stopped at my face. His expression gave nothing away.

I almost jumped when he spoke. "Good luck tomorrow. You deserve this."

He left before I could take another step or even think to respond. I was alone with the sound of water rushing in my ears.

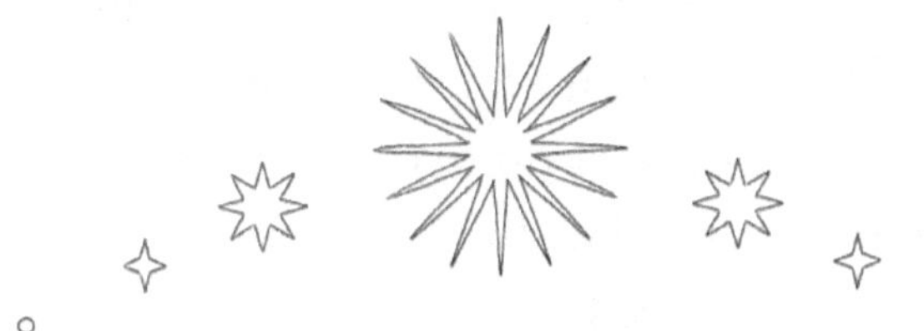

3

The Preparations

*D*ark winged humans fly above Polaris and I can tell from their scaled wings that they are not Deities. Smoke surrounds me, growing denser the longer I stand on the cobblestones. I move to find the source of the fire only to see piles and piles of paper burning in the plaza. The closer I get the more I cough. I try to blink the smoke out of my eyes as tears fall out of them. Then, I am blinded, the smell of fire still in the air.

I woke with a gasp.

The dreams vary slightly, sometimes I was in the sky, too. Sometimes I was at the walled border of Polaris, trapped outside as the interior burned. I always saw those winged creatures and I always woke before I could figure out what was going on.

For the past couple of years, I had gotten very little sleep.

Now awake, I spent hours tossing and turning in my bed. When that became too tiresome, I stared up at the sheer white fabric of the canopy and begged my eyes to remain closed. When they didn't, I let my mind wander. The hours between the time I laid down and dawn felt like years.

Last night I left the waterfall not long after Ezrah. I had tried to put my feet into the water to relax, but even as the mist hit my cheeks, my shoulders would not let go of the tension. The place seemed tainted somehow, like the energy there had shifted. Even after Ezrah left, I could not shake the feeling that I was being watched. The place no longer gave me the sense of solitude I craved.

I returned to the palace, took off the mud-soaked cloak, and tried to rest. When that proved to be frivolous, I laid my head on my pillow, letting my mind become a prison of my own thoughts. My heart beat heavily, like it knew something I didn't.

Something.

Thump.

Is.

Thump.

Wrong.

All that restlessness led to my mother entering my room hours later, opening the curtains, looking at me, and asking, "Adenne, what in this world have you done? Your under eyes are so purple it looks like you've been punched in the face." Then she shoved me out of bed and into my bathing chamber, insisting I hurry and wash before people came for preparations.

Overall, a charming wake-up call after a very pleasant night's rest.

An onslaught of people had been through my room since

then. Some I recognized, but most I did not. On a typical day, I would not need help to get ready, as I did not have duties I needed to be presentable for.

This was a unique day.

The young woman that came with a bag full of cosmetics grimaced at the sight of me. It was risky for her to judge her future Ruler, but I did not blame her. I had taken a second to look myself over in the mirror of my bathing chamber. I hoped she was good at her job.

She sat me down at the vanity in my bedroom and came around in front of me. A skin tone stick was applied under my eyes to hide their darkness, then a different stick of dark coal was applied more neatly along the lines of my eyes.

Someone came to tackle my hair, pulling and twisting it until my light blond strands tumbled down my back in elegant curls. She did not use gentle hands to bend my hair to her will, but the pain was necessary to get a presentable result. My mother was preparing last-minute details. Occasionally, she would come back to the room, give a noise of approval, then leave again.

None of the people working talked to me. They would barely meet my eyes. I expected it to happen soon enough; from my blessing to the end of my pilgrimage, no one was to meet my eyes. I was to be walking in The Light alone for those days, using my solitude to enter a state of introspection. I was to absorb the wisdom and guidance given to me by the Deities.

For the Ruler alone is responsible for their people.

The next few days would be lonely. I just didn't expect the averted eyes and whispers to start so soon.

Sage was the only person to treat me like a human being.

She came in not long after my mother had left and watched as I was pampered and prodded until I looked acceptable. She didn't say much. Most of our conversations weren't the kind just anyone should hear, but the smirk on her face from time to time told me she knew how much I hated this. Despite my mother's best attempts, I have never been the kind of girl that liked to dress up.

Too many girls are taught to be remembered for their appearance rather than their mind.

Once the cosmetics were applied and there wasn't a hair out of place, everyone other than Sage and I cleared out of my bedroom. I took my first deep breath of the morning and slouched into my chair unbecomingly.

"Adella hasn't been around much this morning," Sage said as she uncrossed her legs from where they were curled under her on my bed. She stood and moved behind the chair I was sitting in at the vanity, resting her hands on the posts at either side of my shoulders, watching me through the mirror. Sage wore her hair large today, the curls spreading far past the edge of her hairline. I wondered when she had time to take out the tiny braids she had in—I knew from witnessing it myself that it was a long process. But today was a big day for everyone, and Sage could command a room with this hair. She was never ashamed of taking up a little extra space in this world.

"She has been doing her frantic setup, as expected. This is the day she's been waiting for, you know." Sarcasm dripped from my words.

Sage snorted. "She has been planning this ever since you came kicking and screaming into this world."

I rolled my eyes at her in the mirror. "Yes, well, it better go as she planned, or she just might take me back out of this world."

Sage's eyes dropped from mine. "She wouldn't. She is your mother." Mothers were a sensitive topic for Sage. "Besides, everything will go as planned."

"You sound so certain."

"One of us has to be." She eyed me suspiciously in the mirror, and somehow I knew where her thoughts were headed. I let her ask her questions anyways.

"And have you introspected? Have you sought The Light?"

I nodded. "Yes."

I told myself that it was only partially a lie. I had sought The Light. I had been seeking it for a long time now. It seemed The Light was not seeking me in return. Sage knew this and took it upon herself to check in, which was the reason I did not tell her about the nightmares.

Sage nodded. "Good."

I looked at my friend again, the person I was closest to in this entire world. We had not always been that way, but Sage's world tilted on its axis two years ago. An oil lamp was left on, a curtain caught fire, and Sage and Ezrah's parents were taken as they slept.

Then, Sage's own brother left her here to deal with the grief alone. Sage lost her whole family within a week.

We had both gotten very good at picking up the broken pieces of one another and putting them back where they belonged. Together we had healed in a way that made us stronger than before we were broken. That wouldn't change.

Everything else would. The truth is I have spent the last

twenty-one years of my life walking towards a precipice, forced to prepare for the day I made it to the edge, to jump or to fall. Today was that day. What was at the bottom of the cliff I was standing on could be a very good thing.

Or it could be entirely unexpected.

Or worse, I could be entirely unprepared for it.

"Stop that." Sage's eye narrowed on mine. "You're overthinking again. Stop. You are not the first Ruler to walk through those Temple doors, and you won't be the last. If they could do it, you won't have a problem." She walked in front of me and leaned against the vanity. "You are more prepared than any of them were. You have earned this day. So stop *thinking* and start *enjoying*. Today is a good day."

Today is a terrifying day.

"Okay."

"Say it with me."

I groaned. "Really?"

Sage was as stubborn as she was right. "Say it. Say that today is a good day."

I rolled my eyes. "Today is a good day."

Sage nodded, pleased with her skills of negotiation over me. "Good, because we have to get you dressed. It is nearly eleven."

The time made my heart jump to my throat, but I tried what she said. I decided to try to enjoy the day. Perhaps Sage was right. Maybe I had earned the right to revel in this a bit. This ceremony was the accumulation of years of dedication.

I was not excited about the gown I had to wear. When Sage pulled it off the hanger, the gold beading illuminated in the light. The lightweight pink fabric moved like water when she brought it to me. Together, the gold and the pink were harmonious. Admittedly, it was beautiful, but it was too traditional.

Women rarely wore dresses anymore, other than special occasions like weddings or certain ceremonies of The Light. Instead, women played a valuable role in society where they needed to be able to move their bodies just as men could. Women had adopted wearing the same trousers as men, but more tightly wrapped around their waist before they loosened around the hips so they gave the same flowing impression that a skirt would have. Dresses had become a thing of the past as women finally gained the right to contribute.

Corsets had been gone for even longer. They had been deemed oppressive, and the extra cost made them frivolous. Tops now often had the same structure as a corset would have, with a bustier style and stitching to emulate the same boning— but were made to be moved in while still looking feminine. I was happy I was not born a hundred years earlier.

This dress, however, was made to uphold the traditions of Rulers before me, so it did have boning up my waist, with ribbons to be pulled tight in the back. Tradition was something that the Deities demanded. It would not be comfortable, although tradition rarely was.

After all of the under-layers were on, Sage helped me slip the dress over my head, then she had me grab the back of my vanity chair, bending slightly at the waist as she pulled roughly at the ribbons. She had been there when I had the fitting, so she knew the routine. She also knew how much I hated this.

"May The Light forgive me, but the Deities couldn't be happy with something that stretches?" I winced as my organs were compressed together. I imagined them all becoming one inside of me.

"No." Sage giggled. "The Deities prefer their women to be tucked into the perfect shape."

I suppressed a laugh, which was easier than usual, considering how tightly my diaphragm was being squeezed. "We shouldn't talk like that."

Her face grew serious, "No, we likely shouldn't."

She pulled again. "That is *tight*, Sage," I exclaimed at her, biting my cheek.

"We aren't nearly done."

"How is that possible? There isn't much more of me to squeeze." I could barely breathe. I felt a bead of sweat drop down the back of my neck.

Sage was biting her lip but not in concentration. "They're supposed to be quite comfortable once they're on."

I hated how much she enjoyed this.

"Says someone who doesn't have to *wear* it."

"You're being dramatic. Women wore corsets for hundreds of years without an issue. You're just not used to them."

I gasped as she pulled again. "That, or you're shit at putting them on."

That got no response.

I was going to sweat off all of the cosmetics on my face. If people envied my curves before, this was about to set a very unrealistic expectation.

Sage put all the little weight she carried into one last pull, rocking back on her heels and grunting when she exclaimed, "Done!"

She tied it together then I stood upright, letting the corset settle into exactly where it would stay. There was no room to budge.

I would be lying if I said the end result didn't shock me. The curve of my waist was significantly different from where my hips were, creating an elegant, steep curve. The pink skirting fell below where my hips started and went to the floor. When I shifted to the side, the fabric followed me. My breasts were pushed up to an unimaginable level, and the beading was centered around the bodice, trailing down the center of the corset and into the skirt. Upon closer inspection, the beads themselves were made of millions of little star and sun shapes, like I was a walking sky. The Light was a part of me, sewn into every angle of this dress, glowing from the streams of sunlight through my windows. The pink fabric complimented my fair hair and skin.

Was it worth the sacrifice of being able to breathe? Absolutely not. But I could appreciate why people used to consider this elegant.

"You look beautiful," Sage said from behind me. I could see she had tears in her eyes in the mirror.

"Thanks," I whispered quietly, running my hands down the front of my dress. "I can't breathe."

Her head tilted to the side, "It is worth it, though. Here." She walked to my bed, where she had put the matching cloak down earlier. Cloak was almost the wrong word. This one was sheer, the same fabric as the dress. It would do nothing more than act as a decoration, but the beading on it put the dress to shame. It was likely the most beautiful thing I had ever worn.

I turned to her and stopped in my tracks. There was someone at the doorway, that same frustrating silhouette. I tried to meet his eyes, but Ezrah's gaze worked its way up the detailed beading of my skirt to the bed of my waist to the way my bodice pushed my breasts upwards. He looked at me the same way he had last night, but this morning it was slower, agonizing. Everywhere his eyes went, a blush followed. I saw him swallow deeply. That was all it took to fill me with pure heat, my chest constricting. It made me furious. I needed to do something to tear his gaze away from me. Redness crept into my cheeks, which only made me angrier.

"You're early," Sage said, now seeing why I had stopped. "We aren't ready yet."

Ezrah looked at Sage like he was shocked to hear her voice. He cleared his throat. "Sorry." His voice was rough.

In an act of pure torture, Sage asked him, "What do you think?" And then gestured to me. I did not care what he thought; she knew we no longer talked. She did not, however, know that I saw him last night or that he spoke to me.

Unless he told her. That thought could have led to more sleepless nights staring at the ceiling.

When his eyes flicked back to me, there was very little else that I could focus on. "You look stunning, Addie."

Finding a voice was challenging. I blamed the lack of airflow. "You shouldn't call me that. We're not children anymore."

Lowly, he mumbled, "That is clear."

His eyes were not on my face.

"Okay!" Sage shouted, breaking apart whatever was happening. "You," she pointed at Ezrah, "wait in the hall."

He nodded and didn't say another word as he left.

Air came back to me, and Sage came around my front,

cloak in hand. She dropped it over my shoulders, the fabric tickling my bare arms, making me shiver as she clasped it together at the base of my throat.

Sage was never one to hide emotions, so seeing the tears well up in her eyes was no surprise. It was more shocking that the same was happening to me. A change was coming, we both could feel it. The precipice.

Even if we would come out the other side together, the next few days alone would be much harder without her support.

"I wasn't lying earlier. You are more prepared for this than anyone before you." She leaned closer to me. "The Deities should consider themselves lucky to bless someone like you."

"I—" I did not know what to say to that. "Thank you."

She pulled me close, head tucked under mine, her arms wrapped tightly around my impossibly tiny waist. "Good luck out there. Stay safe."

I nodded above her head, wrapping my arms tightly around her. "I will see you in a few days," I reminded her.

"Yeah," she whispered. Stepping back, she wiped away all her stray tears. I had a feeling there would be more when she left this room.

"Bye," she choked out. All I could do was nod. Any more words and the cosmetics would surely run down my cheeks.

She left, and I heard two sets of footsteps move away from me.

4

The Day I Prepared For

I was not alone for long before my parents came to collect me. As tradition stated, I would walk through the plaza from the palace to the Temple Minora at noon, when the sun was at its highest.

They stood in the doorway and looked at me before entering, not saying anything. My heart skipped when my mother stared at me, speechless. Then, it stopped completely when I saw my father begin to cry. I grasped my fingers in front of me.

"I—"

"You look beautiful, darling." My mother had tears rolling down her cheeks now, too.

My poor, stuttering heart swelled. She was a good person, one of the best in my life, but she rarely had time for affection; her duty was too important.

I flushed all the way to my ears. "Do you think so?"

She came to me, her navy cloak dragging behind her on the floor. When she stood in front of me, she grasped both my cheeks. "Like a Ruler."

Her golden eyes were shining, the proof of her blessing. Mine would have that same color soon enough.

They glowed with their luminescence, moving on their own accord when the light hit them. They were difficult to look away from. As a girl, I thought they resembled the sun itself.

My father stood beside my mother, now placing a hand on her shoulder. His eyes were a deep brown, almost black like mine were now. He was married into this life, not blessed into it. His hair was fair like mine too. I was always told I looked like him, down to my prominent nose. Once my eyes changed today, I would resemble them both. My heart swelled again.

"Are you ready, Adenne?" My father asked. He never had to do the ceremony himself, so he wouldn't understand why his question made my hands shake. My mother did, though, and her grasp moved from my cheeks to my hands, stilling them. I looked down at where they were joined and took as deep a breath as the corset would allow. I squeezed her hands in reassurance to tell her not to worry. She worried anyway.

"I am ready," I said, power in my voice. The ability to speak with more conviction than I felt came from my father. He did a lot of that when he was first thrown into this life. Sometimes I would catch him doing it still.

They both moved to my side, linking their arms through mine.

Leaving my room made my stomach flip. Instinct told me to stay right where I was. I was grateful for the extra support to stay standing as we walked toward the main entrance.

I grew up in these hallways, where the stonework went well above my head, and noises echoed from every corner. The sconces on the walls created a flame with oil, maintaining The Light even in the darkest passage. This place was my home and would continue to be my home. I would be here forever.

When we were children, Ezrah had once tried to convince me that the palace kept a piece of each Ruler in its walls.

"*Like a body part?*" I had asked him, disgusted but intrigued.

I could remember him leaning in to whisper, "No, like a piece of who they are. When they die, some of them are *stuck* here." He was older, and he always loved to tease me.

"That isn't true. When we die, we go to The Light." I replied.

"Do we?"

"Of course we do." I giggled.

His voice stayed serious. "Then how do you explain why the hallways echo when no one is around, or the feeling that there are eyes on you everywhere you go? It is part of the Rulers that are still here."

I had believed him then, probably for far too many years. If I heard an echo with no cause I would follow it until I hit a dead end, trying to seek out the part of the Ruler that remained here. I had even spent time in the library looking for any evidence of what he had told me was true, to no avail.

Still, if Rulers were stuck in these halls, I hoped they were happy about it. I hoped that I would be pleased about it.

Closer to the front door, I could hear the people outside. The blessing ceremony was an important day for the people of

Polaris. Many had never seen it in their lifetime.

I hadn't.

The only other time people gathered in a crowd like this was at the solstice when they came to celebrate the longest day of The Light, but today was different. It would be a celebration, although now they came for a specific purpose. They came for me, and my mother said today's crowd would be even larger than the solstice. Based on the roaring sound I could hear through the walls, I knew she was right.

The texts state that the people are to donate to The Light on days of ceremony, and at a blessing, they expect the most. People would come from all across the countryside to bring their worldly possessions to Polaris for The Light. The texts say the more brought, the better blessing is given.

For The Light must know the people are willing to give everything, and they will receive good fortune in return.

People would come with carts full of goods, from food to fabric and weapons, and leave them along the roads of Polaris for the Devoted to collect for the Deities. Anything left behind would be burnt, the flames giving energy back to The Light. My mother once told me that when she returned from her pilgrimage the ash of the donations still coated the streets, proof of prosperous years to come.

The sounds of people outside only increased as we made our way, arm in arm, to the main entrance. The ceiling opened up here, letting these doors become a looming and humbling size. The size of these doors put my small escape at the back of the palace to shame.

As the roaring outside swelled, I stopped in my tracks, making my father trip over himself. I could feel my heart hammering against my corset like it was trying to escape. The pounding mixed with the sound of the crowds as if they were competing to be the loudest. Suddenly, my lungs began to fight my pumping heart. Both needed room to move, and neither had it. My stomach twisted together in a knot, trying to make space, but all that caused was burning up my throat.

I didn't realize that both my parents were looking at me now. I didn't feel where my father held my elbow, keeping me upright. My legs were weak—the corset must be cutting off my blood supply—and my heart needed space. I couldn't fucking breathe. All I could hear were the people outside. They were here for me. I was theirs now. My eyes went to the doors.

My father stepped in front of me, bending to meet my height. "Adenne, look at me." My eyes wouldn't focus on him. "Adenne, look here."

I looked back at the doors. The height of them loomed over me. I have never felt smaller. I couldn't breathe.

"Adenne," he said again. I pulled myself to look at him. I saw his mouth moving and was able to match the words to it. "Watch my breath, okay? Breathe with me." He took a long slow breath in, then even slower out.

I tried to do the same thing, but it came out with a shudder. I felt like a child again, a useless little thing. The sound grew from outside and my head pounded. I couldn't do this. I was not ready, I was too little and I would fuck it up.

Something was wrong. I was wrong.

"Adenne, breath." He said again. His brows furrowed as concern concreted itself in the creases of his skin and I knew I was letting him down already.

I tried to breathe and it came out in a pathetic shudder.

My vision blurred again, but I saw him smile. "Good. Again, Adenne." His hand came up to cup my cheek as he repeated the action. He did it again. And again. We did that until my insides stopped fighting each other. I realized now how hard I was shaking and that my mother had my hands in hers again. She squeezed them tightly.

My eyes looked past them, and I saw my grandmother standing at the side of the room, barely out of the shadows of the giant pillars. She watched me, then offered a small smile. I saw her take a deep breath with me. We released it together, and then she nodded.

I looked back at my mother and father. When I found my voice, I tried to explain what was happening to me, it came out as, "There are a lot of people out there."

My father shook his head. "It is not about them. Today is about you."

"Today is about the Deities."

One corner of his mouth went up. "Them too, but mostly you. Adenne, today is the day you have been waiting for, and we couldn't be prouder of you."

Tears threatened me again. Pride was always the emotion that could push me to the brink the fastest. It was pride that I craved the most.

My mother squeezed my hands. "Today is the day you become who you were meant to be. You were meant for this, Adenne. Are you ready?"

Numbly, I nodded my head even though I didn't believe them and both of my parents smiled. I took a moment to look them both in the eye. This would be the last time I would see them until I returned from my pilgrimage. It would be the longest I had ever gone without them.

I looked at my mother. Her dark hair framed her pale face. She was one person who would always push me to be better than I was and the one person who had never doubted that I was born to do this. As the most dedicated woman I have known, I would be honored to become just like her. I looked into those eyes that looked like the sun, and they were filled with tears. She smiled at me, and a smile pulled at my lips in return.

My father's composure was slipping even further. He must also be thinking of how long we will be apart. I looked at the face that mirrored my own, into his dark eyes that mine would no longer resemble after today.

I took in every detail of them so that I could carry them with me for what happened next. It was because of them that I knew I would survive the next part without them, but at the same time, I didn't want to *be* without them. I did not want to be alone.

We did not say goodbye. They nodded at the person standing next to the large doors, and then the brightness of high noon blinded me. My mother's crown glinted in the light. They both leaned in and placed a kiss on the top of my head before going out the doors to address their people. My grandmother followed, winking at me as she passed and stood a few feet behind my mother and father.

I watched from the shadows as my parents stood there until the murmur of the crowd stopped all together.

"Today is a blessed day," my mother's voice cut clear across the plaza. "Today we usher in a new generation of leadership. As The Light decreed long ago, your future Ruler will meet with the Deities, our protectors, in the Temple. There, they will bless her with all the knowledge and guidance needed to keep all of Rhea prosperous and safe. Thanks to both your donations and the preparedness of our daughter, Adenne, we believe that the coming years hold a bright future for you all."

The crowd was quiet, starkly contrasting how they were before. It took a few seconds before someone cheered. Then the roaring resumed. My parents stepped to the side, and I passed through the doorway, allowing both the sunlight and the gaze of thousands to meet my skin.

From the top step of the palace, I could see that the streets were even more full than they sounded. People packed along the entire main road that ran through upper Polaris, and there was no space between them.

The people screamed even louder when they saw me exit the palace, and the sound was gut-wrenching—it sounded like an oncoming storm. If this weren't a celebration, I would think they were in misery.

I walked down the steps slowly. I indeed looked becoming of a Ruler, dignified, but I was far more concentrated on not tripping over this ridiculous skirt. The solid ground beneath me at the bottom step comforted me, as did the piles of donations. The Deities would surely be happy with the amount that the people were able to give.

They filled the plaza, leaving only a narrow path for me to walk directly to the doors of the Temple Minora. Piles of wheat and various green crops took up most of the space. Silverware and cookware were there, too, reflecting the sun off their shiny surfaces. Silk fabric was laid in rolls. I saw a wedding dress with layered white fabric and lace. Anything of value that the people of Polaris, and the rest of Rhea, had was here. Their generosity would shine back to them in good fortune. There were wooden chests that I assumed were full of things too valuable to be left in the open. Not that it would have mattered. No one would risk stealing them. The punishment for being caught was too great.

The piles were so high I was certain that I would receive a good blessing. I would help my people because of what they have given me. Pride filled me again, knowing I was off to a good start.

They were also high enough to block the people from my sight, which I was grateful for. My breath had just returned to me, but when I thought of the size of the crowd, I was in danger of suffocating again. Too many eyes, too much pressure.

Slowly, my feet moved across the stone mosaic cobblestones under me. The whole mosaic could be seen from the top floor of the palace. The rocks painted an enormous sun, its rays reaching beyond the plaza and into the surrounding streets. It represented that The Light was always here, even on the ground I walked upon. It had always been that way, although the only real place it could be seen was from the palace. I wondered if the rest of the people of Polaris were aware of the beauty they stepped on.

Looking up, I could see the doors of the Temple before me. Unlike the ones at the palace, these were made out of gold, the ornate details lost in the reflection of the high noon sun. But late in the day, they could be seen clearly; pictures depicting when The Light first came and when the Deities were created. It is a mural of creation made in gold.

The three Deities were carved faceless, but they could be distinguished by the power that surrounded them. Each had their own division of light that they were skilled in. On one side Hebera was surrounded with crops, giving them life and growth. On the left Manumit was surrounded with texts, a wealth of enlightened knowledge. In the middle was Justus with a sun depicted above his head and flames at his feet. His power was almost palpable, even in carved gold.

The rest of the building was stone, made in the same simple beauty as the palace, with large arched windows filled with stained glass. Shapes of yellow and orange filled those windows, sometimes depicting stars, sometimes fire. The window at the back of the Temple was my favorite; it looked like a giant sun.

I heard screaming beyond the donations still and I wished they were as comforting as I was sure the people meant them to be. Likely, they were wondering how far along the walk I was.

There was a scuffling on the other side of a pile of wheat near me. Someone shouted, "No!" and the pile pushed closer to me. My heart jumped.

A guard yelled above the crowd, "Get back!"

"Get him out of here!" Another yelled.

The guards were there, and I was safe. That, and the people of Polaris, meant me no harm, not on a day of celebration. But the shouting made me miss a step, almost tripping on the pink fabric before me. Heart pounding, I watched the wheat for a second longer, listening to see if I could hear any more shouts that seemed out of place. When I didn't hear anything, I stepped forward. Lifting my chin, I picked a point on the doors of the Temple to focus on for the rest of my walk.

Closer to the entrance, the piles faded away and were replaced with people. The Devoted stood on either side of the doors, their white cloaks reaching the ground. They looked almost like a long shapeless dress until they moved, the fabric parting in the middle when they walked. Now, though, they stood still, creating a sea of white before me.

They kept their eyes on the cobblestones, hoods up so that one was not distinguishable from the next. None of them looked up to watch me pass. They treated me like I was already on my pilgrimage. A shiver rolled down my spine. It made me feel inhuman.

As I ascended the steps on the other side of the plaza, the crowd's screams grew louder again. I knew better than to look at them. Instead, I stood before those huge golden doors and waited for them to open. Beyond was a Temple I had stepped foot in many times before, except this time, I was alone.

Well, not for long.

I walked in, my shoes echoing as they had before in the palace. Just as the fabric train behind me cleared the doorway, I heard those large doors close behind me, sealing me in.

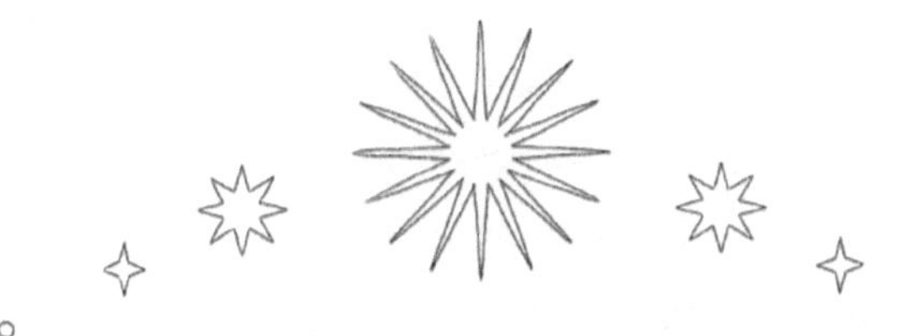

5

Sealed In

The Temple Minora sat in ghostly silence, shadows cast eerily over the walls.

When I used to ask my mother how I would know what to say to the Deities, how to treat them, she would reply, "You will just know, Adenne. It is instinctual. They demand respect that you will naturally give. It is their energy."

I did not know what the fuck to do with that information.

But this lack of knowledge also made the fact that the Temple was entirely empty confusing, to say the least.

I walked forward, the walls blocking out the noise of the crowd outside. The crowd was likely clearing out now, preparing for when I would leave the Temple and begin my pilgrimage alone. I could not hear them, though. The only sounds here were my own footsteps and shallow breaths. I moved to stand under the high arched ceilings. When I looked up at them, I instantly felt dizzy. There was artwork painted on the ceiling depicting stories I had heard repeatedly. When The Light first came and brought life to Earth. The creation of the Deities and then the first people.

There were small, padded benches that sat low to the ground around the perimeter of the room. It was where the people of upper Polaris would kneel for their introspection, seeking guidance from The Light. Sometimes people would reflect here for hours, searching for something, be it an answer to a question or admitting guilt for something they had done wrong. With enough introspection, people would feel The Light enter them, and they would know what to do. They would act as if they were glowing and The Light could be seen on their breath when they exhaled. They would leave the Temple Minora feeling much less troubled than when they entered.

I had not felt that in years.

In the time leading up to my blessing, I knelt for hours in the palace Temple. I would sit there until my knees ached, the padding on the bench no longer giving me any comfort, and I asked for any assurance I could get. No Light filled me.

I walked past the benches on the wall and toward the center of the room. My footsteps echoed back to me. The sound was taunting. I felt like I was being watched as I went toward the stained glass window on the opposing wall.

Tilting my head back, I still could not see the whole thing. The sun was as beautiful as I remembered it being, detail even in the smallest part of the window. Orange and yellow glass reflected the color back to me, and when I looked down at my arms, it painted my skin.

I stopped in the center of the room, listening, and was met with near silence—the only sound was the low ringing in my ears. Going from the loud sounds outside to this was jarring. I turned in a circle, looking for any sign that someone else was there because someone else *had* to be there. The Deities had to be here, somewhere. I looked at every bench along the walls, taking my time to complete my turn and making sure my shoes were as silent as I could make them. When my gaze returned to the window, I didn't move another muscle.

I did not know what to expect, but something was wrong. *They should be here.*

I could feel my skin buzzing, begging me to let the panic sink in. If my mother had been allowed to tell me what happened to her when she got her blessing, I would know if this was normal. She had only ever let one thing slip to me after a bit too much wine.

"The Deities glowed like light came from under their skin. They *glowed*, Adenne," she had said.

I never brought it up, and it was never talked about again. It would not be worth risking angering the Deities by breaking tradition. That did not stop me from thinking about it constantly. I wanted so badly to see that for myself.

Beyond that, I knew nothing about the ceremony. Still, I was surprised to be waiting. I expected them to be here when I arrived, but I supposed that was an assumption made from no real evidence. This was likely how it was supposed to go.

Time kept moving as I stood facing the window. I stood there, still, until my legs started to ache. I didn't move an inch as I watched the sun enter the window and paint the floors with the color it created. I ignored the way my legs shook with anticipation.

"Hello?" I gently called into the empty room, my voice

cracking.

No response.

Over the pounding of my heart, I spoke louder, "Hello?"
Silence.

I cleared my throat. "I am here. Here to be blessed. Blessed by the Deities and under The Light."

My voice echoed off the walls and came back to me. As my cheeks flushed, I decided not to speak again. Instead, I stood still for what felt like years, and waited as time passed. I could feel the ache from standing for so long as it settled into my legs. Hours must be passing and I just stood there waiting for something to happen.

Something was awry. I could feel it down to my bones. It was instinctual. This day was not decided upon on a whim, it had been set in stone since I was born. I always knew it wouldn't be easy, but I lived with the certainty that it would happen. That certainty was slipping out of me. My gut rolled over itself, then clenched together hard. If the corset hadn't held me upright, the pain would have made me bow over. Instinct beat quickly in veins, screaming.

Something is wrong. This is wrong.

Panic held me completely still as I tried to clear my mind. Thoughts tried to spiral as I fought desperately to control them. Most days I could, but I would certainly spiral now if I thought too deeply about these empty halls.

Or why they were so dark.

Why is there no light in here?

Light came through the windows of course, but none of the oil sconces had been lit. It looked like a Temple where they didn't expect anyone to show up.

Which, of course, was ridiculous. They knew I was coming. The Devoted knew the Deities were coming. There was a crowd outside, for fuck's sake. There was no reason the sconces should remain unlit. I could use all of The Light that I could get.

Maybe it was some kind of test, A puzzle I had to solve to prove I would be a wise Ruler. Perhaps I had to light the sconces to prove… something.

Slowly, I picked up the front of my skirt as I padded to the wall. I was tempted to take off my shoes to stop the mocking of the echo coming back to me, but I resisted. It would not look dignified if the Deities saw their new Ruler shoeless and walking in circles in a Temple. Still, it felt like the echo was growing louder with every step.

The sconces lit easily with a small switch at the bottom, and, one by one, I lit them, feeling more grounded once there was more light. Slowly, It chased the darkness away and made the Temple inviting. Having a task stilled my mind, but it did not lessen the shaking of my hands.

I stretched my fingers out in front of me and watched them, willing them to still. When they did not, I clenched them into fists and tried to restart the nerves in my hands. I wondered how long my hands had been doing that, if they had stopped momentarily between when my mother had grabbed them in hers or if it had been ongoing. The more I thought about it, the more sweat coated my palms.

Sweaty palms were also not dignified.

I gripped my skirt instead.

It took a while for me to make my way around the large room. The effort of walking alone made my chest try to stretch against the constraints of the corset. When the fabric would not budge, I resorted to shallow breathing. I weaved behind the benches and against the walls. The light through the stained glass grew longer, stretching across the Temple floor. The day was growing late, and I was still alone.

This is wrong. This is wrong. Something is very wrong.

I could hear the ringing in my ears even louder now.

Eventually, I circled back to the center of the room and waited. The room had more light inside of it now that the sconces were lit, but it remained dark because of the setting sun. I looked behind me and saw how long the window's reflection had stretched. It almost touched the entrance. I waited. I listened. Both of those skills were becoming increasingly difficult. That same feeling tingled on my skin. I felt panic taking hold of me more and more. When no sound was heard my body took over, making me kneel.

My knees cracked on the marble at the force of it, but I did not fall over. I would have liked to believe it was because of my composure, but it had more to do with the corset holding me up. The tight fabric was holding me together.

I wondered if that was why women wore them; to keep them from falling apart.

There was no reason to fall apart yet. For all I knew, this could be normal. Perhaps the Ruler was meant to wait. It could be another type of introspection, that The Ruler did not know about beforehand. This could be normal. It was not my place to assume I knew how this should go, nor was it my place to demand the Deities were here on time. I should grant them patience.

The concept that they were late was almost laughable. It

was not as if they had something else to do today.

Immediately, I cursed myself. It was also not my place to assume the Deities had time to spare. They are certainly very busy. They watched over us, our one true connection to The Light. It was a role that was likely very time-consuming.

So, I waited on the marble floor until its coldness seeped through my dress and into my knees. The sun from the window kept stretching across the floor. I had to force myself to not look behind me and see its length. I looked ahead instead and stopped my mind from wandering by counting my breaths.

One breath in, one breath out. Two breaths in, two breaths out.

My breaths were quick. That couldn't be good. It could just be because of the corset. That was most likely. Or it could be that this was not going the way that it should be. My instincts were telling me that. My mother told me to always trust my gut. Was this what she meant? All good Rulers trusted themselves, but all those Rulers were also blessed. That hasn't happened to me yet. My breaths sped up even more. Why was I breathing so quickly?

Because something is very, very wrong.

I closed my eyes shut tightly, blocking out everything around me. The tighter I closed them, the more ringing I could hear. I thought of how great it would be to open my eyes and have the glowing figures that my mother told me about in front of me. Would they explain what was happening? Would they ask me to stand?

How would they bless me?

Would they bless me?

Air stopped in my lungs like it was a living being, and

even it did not want to come out and face that reality. When it finally escaped, it was a gasp that echoed off the empty walls. I opened my eyes to the dying light from the window.

Of course, they would bless me. There has never been a Ruler that came for a blessing and didn't receive it. Not to my knowledge. I would be blessed. It was my birthright to do this. It was why I trained so hard. I was made to do this. This was the only thing I was made to do. They had to come bless me. They didn't have another option. I had no other choice.

Then why are they not here?

I needed to focus. I needed to calm my mind and go inward. If I started my introspection, then maybe I could find The Light. Maybe that was needed to make the Deities come.

Why the fuck had I not thought of that earlier?

Why would they come for someone who couldn't even find The Light within?

I closed my eyes and focused on my breathing. When I breathed in, I pictured light filling me. When I breathed out, the darkness left me. Breathe in the good, out the evil. I did that until my hands stopped shaking, and my skin tingled in a new way. There was a long period before today when I would do this process and feel nothing. I would try and try and feel nothing from The Light. One day, I stopped trying. I did not try it again until my ceremony was fast approaching.

Maybe that is why they were not here.

I let my mind wander to anywhere but this day or any days to come. If I thought about the future, I would have to calm myself all over again. That old habit of letting my worries spiral could easily pull me under. Instead, I thought back to a place that brought me peace.

I could practically feel the heavy air filling my lungs. If I concentrated hard enough, I could feel the mist tickle my skin. The sound of water crashing down was almost tangible, too. I was back there, in my mind, standing under the waterfall. Back to when that place filled me with The Light by just being there.

It had been a long time since I had felt The Light. Maybe that was a sign of what was going to happen today. I should have done more to find it when it had first left me. Instead, I watched it leave, more concerned about nightmares and preparing to rule. When I should have been looking to it most I instead learned how to cope without The Light.

Hours passed as I introspected and I felt no different. I did not feel the glow others did or enlightened in any way. Instead, I sat on sore knees as I tried to concentrate for hours, begging to be blessed.

When I finally opened my eyes the sun from the window stretched long across the floor. The day was almost over. The light was gone. Reaching up, I could feel dampness on my cheeks.

I stared at the window in front of me for a long time. My eyes burned, but I did not look away. My limbs grew numb. It felt like every bone in my body was hollow like nothing was left in me.

Light faded from the window, leaving only the sconces casting away dimly, the flames making shadows across the empty room. Night had fallen in Polaris. I was officially twenty-one years old.

Today was supposed to be the biggest day of my life. It was the day I had trained for since my birth. I was supposed to do something that only one person in each generation was to do.

I was to follow in my mother's footsteps. I was to become her legacy. To lead the people. Today was the day that I was supposed to meet the Deities and take my rightful place. I was supposed to become blessed.

The truth settled in me like a weight was put into my heart, making it sink all the way to my gut. I choked on the next breath that tried to come out. A shuddering gasp of air left me. Tears fell again.

Today was not the day I expected it to be. I would not meet anyone in this Temple. I was alone here because I could not find The Light. This is my fault. I am not blessed.

The Deities do not want me to become their Ruler.

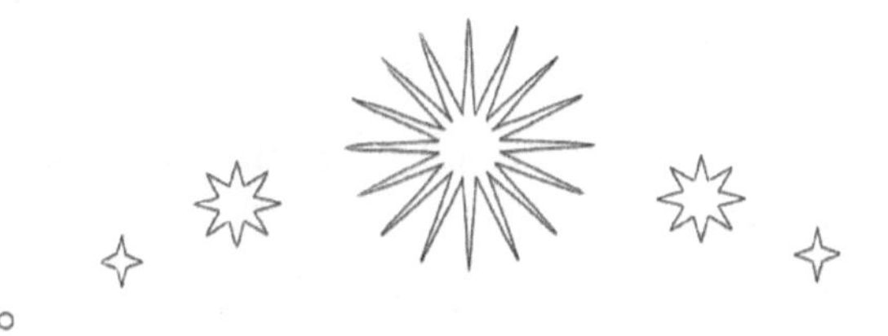

6

Not Worthy, Not Blessed

Hollow legs carried me, knees aching from how long I had spent on them. They still felt cold from the marble floors, but I welcomed the feeling.

I didn't remember walking to the doors, but I knew they were heavy to push open. My muscles ached from the effort.

Cold night air engulfed me. Outside, it was quiet and dark.

The street was silent. Just hours ago, it was filled with people screaming my name, screaming in joy for what I was about to do. The ringing in my ears still sounded like them.

People who would depend on me to rule and protect them under the blessing of The Light.

That was what I was supposed to do.

The world tilted when I reached the bottom of the stairs, the plaza before me twisting, buildings taking on new angles. Acid came up my throat, burning a path through me. I pressed the palm of my hand into my chest. I pushed against my skin until it stopped—until I could breathe again.

Breathing was difficult when my lungs had to share their space with panic.

Panic. That's what this was.

My heart pounded against my palm. My lungs fought for space, only having room for shallow breaths. Not enough room. Panic rose. It made my skin tingle as the world swayed. Panic filled me. My hands shook. Panic shook me. It showed me the truth.

This was all my fault.

It had to be.

Not blessed.

Not worthy.

There was a plan.

My plan.

None of that would happen now.

And it was my fault.

When I looked up, my home loomed over me. The palace's tall turrets were almost invisible against the dark sky. From this angle, they looked like talons reaching over me. The windows on the towers that usually were filled with light were left empty, like barren eye sockets in a skull. No one was looking.

Slowly, I stepped into the night. No one was around, and windows were closed tightly. No one was supposed to see me until I returned from my pilgrimage. I would receive my title and come back to rule. That was the plan, and now none of that would happen.

My weak arms crossed over each other, circling my waist

that had become impossibly small in this corseted dress.

It was supposed to be quite simple. It really should not have been hard. I failed the simplest plan, which had never before had room for failure.

As my feet navigated the cobblestones, I realized this sick feeling wouldn't leave me. I made a friend of it, letting the burning sensation consume my insides. It was a pain I surely deserved to feel.

Everything I wanted was gone, and it was all my doing.

Panic and truth were one and the same. Both filled me, and both weighed me down. They were things I could not let go of.

I was grateful for the tradition of isolation, that no one could see me. It made it more bearable. I couldn't stomach what a sorry sight I would have been—a broken Ruler. My steps were slow and uneven as if my body was giving up on me. It no longer wanted to move, and I couldn't blame it. I clutched my arms tighter to myself, trying to hold something intangible together.

I moved as fast as I could, which was painfully slow. Numb legs did not move quickly.

Thoughts screamed at me, a jumbled-up mess of noise like the crowd from this morning. I wish I could go back to the ringing. That had hurt less. I wish I couldn't hear what my thoughts were saying.

I had a plan.

The only thought that made it through the mess. It echoed off the walls of my brain, making my heart pound back to life. It still had that same weight, but it was pumping my blood furiously. The sound of it roared with the mess of thoughts. It made me dizzy.

For as long as I could remember, I knew exactly how my life was destined to be. I would follow the path of my mother, I would protect my people, and I would lead in peace. Train, bless, and Rule.

It was told to me in my bedtime stories as a child. It was said to me by my instructors. Everyone in my life knew exactly where I would end up. There was never debate about it, never a choice. This was what I was to do. It was what I wanted, what I fucking planned.

My hands gripped my waist harder.

Fire rose in my throat again. I stepped forward. My ankle twisted on the uneven cobblestones, but my feet righted themselves just before I fell.

The flames splashed up my throat with a vengeance. I didn't care.

I used to spend hours up at night staring at my canopy and picturing those exact moments. How they would feel when they finally happened—The Light would fill me. I would be doing exactly what I was supposed to and what was expected of me. I would picture the first time I passed a law that would benefit someone and the pride that would fill me. I imagined the day I would marry. Even without my choice of who, the idea of having someone to help me Rule filled me with joy. A constant partner by my side. I imagined the day I was crowned the Ruler of Rhea. I would know at that moment that it was all worth it. The training, learning, marriage, sacrifice, and planning. It would be worth it when I felt The Light fill me again.

This was a sick joke. It was cruel.

It made me feel ridiculous.

This had not happened to anyone before.

Not to my mother or grandfather—All of them were blessed without falter. They were worthy without trepidation.

I was the first.

The first to fail.

What am I going to do?

The girl that imagined this day felt ridiculous inside of me. That girl who had trained for hours and studied harder than anyone was embarrassing to think about.

Even after all of that, I was not worthy.

After all of that, I messed up.

Now I was not blessed.

My feet stumbled, either on the uneven cobblestones or this ridiculous dress. My hands were still wrapped around my waist, my bones too numb to move quickly enough to catch me.

I fell flat on my face, gasping as the cold stone scraped my skin. My arms were useless, trapped under me. I started to cry, curled up on the cobblestones in the middle of the plaza. My body pulled in on itself like it was trying to disappear. My knees pulled inward, and my back tried to arch. I strained against the constraints of the corset, my cheek still against the stone.

The wails that pushed their way out of me were still silent, as if I still was trying to follow the tradition of not being seen. Did I want to be alone or did I want to be invisible?

Did it matter what I fucking wanted?

Slowly, I pulled my arms out from under me, pushing up on my hands and knees just as that acid burn returned.

I didn't have time to think about stopping the vomit that came out of me. It was a clear, thick liquid. Pure bile coated the stones, and I held myself on weak arms.

It likely coated my dress.

I did not care.

My chest heaved it out until I was empty, and it tried some more. I choked on the burning liquid that was coming out of me. It was trying to clear my stomach. Trying to empty me.

My body wanted nothing left in it.

Tears streamed heavily. I lifted one hand to wipe at them, and it came away black from the cosmetics someone had so delicately applied. Now, this was what was left, a broken Ruler on the ground. Smeared with cosmetics and covered in her own vomit.

Come tomorrow, everyone would know.

I wished it would stay the night. I wished tomorrow would wait for me to prepare myself.

It would not wait.

I would have to be ready.

Another sob heaved its way out.

I don't want to be ready.

I tilted my head upward to where those talons made of turrets loomed over me. My home seemed so far away. The space between who I was this morning on the steps of my home and who I was now was growing.

My numb legs could barely pull me to stand. It took me a very long time to become upright. Or it could have been no time. I was no longer walking; I was stumbling. Making it to the palace would be an achievement that I would be astonished if I accomplished.

I would not let the people find me here, though. I had *some* dignity still.

Not that dignity would matter. Why should it matter what my people thought of me if I would not rule after all?

Not my people, *the* people. They were not mine, and I could not be theirs.

My gasping breaths quickened.

What was I going to do?

There was no plan. Not for what happens if the Ruler can't rule. This was never an option.

For a second, I thought to myself that my mother would know. She always knew what to do. For a second, I let the thought that my mother could help comfort me.

Then I thought of what her face would look like when I told her. When she saw that my eyes were not golden like hers.

They never turned golden.

What would she think of her daughter becoming the first not to be blessed?

What would my father do?

He had been so proud, so sure of me. Always confident that I was on the right path and capable. He may have never had to get a blessing, but he was sure I would. Everyone was. That was simply what happened until me. Now I would have to go back there and tell them.

This would destroy him. It would destroy both of them.

They would take one look at me and know that all of this was my fault, and the look they would give me might kill me.

I barely caught myself when I tripped up the steps to the palace. I crawled my way up the last few steps like someone in the last seconds of their life. Grasping the handles of the door, I hauled my body upward and pulled it open.

When I stepped back into my home, it felt different. If the walls had eyes, they were staring at me. They peered into me like I didn't belong.

Had the walls known all along?

Maybe it wasn't the walls. Perhaps it was the pieces of past Rulers left behind, as Ezrah had said.

What did they think of me now?

I had no plan. I did not know where I was going, but my legs moved and I let them lead the way. Within these walls, they had become steadier. My body was taking comfort from this familiar space. My hands didn't shake either, but that was likely because they held my hips again, trying to keep me together.

I pushed forward toward a plan. To any sort of plan. Forward to *something. Anything.*

It was instinct again. It pushed me.

More sure-footed than I was before, I moved forward. There was less echo on these walls. I felt less mocked. I didn't realize where I was going until I stood in front of the palace Temple doors.

Even through this sickening darkness, something in me still sought The Light.

These doors were open, and I walked through them. The echo was smaller here, leaving me with some dignity.

Unlike the Temple Minora, this place was private. It was in the palace and only used by the Ruler's family and the Devoted who lived here to maintain it. I felt safer here than I did outside. The small room enclosed me in a way that made me feel protected rather than exposed. I took a deep breath.

I walked until I stood in the center of the room, just like before. This time though, I wasn't filled with the false hope that someone was coming.

I didn't know what I was supposed to do now. I had no plan. I needed a plan.

Glancing up, I saw my bench where I would do my introspection. I walked to it.

The bench itself had been replaced. The fire in this Temple had destroyed everything in the main room.

More than that, it destroyed people. It had destroyed lives that day.

Sage and Ezrah's parents died. They were Devoted to The Light, and The Light took them in its flame. They died with dignity.

Every day since then, this room felt different. That day changed almost everything for me, but even more so for Sage and Ezrah.

It had been just over two years since The Light took them. Two years since it left me.

Before it had been replaced, the fabric on the bench had been worn, showing where I used to kneel as a child. I would come here and line my knees up to where they had been so many times before. The Light would fill me, it was easy then.

I was tempted to try again. I practically begged my legs to fall back to that familiar place, but it wouldn't change anything.

If I knelt there, I would not be able to find The Light.

I pulled my hand back from the bench.

My eyes ached, I could feel that they were puffy, and I knew if I looked in a mirror, they would be red. The rest of me ached, too, like I had been pushed down a flight of stairs but was somehow still breathing. I wanted to lie down and accept what had happened. What was going to happen?

I could already picture myself being found here in the morning, likely by a Devoted. I could see their faces when they first saw me and thought I was dead. They would flip me over and look into my eyes, which were very much alive. I could see the realization hit them that my eyes were still brown and hear their footsteps running out of the room, away from me. I would just lie there.

I stared at the floor. My body wouldn't move. It refused to give in to the fantasy that my mind had spun for it.

Instead, I wrapped my arms around my waist again, taking comfort in making myself as small as possible. Finally, my breaths were slow and deliberate.

No one was coming for me here, neither Devoted nor Deity nor The Light.

I was not blessed. I would not be blessed. My eyes were not gold. I was not blessed.

The more times I said that the more I grounded my feet into this cold, dark reality. It gave me legs to stand on.

I was not blessed, my eyes had not turned golden, and I had no pilgrimage to go on. In the morning, everyone would know.

Unless I had a plan.

Squaring my shoulders, I looked to the side, where behind a tall velvet curtain there was the door to the palace Temple's library.

If there were any answers as to what I had done to cause this, they were there.

And I had until daylight to come up with a plan.

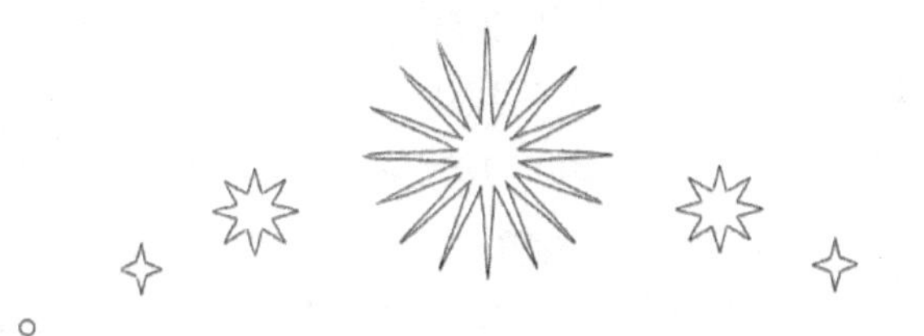

7

A Plan

The library was a small room, smaller than the Temple outside. It could barely hold the large wooden desk that rested at the center. I went to the desk, running my hand along its smooth edge. There was a small lamp there that I lit, illuminating its surface.

If I walked around and looked underneath the desk, I would see two names carved into it. A stark reminder of a very different time. I could almost hear the laughing voices of two younger children with much less to worry about.

"We shouldn't be doing this." I giggled.

He smiled at me. "You have to learn to break the rules, Addie."

Blinking, I forced the memories out of my head. Now was not the time to become distracted by the past.

It was time to find some answers and make a plan.

Now that I had stopped shaking, I knew it was unlikely this had ever happened before. The history of my family was long. I could not be the first to have trouble being blessed. Although I did not think my ancestors had trouble finding The Light, either. And I had never read about anyone else struggling as I had. So there must be something I missed. I could not be the first.

Somewhere in these texts, there was an answer. This would all make sense soon. By the morning, I would know what had happened and what to do—I would have a plan.

I unclipped my cloak and lightly placed it on the desk's surface. My dress may be ruined, but I could still salvage the cloak. The stars and suns beaded into its delicate pink fabric winked up at me.

This was a small room with four simple walls, different from what one would expect from a library holding centuries' worth of texts. The dark wooden shelves seemed to go up the walls forever. I had always thought the first people who built the palace did not know we would survive so long. This room was not made to hold the amount of history it did.

Instead of relocating, they expanded the shelves upward, with tall ladders eventually turning into scaffolding to reach the oldest texts. As a child, I was confused about why they didn't find somewhere new. Plenty of rooms in the palace were larger, but I know now that tradition is not to be questioned. If the texts had started here, when The Light first came, this is where they would stay.

In between these congested, looming walls, I felt calm. My hands did not shake as they had before. In this room, I could pretend that nothing wrong had happened.

I took my panic and pushed it down deep. My mouth still tasted like bile.

I spent a lot of time within these walls, learning my history and how to rule. I must have read every book in this room. Every second I was here, I wished I was in the regular school, learning with the children of high Polaris, like Leon.

Leon.

For a moment, my heart stopped. Leon was a kind man, he always had been. I knew he had planned on our marriage as much as I had, even if there was no official announcement yet.

If I really was the first to fail, he would not want me and I wouldn't blame him. His reputation had value, and there was no point tarnishing it on something like me. It was a stain that would never come off.

The walls seemed to tower over me, leaning inwards and caging me in.

Usually, I would get someone to retrieve the texts I needed to avoid climbing all that way. There was always a Devoted in the palace Temple. Other than tonight. Tonight, it was tradition for everyone to hide from me. Tonight, asking for help was not an option. Perhaps that was for the best.

I would start with the oldest texts and forge my way forward, looking for any titles that spoke of the blessing. Of course, I had already done this. It was all I had read in the past year. The chance of there being a text that I had missed was slim.

My stomach flipped.

There wasn't much other option, though. I could introspect and seek The Light, but I knew deep down that I would spend hours on my knees and feel nothing. I could come clean and *ask* for help, but by morning, my parents would know anyway and that already felt impossible to face. I might as well spend these last hours of the night looking for a solution myself.

Even if these texts contained nothing new. Even if there was no history to lean back on.

I told myself determination made me grip the rails on the first ladder so hard. That the shaking of my legs had everything to do with the hour of the night and nothing to do with the height I was climbing. If I fell, I would only maim myself. It was nothing.

At the same time, I was grateful that my legs were trembling with purpose now and not fear.

Halfway up the ladder, I was ready to give up, instinct telling me that people were meant to be on the ground. People were never meant for heights, but I had to do this. I could do this.

I had my eyes closed for the rest of the climb, so I had no idea how I made it to the top, but when my weak legs stepped onto the scaffolding, it was only a slight relief. This high up, it was dark, so the Devoted had oil lamps placed on the scaffolding that they could carry with them to explore the shelves. I grabbed a lamp by the handle and flicked the switch to light it.

I didn't look down as I ran my fingers over the texts on the top shelves. Dust came off them in clouds, making me cough. These texts were ancient, frail to the touch, and most of the spines were coming off in pieces. The Devoted do their best to preserve them, but time hurts all things.

These texts were written just after The Light first came. The Deities wanted our history preserved so they dictated anything and everything to the Devoted to scribe down.

Despite their age, the smell from the older texts could very well be my favorite in the entire world. Behind only damp air after it had rained. It felt like The Lights energy came off these Texts. The energy of stories from people way before me. I breathed in deeply despite the dust, craving their power.

I smelled ash and instantly I was brought back to the nightmares that haunted me.

Burning piles of paper littering the streets. Pages blowing towards me in the wind, landing at my feet. One by one they swirl at me as if they hold a message that is trying to reach me.

I shook away the dream and willed myself not to be distracted. They were just dreams. Instead, I focused again on the texts in front of me.

I had spent hours studying the complicated history of Rhea until it made sense. I had read nearly all of it. I vigorously memorized what these texts told me until my instructors were pleased with how I could recite them back to them. I knew exactly what the Devoted and the Deities wanted me to know.

Being in this room brought me back to the years of solitude while preparing. I used to dream of reading regular books. Ones of fiction and romance that people wrote purely for entertainment. I was to read only what was expected of me, texts to prepare a ruler. Most of the time I studied was lonely, but not always. Ezrah didn't learn with the children of upper Polaris because his parents were Devoted. A lot of the time, children of Devoted were expected to follow in their parent's footsteps. Neither Sage nor Ezrah wanted that anymore, as far as I knew.

But because he didn't study with them, he would come here with me while I did my work any time he could. Even if it was not as frequent as we would have wanted, his company kept me sane. More times than not, he was more distracting than helpful.

Still, these texts had bored me much more than they had thrilled me. I told my mother that once, and I still remember the speech she gave me.

"These texts are our history. The Deities had all of this recorded for us, for the Ruler's family. We study them to know how to avoid repeating the mistakes of our ancestors. They are integral for ruling."

I told her it was integral to my boredom.

That week I had a bigger stack of reading than usual.

All of the hours I spent here felt wasted now. They were in vain.

If I had known this was coming, that it was inevitable, I could have done so much more with that time. I could have been preparing myself for a very different life. With practice, I could have made myself a life full of joy.

Instead, I had neither. No life of joy, nor one of purpose.

The acid inside of me earlier lowered to my guts. Burning away at me, it made me almost hunch over. Having a task at hand had let my brain focus on other things, but the truth always had a way of finding me.

I ignored the burning the same way I ignored the shaking of my legs and the pounding of my eyes. I embraced that numbness instead of pushing it down to try to focus.

As I made my way shelf by shelf, finding nothing new, I became increasingly aware that I was on a fixed timeline. I could not be found here in the morning scouring the shelves. Not when I was supposed to be long gone.

I needed to find a solution tonight. Either that or I was out of time.

Exhaustion crept into me, but by the time I had checked every shelf I could reach from the scaffolding, I felt like I could roll over and sleep. It would take them a while to find me up here the next morning, where no one expected me to be. Maybe I could live up here.

My mother would say that delaying one's problems was only delaying solutions.

I went up and down ladders next, looking at all the shelves within reach. I was not shocked I had not found anything new, but my lack of surprise did nothing to stifle my disappointment. The texts I had already studied lay on the desk below, left from my late nights of preparation. The Devoted had not had a chance to put them back where they belonged. I remember having them double-check the shelves more than once to ensure I had read everything about the blessing.

I knew for certain the texts on the desk said nothing about a Ruler before me not being blessed. The closest they came was some testimonies from people before me, but they only discussed how the Deities were pure. They spoke of feeling The Light more that day than they ever had the rest of their lives and how now they knew exactly what to do and how to rule. Nothing specific, nothing helpful.

I poured over those testimonies. I devoured them, so excited to someday write one. I used to think about how a Ruler generations after me would take comfort in my words.

My heart quickened against the corset, pounding in my ears.

No one would find inspiration in a story like this.

I gripped the ladder tighter. I would not get to be the Ruler I expected myself to become, even if I found an answer. Things would be different for me. The weight of that sunk into me. I tried to lift my hand to continue my search. I failed.

When I tried to move, the shelves swayed before me. Or I was swaying.

I gripped the railing tighter, my nails denting the wood. My eyes were closed shut. If I couldn't see the shelves moving, I must be still, right?

I could still feel the room swaying.

Eyes closed, I tried to step down the ladder. I made it down the first rung, but then I slipped on the second, the fabric of my dress getting caught under my feet. The only thing worse than being found here in the morning would be if I was found dead in a big splat on the ground.

This ridiculous dress. A ridiculous tradition.

The acid rose again, coating my throat. I wanted to spit it up. Or I wanted to suppress it.

I didn't want it. I didn't want any of this.

What I wanted didn't matter.

I squinted my eyes open enough to proceed more cautiously. The fact that I made it to the bottom was the only thing telling me that The Light may still be out there, even if it wasn't there for me.

The hollowness of my bones wouldn't support me. I fell to my knees, which were likely still bruised from my time on them earlier. I didn't feel the pain. I didn't feel anything.

Breaths were coming out of me far too infrequently. When they arrived, they shuddered. They made me feel dizzy— an invisible hand gripped my throat, trying to close it as I tried to breathe.

I just wanted to breathe.

I don't get what I want.

Gasping. That was what I was doing. And spiraling. Away and away.

The grip on my neck tightened. I was helpless. I fell to my hands, looking down at the wooden floors, my back stiff. My stomach was being gripped, too.

By the corset. The corset was tightening around me. I reached up and pulled at the bodice, trying to force it away from me. It did not budge.

I used both my hands now, righting myself in the process. I reached behind me, seeking the strings that I knew were there. I grabbed at anything I could find, tugging at it. The more I struggled, the less air I got.

"Fuck, fuck, fuck," I whispered to myself.

Has anyone died from the suffocation of a corset before?

Short, panicked breaths came out of me as I frantically pulled until something loosened behind me. I pulled harder. Air entered my lungs.

The breath I took then was the deepest one I had ever taken.

It was the only thing my mind could concentrate on doing. Breathing in and breathing out. I wanted it to stay that way. The air cleared my mind as I sat there, a crumpled mess on the library floor.

Every time I felt shame for myself it cut deeper, and every time I was convinced that was as deep as it could get. Every time I was proved wrong.

This was pathetic. I was pathetic.

Someone in my state should not rule. Someone who cannot solve their own problems should not be responsible for finding solutions for other people.

I needed to prove I could do this or decide that I wouldn't.

My knees didn't shake for the first time in hours, even when reached to the tallest point of the ladder again. My body must be too tired to shake now. I went from ladder to ladder, shelf by shelf. If there wasn't an answer here, then it was done. I would not rule. Finding an answer in this room was the only solution I had, my last chance. My head ached.

With every passing shelf, I knew the inevitability of what I faced. Still, I looked, trying to suppress the rising anger in me. If I could meet that anger with acceptance, then maybe I could scrape some dignity out of this situation. Even if it killed me.

There was no fucking dignity in this.

I did not know why The Light would choose this path for me, but I would meet the answers with the assurance that it happened because it was supposed to.

For one reason or another, I deserved this.

I fucking deserved this.

There was no one else to blame, no accusations I could make other than the one that stared right at me. This was all about me.

Back on the ground, the bottom of the last shelf had eyes, and it looked back at me. I could feel them on me as I moved from one end of the shelf to the other. When my hands skimmed the last text, and I found nothing useful, it felt like someone had grabbed my heart in their fist and squeezed.

There was no plan for me.

My hands shook again, but not in the same way as before. I walked over to the old wooden desk. It was likely made at the same time this room was, its elegant woodwork matching the shelves. I could feel the eyes of the texts on the shelves watching me. Texts that I had spent years studying. Years of wasted time. I looked at the texts on the desk that I had read so many times I could practically quote them. I studied them and prepared. That was what they were supposed to do. They were supposed to prepare me. They failed.

I failed.

The dust coated my fingers as I picked one up by its frail pages. I breathed in the scent, taking it in like it was my last chance.

Then I lifted it over my head and threw it against the wall.

The text bounced to the floor. A page shook loose from it. It may be ruined, but I felt just the tiniest bit lighter.

I picked up another and followed suit. And another. Now with room to breathe, my chest opened wide.

Thud.

Another.

Thud.

I kept throwing them until the history of my people was strewn across the floor.

I thought I was crying, but I could have been screaming. Likely it was both. With every throw, that weight in my gut lost its prominence and gained purpose.

I laughed at my discarded history. It came out in a gruesome gurgling mess that I didn't recognize.

The end of the pile was near. I would have to find more.

I wouldn't stop until the damage done to this room felt equal to the damage I felt. I wouldn't stop until I was healed. Until I was light again.

I lifted the next text above my head, gripping it tightly. The pages crushed together in my hand.

Instead of launching it forward, a force pulled it from me.

I hadn't heard anyone come into the room, but the presence from behind me was undeniable now.

"Addie," Ezrah said, with a curious tilt to his voice, "What the fuck are you doing?"

8

Caught

I thought my heart had been racing before, but it was nothing compared to how it beat now. I could not hear past the sound of it hammering against my ribs like it was trying to get out. My heart was trapped here, and so was I.

He was here, directly behind me.

Ezrah was here.

I wasn't supposed to see anyone tonight. No one should have even known I was here. Ezrah was the last person in all Polaris I would want to see, yet I could feel the smugness radiating off of him already. It was in the way he towered over me with an amused lilt to his voice. That and that stupid childish nickname.

No one else would have been brazen enough to nickname someone in the Ruler's family, but Ezrah was his own unique kind of stupid. He had called me that for longer than I could remember, and that name became reserved for him.

It was another claim over me, and he used that name now like it still held power, but I would not let my heart get the same thrill at the sound of it as it used to. Ezrah lost all the power he held over me when he left. He gave it away. It was arrogant of him to assume that his claim still remained, and it was fucking obnoxious of him to call me that.

We were not friends. We were not… anything.

Yet, he was the one who found me here, hurling books at the wall as if they had wronged me. Had he heard me screaming? Crying?

"You can't be here." It was barely a whisper, and my panic came out like venom.

Venom never scared him. "I can't?"

Again, I found myself on a precipice with no good choices. There was a long drop before me, a fall into countless unknowns. He stood behind me, blocking my exit. If he saw my eyes, everyone would know exactly what had happened by morning. If I ran… I couldn't. I didn't have anywhere to go.

I shifted farther from him, narrowly missing the corner of the desk. The space felt good. The further I could get from him, the more room I would have to think, but the library was small.

"You need to leave." I tried to force my voice to fill with conviction. That was difficult when I could imagine him standing on the other side of the door, hearing me scream and cry. Any dignity I could muster would be false.

"You didn't answer my question, though." His voice was still irritatingly light.

"You're breaking tradition by being here."

"I'll go as soon as you answer my question." He spoke as if this were a joke to him.

My skin prickled, and my teeth clenched. My mind refused to focus. "What question?"

His footsteps thudded loudly as he stepped closer, the sound almost louder than the pounding in my veins.

"What," he spoke slowly, "were you doing," way too slowly, "throwing books at the wall in the middle of the night?"

I was going to hit him.

I could feel his breath on me now. It danced down my neck, making a cool path where my skin was heated. This was officially the closest we had stood in two years and precisely fifty-seven days.

I would have preferred to stay away from him.

I would have preferred if he had never returned.

Maybe if I stayed here long enough, ignoring his question with my back towards him, he would leave me alone. There was only so long someone could wait for an answer, but Ezrah was not one to admit defeat easily. He was as persistent as he was a fucking asshole. When we were younger, we made quite a stubborn pair; while I had grown since then, he had not. Ezrah would not leave this room because I refused to answer him, nor would he because I asked him to, not when he knew he had me cornered. He had always gotten pleasure from tormenting me. Ezrah knew when he had the upper hand and when to apply pressure, and always knew which parts of me to push.

That was the danger of having someone that close to you. If they decided to leave you, they still knew how to play games with you. Everything was a game to him, even me.

But he was not the only one who could play those games.

"I could ask you the same thing—"

"I wasn't throwing books at a wall."

"But you were wandering the halls of the Temple in the middle of the night. Not just any night either, the night of my blessing." I swallowed the knot in my throat before it could swallow me. "The one night it is tradition to have your eyes closed in your room. What were *you* doing?"

Pressure applied properly. Men with secrets would do anything not to share them. I stepped away from him again, running my fingers along the shelves as I had before. Dust came off of them, and I watched it move through the air. Every extra second it took him to answer meant the scales were tipping in my favor. I moved to the next shelf of books. If I acted nonchalantly, he might think I was calm. Unless he noticed how my corset hung off me or how my breathing was uneven.

"I was visiting Sage." I could tell his guard was going up by the tone of his voice alone. Ezrah had been the kind of boy that did not like to answer for his actions. As children, we got ourselves into many situations that neither of our parents would approve of, which led to numerous lectures. He used to do anything to avoid ownership of his actions, creatively spinning a story to put the blame elsewhere. I wondered if he had the same qualities as a man.

"In the middle of the night?" I pushed myself to not sound as trapped as I was, letting a playful tone emerge instead of the panic I felt.

I knew I could talk myself out of any situation, it was a skill I learned from my mother, a skill any Ruler should have, but this situation was high stakes. My palms were sweating, and my stomach twisted.

If he knew why I was here, the rest of the palace would know soon enough. His words would spread a rumor that would grow like wildfire.

He could destroy me if he knew what had really happened.

"I had something to tell her." He was defensive now. I was one step closer to getting him to leave me here.

"In the middle of the night?" I repeated myself.

"Yes."

"Seems like inconvenient timing."

"It was an important message."

I did not care about the importance or unimportance of his message. "Must have been. You need to leave now."

He heard the crispness in my voice. Against our playful words, it was jarring. My cold tone gave me away. I could feel him calculating from behind me, planning his next step. He sensed something wrong and was now trying to decide where to apply pressure.

"Why?"

Because if you see my eyes, I will be ruined.

Because I am out of time.

"Because this goes against tradition."

"Tradition?"

"No one is supposed to see me the night of my blessing."

He laughed. He actually laughed. "Tradition says no one is to look into your eyes. I'm not because you refuse to turn and face me."

"I—"

He interrupted me, "Don't argue, Adenne. I know the ways of The Light. Maybe even better than you do."

Heat rose to my cheeks because he likely did. I may have used this library to study and the Temple to introspect, but he was born within these walls. The people who raised him dedicated their entire lives to these traditions. Ezrah knew the punishment for looking into my eyes before I returned from my pilgrimage and was here, anyway.

"You still need to leave," I said instead.

"Why?"

"Is my asking you not enough?" My voice cracked. I tried for conviction. I tried to sound like a Ruler that no one would question. But I fell short. Again.

Ezrah knew something was wrong when he followed my screams to this room. He had the upper hand this whole time. Seeing the pile of books on the floor, crumpled and ruined with pages bent at unnatural angles, would have only confirmed it for him.

I could feel him calculating again. "No, it's not." His voice was soft, and he stepped toward me.

The tension in my shoulders relaxed, but I refused to acknowledge that it may have been because of him. I was no longer as comforted by him as I once was.

It was pure cruelty that The Light sent him to me now. If it had been two years ago, he would have been the first person I went to after the Temple Minora. He would have talked to me in that same soft voice. It was unlikely he could fix the problem, but he would have made it better.

It made his presence intolerable now, irritating. Having him here was exhausting. It pulled me in too many directions when I already had nothing left. The Light was taunting me.

I had one last chance to gain the upper hand, and the words came out of me easily.

"Fine, Ezrah. You need to leave because I don't want you here. Not in this library or in Polaris or in my life. I don't fucking want you taunting me, teasing me like nothing happened. Not when *you* fucked everything up between us. I can't stop you from coming back or joining the Rulers guard, but I won't let you treat me like things are the same. The only reason I tolerate you is for Sage's sake. I don't want you here and I don't want your help. Even if things are…" My voice cracked and I felt tears well in my eyes.

I could hear deep, steady breaths coming from behind me as he took in what I said. I hoped he was deciding to leave, that my cruel, honest words would be enough to deter this determined, annoying man.

"Things are what?" He had that same gentle tone.

Things are fucked. Hopelessly fucked.

My heart dropped. I had fallen over the cliff and hadn't even realized it. Now I was hanging off the edge, and The Light sent me the one rope that I couldn't use to pull myself up. The one rope I refused to use.

It would be easy to turn around and tell him what happened. The mere thought of doing so felt like a weight lifting off of me. I didn't have a plan. In the morning, I would have to tell everyone the truth anyway. I had no alternative. The walls felt like they were collapsing around me. If I managed to leave this room, I would bide my time until the morning. I didn't even know where I would go. I pictured myself wandering the halls of a place that used to feel like home, my corset falling off of me, my face smeared with last night's makeup. I would look like one of the dead Rulers still stuck in these walls, the same ones we used to joke about. The only difference would be that I would not be a Ruler.

I would wander those hallways until someone found me in the morning. They would summon my parents, and I would have to see their faces as they realized what had happened.

It would be easier to turn and tell him first.

Except I wouldn't have to tell him. He would know right away when he saw my eyes, dark brown instead of golden. I would have to watch as he realized what had happened, that I was not worthy of a blessing. That I was no Ruler.

Would seeing his face contort with the realization be worse than my parents? Which would hurt me more?

"Addie," he said again, stepping closer. I breathed him in, my chest moving freely inside my loose corset. The scent was familiar, but now with something more profound. Woodsy. I wanted to fall into it. I wanted to run away from it.

"Please go." I was so quiet I was unsure how he heard me, even when I could feel him standing behind me. His breath danced down my neck again, but this time it was hot. Somehow the heat spread to the rest of my body.

Hot tears also ran down my cheeks. I was shocked I had any left inside of me.

"No," he said. I was shaking, but my heart was calm. Maybe it had given up on me. "Something is wrong, Addie. Tell me what it is. I can help."

No, you can't.

I wanted to scream. There was no way he could help me, even if I wanted him to. Even if I asked him to. He could not help me. I couldn't even help myself.

I could turn, reach out and grab the rope being handed to me. All I had to do was turn. I would not even have to use my words. What happened was printed on my face and in my eyes. That was all that would be needed to let the truth out. He would tell the world. I could just turn. Then, hopefully, relief would hit me.

The relief felt too close like it was just around the corner of this one last decision. It was in the way my lungs breathed without restriction, and the woodsy scent that surrounded me. The relief would make me feel weightless.

I wanted that. I wanted to give up, but my legs were like cement. They stood solid, stubborn, refusing to move.

Because even if that relief called to me, I would not let Ezrah be the one to give it to me. It brought him joy to watch me dangle now. Even if his voice sounded genuine, I would not let him fool me again. Two years ago he had made it clear to me that very little was genuine about him. He didn't only hurt me then. He manipulated me to make the hurt worse than it already was.

I did not have a plan, but I would not let my destruction be in his hands. He would not be the one to take me down.

I gave my last effort. "Please." I hated that I begged, but there was no denying the pleading in my voice.

He didn't move. Instead, he said my nickname again, with enough compassion to make me wonder, then he placed his hand on my shoulder.

It only took a second to realize he was going to turn me to face him. If I was any slower, I would have let him do it.

Spinning the other way, I tried to go around him. The

movement pushed him into the desk, and he gripped my arm. I tripped while he pulled at me, my ridiculous dress tangling around my legs, and I fell into his chest, knocking us both backward.

My face was against his chest. I breathed in that woodsy scent deeply, feeling his breath move in and out heavily. When he let out a breath, I fell even further into him. His thumb moved up and down my arm in the smallest motion.

We had not touched since the day before he had left. I remembered every second of what we did then, even though I tried daily to forget it.

His skin still lit mine on fire.

I looked up at him, wondering if he felt this too.

My instincts had betrayed me.

I saw him look at me, first with sympathy. His hand moved to my cheek, wiping away tears stained black. He took in how broken I looked, how unbecoming, but there was no disgust in his gaze. Instead, he gave me as much dignity as sympathy could hold.

His head tilted to the side. I saw his eyes change, becoming curious as to why the tears were there in the first place. What had happened to break me?

He came to a realization. The connecting of the dots. I could almost see his mind running through the events of the night.

His eyes shifted quickly between mine, registering the one thing that could give me away without words.

My eyes were still brown when they should be gold.

He stepped back from me, his mouth falling open with shock. Ezrah was shocked.

He dropped the hand on my cheek back to his side. I felt no relief when his touch left me.

Ezrah stood there, unmoving. My insides turned cold, and shame rose in me in the form of a red-hot blush. It started at the top of my head and moved all the way down to my feet.

This was not what he expected to see.

It was not what I wanted him to see.

I stepped around him. I picked up my skirt and ran as fast as I could.

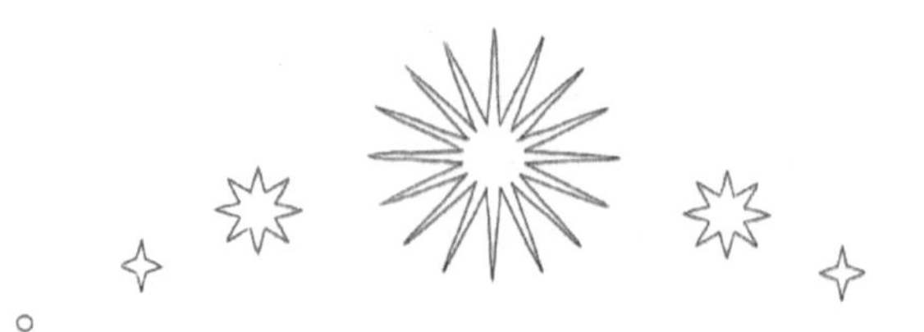

9

Out of Time

Even though the rest of my body seemed to be shutting down, my feet knew where they were going. They pulled me through the hallways of a place that no longer felt like home. The tall stone walls felt closer to me now like they were caving in over my head, warning me to get out or be buried beneath them.

My surroundings blurred past me, but it wasn't until I saw the small door ahead that I knew where I was going. Seeing the door did not bring me the relief it would have if I had been alone.

In a far back section of my mind, I wondered if it was wise to go there. Shouldn't I avoid any place he knew? Was I genuinely trying to avoid him? Most of me simply didn't care anymore. Caring about such things required energy I no longer had.

I broke through the door and into sticky air. My lungs filled as much as they could. At the edge of the cliff behind the palace, I could see above the tree line to the water. The stars were out, and the world looked huge.

Thankfully, I had loosened the corset, allowing my chest to heave up and down freely. I took a second to surrender to the fact that the world made me feel very small.

I never thought I would want to be small again.

When footsteps echoed behind me, I took off, lifting the fabric to make my descent down the staircase that nature had created just for me. The slippery moss ruined my dress as I twisted to slide down to the large drop on my stomach. I didn't care about the soiled fabric.

My feet sank into the soft earth at the bottom, but I could barely feel it, the numbness still running through me.

The next part was easy. I jumped from rock to soft soil, avoiding the deeper puddles of water. I ducked between large rocks as I navigated the twists and bends of my favorite place. My only sanctuary. The only place I could be without prying eyes, the place I could let truths come to me.

I ran until I heard the water falling and then broke into a sprint.

When I finally saw it, the smile felt foreign to my face. My skin cracked at the stretching like dry paint chipped off an old, forgotten painting. My chest heaved again to let that air in. On soft feet, I walked forward, feeling my muscles relax.

I walked until the waterfall misted my face. The sound drowned out everything here.

Then I screamed. I screamed and released what little was

left of me. My lungs burned. I screamed at The Light, I screamed at the Deities, and I screamed at myself.

That is how he found me, screaming at the water, collapsing into myself. Buckling over as my lungs broke down, involuntarily bent over at the waist. Holding myself vertically took energy I didn't have.

Mist coated my face, mixing with the tears. I wanted to lower myself fully in the water, to wash this away. I craved the silence that would come if I were fully submerged.

He stood a few feet behind me and he watched but did not interrupt. He likely thought I had gone insane, but I didn't care.

Ezrah didn't interfere until I started collapsing. He caught me from behind, stopping me from falling into the deep water at the bottom of the falls. His large arms circled me, and I was so small in them.

Hauling me back against his chest, he pulled us backward, letting me fall onto his lap.

Turning, I hit my fists into hard flesh, and he held me there. Limply closed fists assaulted him while I cried.

Tomorrow I would be embarrassed, ashamed at how he saw me break. Tonight, I did not care.

I had given The Light the first twenty-one years of my life, and now they could have the rest of me, too. Even if I couldn't serve it, even if it didn't want me to. I would empty myself in its name. Maybe that would be enough.

At some point, my fists stopped hitting him and started shaking. I clutched his shirt to stop them, my fingernails piercing through the fabric and into the skin of my own palms.

My body fell forward, my cheek landing on his chest.

Sobs racked my body, and my chest moved up and down on its own accord.

Ezrah did not say a word as I clung to him. I felt this hand come around my back and stroked it slowly, moving up and down. The feeling took power out of my harsh breaths and left me shuddering.

I welcomed the numbness when it returned. I felt it sink into my bones in a way that felt familiar. My mind was making the same noise the water did, but at a higher pitch. It rang in my ears.

After one long inhale, the first one I had taken that was steady, I pulled my face off his chest, staring at the small patch of water left behind by my tears. I didn't look him in the eye as I pulled back and stood up. I heard him stand behind me as I took a few paces away from him, putting space between us. He didn't look at me either for a few seconds, giving me a moment to collect myself. Ezrah was a selfish man, but he granted me enough dignity to let me stand on my own.

I turned back to him, and when he finally looked at me, there was almost no pity in his gaze. If that was what he felt, he hid it well. Mentally, I thanked him for that. He knew me well enough to know that is not what I wanted.

After a pause, he spoke first, "You didn't go?"

"What?"

"You didn't go," he paused like what he said should be clear, "to your blessing."

My eyes narrowed on him. "Of course, I went. You saw me walk through those doors. All of Polaris did."

His eyes narrowed back at me, filled with suspicion. "I don't understand."

I breathed deeply. "I went. They weren't there."

I thought those words would be much harder to get out, but they came easily. I was unsure if it was because they needed to be said or because I said them to him. As much as I tried to ignore it, years ago he was my person. He knew my secrets. Sharing this one with him was easy. As soon as the words left me, I felt lighter, my stomach unclenched, and I could appreciate the heavy, damp air in my lungs. I breathed deeply again.

His face hadn't changed. "I still don't understand."

It only brought me a little joy that Ezrah was confused. "I went into the Temple Minora today, and no Deities were there."

He shook his head, and his eyes widened. It was a difficult task to shock Ezrah. He looked like he thought I was pulling some elaborate joke on him.

My joy increased when he said, "That doesn't make sense."

"Yeah, no shit."

"Addie."

I resisted the urge to roll my eyes. "What?"

He looked at me like he was waiting for the punchline.

When I said nothing, he said, "You must be mistaken."

I laughed. It came out in one sharp sound. It was out of place. Nothing about this was funny.

Except for the bewilderment on Ezrah's face, that was slightly funny.

"I don't think I could have missed three glowing, winged Deities walking around a Temple." He still looked confused, clearly not seeing the humor in all of this. "They weren't *there*, Ezrah."

I watched his expression change. His brows went from furrowed to raised. I saw his eyes move back and forth like he was looking over a puzzle only he could see. Then he looked me over at my state and factored that into his calculations.

"You're not fucking with me." Finally, he came to that simple realization. As if he thought I would have played this elaborate prank on the most important day of my life. I saw his lips relax with understanding, then his expression settled on pity. "I am so sorry, Addie."

"I don't want your pity." He winced at the clipped tone of my voice and didn't say anything.

Apologizing for something he didn't mean was not in his nature. He wouldn't say sorry for giving me pity because it was inevitable that he would. Who would not pity this? He didn't speak, he knew better than to do that. Still, anger filled me with heat. I felt it wash over me and then back out.

"How did this happen?"

Because I majorly fucked up.

"I don't know."

"What does it mean?" he asked, quiet now.

I shook my head, lifted my arms in defeat, and gave him an answer he must have expected. "I don't know."

The fact that I had no answer brought tears to my eyes. I always had an answer. I swallowed the tears, and they burned down the back of my throat. He had seen me cry enough for tonight.

Ezrah was wrapping his head around my words, calculating the events of the evening. He had the kind of eyes that you could see processing. I remember if we were close enough, it was like I could see his brain working behind them.

His eyes would turn darker when he thought deeply about something. I used to get lost in them.

I didn't understand why he was working so hard to understand this. It was not the kind of situation most people would want to be brought into. He worked away at what was happening like he thought he could solve it. If I was him, I would have left by now. If the roles were reversed, I would not have chased him here in the first place.

"Is that why you were in the library?"

I nodded.

"And?"

"And what?"

"What did you find?"

I shook my head. "There are no answers there."

"None?"

"As far as our texts say, this has never happened before. Every Ruler before me has gotten their blessing. I don't know what I did wrong." My hands shook again, so I squeezed them into fists.

"Who says you did something wrong?"

That sharp laugh erupted from my chest again. "I have done plenty wrong."

For a second, I thought he would try to convince me that I hadn't. When he had known me, that may have been true. I did not want to convince him that I had changed.

His mouth tightened. "We have all done things that are wrong. That doesn't mean you wouldn't be blessed." When I didn't respond, he asked, "Do you honestly think it was something you did?"

I didn't answer.

He stepped toward me. I would have stepped backward if I could, but I was on the water's edge, leaving us closer than either of us would have liked.

"There has never been a Ruler more deserving," he said, his words mirroring Sage's this morning, making my heart twist again. "You have given up your life to them. This isn't because of you."

If only he knew how many hours I had spent on my knees seeking The Light and how every time I only found darkness. Still, his words made my heart twist further. I filled with heat again, that red tone creeping into my cheeks.

It had been a long time since I had talked to Ezrah. I had forgotten how much his words could affect me. They took the sting out of what happened today, calming me. He always had the ability to say precisely what I needed to hear, even if I didn't believe his words.

We were acting like we were younger again like no time had passed. I cursed myself at how easy it was to slip back into that old habit of having him. I was far past needing him.

There was a time that I was ready to disregard the rules, to ignore the fact that I was expected to marry someone from upper Polaris. Back then, I believed I needed him so much that I would have risked it all by breaking tradition. Then he taught me I did not need him after all. I could do it alone. Even if the lesson was unintentional, I was no longer dependent. Not on him or anyone else, and I refused to go back.

"You should go."

His head tilted to the side, "What?"

I crossed my arms in front of myself. "You need to leave. You shouldn't have followed me here."

He didn't move.

"Go, Ezrah," my voice cracked.

"Adenne." His voice was so soft I could lean into it. "Don't do this."

"Do what?"

"Push me away."

I tilted my head back and let out a sharp laugh. "You pushed yourself away the moment you decided to leave here. You don't get to twist that around on me."

My words were a blade to his gut. "I know that, okay? I get to feel guilty about that every day and I'll live with that. I'm not trying to blame you."

"Then what are you trying to do?"

I looked him right in the eye and waited until he looked away.

When he looked back, his expression had changed, hardened. "I'm trying to help you," he said.

The offense in his voice shouldn't have stung me so badly. I should feel nothing about hurting him. The Light knows he feels nothing when it comes to hurting me.

"I don't need help." I felt my lips tighten unbecomingly. My tone was biting. My palms sweat at the lie.

"So, you have a plan?" His walls were going back up, too. This was a territory that I was much more comfortable in.

I couldn't admit I had no plan or clue what to do next, that I had used all my resources to figure this out. There was no more time. I felt like an animal backing into a corner before it was slaughtered. Nowhere to go. I had tried to find an answer, and I failed.

Still, I wouldn't admit that to him.

"I need answers." It was the best lie I could muster.

"You're going to Temple Majora, then."

He said it so simply, like it was obvious. It should have been for me, but it had not even crossed my mind. Heat filled my cheeks again, but I pushed it down.

The Temple Majora was the largest Temple we had. It was said to be in the same spot that The Light first touched the world and made the Deities and the first people. It was the most sacred place in all of Rhea, and its library put ours to shame. Devoted went there to study and learn the ways of The Light. It is north of Polaris by a few days' journey, but not much further than what my original pilgrimage was to be. I could leave for there instead of the Sisters, and no one would be the wiser.

Why hadn't I thought of it?

Shame almost stopped me from nodding, but I did it anyway. I took his idea and claimed it as my own. He nodded like he believed me, like I assured him I had this plan all along.

Then he said something that I should have seen coming. I would have expected it before, but now it was exactly what I was avoiding.

"When do we leave?"

"We?" My voice was shrill.

He nodded.

"No," I replied.

"I want to help."

The earnestness in his eyes almost broke me down into that old role we used to play for each other. The parts we had before we grew up and became these morphed versions of ourselves. He looked genuine, and I wondered if he felt himself slipping backward, too. Was he trying to resist it as hard as I was?

"There is a death penalty for looking at the eyes of a Ruler on their pilgrimage, let alone helping one."

"I don't care."

I couldn't tell if he was kidding. "You want to be strapped down and left to rot in the streets?"

My gut twisted at the thought of it. "I want to help," he repeated.

I hated him, but I wouldn't risk it. "If you want to help—" I paused, the words almost getting caught in my throat like my body didn't want to release them. "Then you can go back to your room and pretend this never happened. Wake up tomorrow, and don't tell anyone you saw me."

Only when he leaned away from me did I realized how close he had gotten. "That's what you want?"

"It is."

His brain was working again, and his mouth drew tight. He was planning his next move. I hoped he wouldn't further this argument. I had little energy left to fight him, and I did not want to discover what would happen if I ran out completely.

Ezrah stepped closer to me again. Close enough that I had to bend my neck backward to look him in the eye. He had grown so much since I knew him. For a long time, I believed that the last time he stood this close to me would be the last time I would see him in my lifetime. I had no idea how we got here again.

"You don't have to do this alone, Addie. I'm here."

"The best thing you can do is get away from me." I closed my eyes, hiding the effect his offer had on me. Before I opened them again, I let them turn to stone.

He nodded but didn't move. We stood a breath apart, and he looked into my eyes like he expected me to break. If I did, he would know the truth about how badly I wanted help, *his* help. But the pilgrimage was still meant to be done alone, and even if I was headed a different route now, I wanted to follow tradition. I had broken enough traditions in the last few hours. Beyond that, the people of Rhea might recognize me on this new pilgrimage, and even with their eyes cast down, someone traveling with me would not go unnoticed. It was not a risk I would take.

And I had to do this next part alone. I would not take other people down with me.

So I kept my eyes cold as he stared at me, offering his help. I let him believe I didn't need it when every part of me wanted it. Eventually, he relented, stepping away from me. He didn't say anything. A small, sad smile pulled at one side of his lips as he nodded. Then he turned and left, his silhouette fading into the place we used to share.

I ignored the guilt that was eating at me. I wouldn't tell him that he had already helped me.

He had given me a plan.

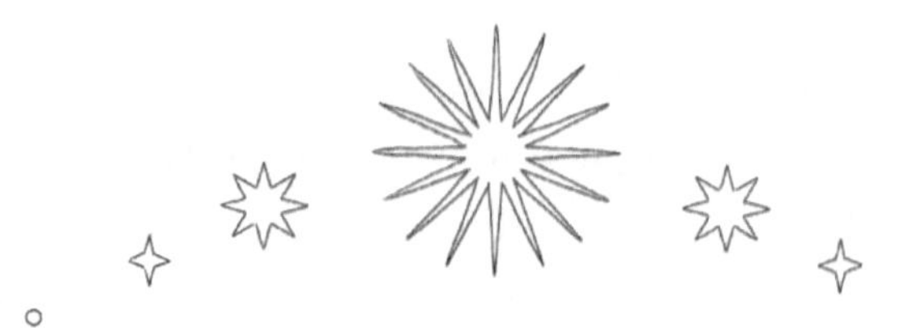

10

A New Path

I didn't bother with sleep. It was too late into the night for that. The sun would be up in a few hours, and I would be gone.

Ezrah was nowhere in sight as I returned to the palace. The halls that were usually filled with workers running from room to room were empty. The silence of it all was a stark contrast to the sound that the water had made. Everyone was sleeping peacefully tonight, thinking they had a new, capable Ruler to take care of them.

Knowing no one was awake, I walked on light feet through the hall and to my room. The moon painted the room in light through the open curtains. The four-poster bed was still made, the vanity in the corner was clean, and the wardrobe had only one hanger on the outside so I could hang up the dress I wore now before I changed for my pilgrimage.

Looking down at myself I saw the beautiful light pink

fabric covered in dirt and mud. The dress's train was entirely coated, creating an awful brown color. Spots of muddy water followed up the elegant fabric, staining in between the beading. The corset hung loosely off of me, and I almost spilled out of the top of it.

The fabric was a pool of soiled pink on the ground as I made my way to my bathing chamber and washed any remaining cosmetics from my face. Then, I took a brush and slowly worked it through my fair curls until the knots came loose. My eyes were puffy and raw, but I felt cleaner now. The reflection that looked back at me in the mirror looked older somehow, it was the small line that creased between my brow and the determined set of my jaw.

Or possibly it was the persistent deep brown color of my eyes.

I went to the wardrobe and pulled out the clothing that had been prepared for me. The corset-shaped bodice was made in an emerald green fabric, the design resembling the outfit now on the floor. Although it had stretch to it, allowing me to breathe. For that reason alone, this style of top was always my favorite. The color was rich against my skin, but it also brought out the red around my swollen eyes.

The trousers were tight around the waist and calves while hanging loose around my thighs, a typical style in Rhea. They were made of brown canvas, comfortable to wear on horseback and breathable. A brown leather belt held them in place. After wearing a dress all day, I was thankful for these pants.

A saddle bag was already packed in the corner of the room by the door. It had rations of food, a tent, medical supplies in case of emergency, and a change of clothes. An emerald green cloak lay on top. It had golden beading that started at the clasp in the front and went around the collar. It was beautiful.

The cloak would also be a dead giveaway about who I was, or at least that I was somebody of status. One person had already seen my eyes and figured out the truth, I could not risk that happening on the road, too.

I returned to the wardrobe, where I knew there was an old cloak of Sages. She had left it here only days ago, and with the rush of everything through the last few days, I had forgotten to return it. The cloak ended at the top of my legs, curving at the back. It was made in a brown fabric, about the same color as my pants. When I clasped it around my neck, I could instantly feel the fabric scratch my skin, but the discomfort would be worth hiding my identity. This one also had a hood on it. I felt more secure with that extra level of protection.

People would not recognize me out there. I would not be on my typical path, and it was not as if my portrait was in every home. They would know my face if they had been close enough to see it in person at a ceremony, but that was it. With Sage's cloak and my dark brown eyes I should be unrecognizable.

I hung the emerald cloak at the back of the wardrobe, hoping it would take a while for someone to realize it was there. Then I turned to the dress. I had to leave it to avoid suspicion, but as soon as anyone saw the state of it, they would know something was wrong. I hung it on the front of the wardrobe, then walked to the stationary I had on the side of the vanity and wrote a note to try to explain the condition of the dress.

I had to go to the water one last time. I am sorry.

I love you, Mother,

Adenne.

I took a pin from a drawer and attached the note to the front of the dress as I convinced myself that omitting the truth was not a lie.

Then I grabbed my pack and headed for the stables.

Other than their pilgrimage, a Ruler never really left the city of Polaris. All of their duties were here, so travel was unnecessary.

The only reason that Rulers learned to ride horses at all was the pilgrimage. The journey for the pilgrimage was demanding and strenuous, so it was the only way of travel that made sense.

Ever since my first day riding, I have loved being on horseback. There is something amazing about having the power over a huge beast, depending on the connection between you and the horse to be enough to convey where you want to go.

Onyx recognized my presence as soon as I walked through the stables. I heard her bristle in her stall at the end of the barn. There were not many other animals in there, only a few other horses, mainly to keep Onyx company. Sage would ride Scout, a slightly shorter horse with a gray-and-white spotted coat, when I wanted company. Sage did not find riding as enjoyable as I did.

When I first picked Onyx as my horse, my mother told me I was crazy. She was far too tall to be a reasonable horse for me. But her jet-black coat beckoned to me—when she looked me in the eye, I knew she was the one.

I walked to her now and saw her tail start flicking once she saw me. When I got close, she calmed, although I could still sense a restlessness under her surface. I stepped into her stall and rubbed my hand down her nose, and her eyes closed. Leaning in, I rested my forehead against hers. Her energy hummed against me.

"Okay," I said to her. "Are you ready?"

She didn't respond. It was going to be a quiet trip. I didn't want to be alone with only my thoughts. I wondered if my mother felt the same way. Did she revel in the solitude or hate it? It was a discussion we had never had. I hoped that when I returned, things would be calm enough for conversation again and that my failure would not damage our relationship beyond conversing. I hoped she would accept me no matter how this turned out.

I walked around Onyx and attached my bag to her saddle. Someone had already taken care of feeding and preparing her for the journey.

I mounted her and leaned forward to whisper, "We are not going where I thought we would. We have a different path to follow."

Onyx silently blinked up at me.

We trotted out of the barn and into the forest that surrounded it. These trees were not as tall as the ones near the water, and the ground was much more solid. The moon was large in the sky, giving me light through the night. I tried taking that as a sign that The Light was with me, but even the thought of it felt tinted in a lie. If The Light were with me, I wouldn't be where I am, nor would I feel this lonely. The Light was as present as the Deities.

As I directed Onyx through the undergrowth, I thought of what Ezrah had said about why the Deities had not shown up. He seemed so sure I could not be to blame. Nevertheless, I could see no alternative answer.

I did not know what I did to anger the Deities and push away The Light, but I would fix it. The Temple Majora would have the answers. I had to believe that. It was the last shred of hope I had.

These were the trees I practiced riding in, so I knew them well. But in the dead of night, the roots seemed wilder, the mossy ground more slippery. Navigating through these woods felt much more treacherous now, or maybe I just needed sleep.

When no one was awake, the sound of the forest in the middle of the night was eerily calming. A slight buzz of insects in the air broke up the silence. The noise they made came in waves, reminding me of how water moved. Occasionally, I would hear what I thought was a frog, then a bird swooping overhead. All that was out here was the animals.

There was a snapping sound behind me, and I pulled on Onyx's reins to stop her. I listened carefully for the sound I had heard to see if I could hear it again and locate where it came from, but the buzzing sound muted my senses. The insects wouldn't silence themselves because of me, so I waited. It felt like I was listening forever, not moving a single muscle. I heard three birds swoop and what I thought was another frog before I almost gave up. Onyx's tail flicked back and forth as her ears perked up, listening too. Then I heard it again. A sharp snapping and a shadow of movement. I couldn't tell if it was small or large, but it was likely an animal. This shouldn't be concerning, but my heart hammered in a warning. I looked over my shoulder like I expected something to jump out at me.

There were no animals here that were a threat to humans. We had killed them off long ago to ensure our safety, but if there was nothing big enough to be a threat, then what had made that loud sound?

I listened for what felt like forever, but the noise did not happen again. Even if it did, nothing could be done. I told myself it was an animal, then squeezed into Onyx's sides to move her forward.

I ignored the fact that Onyx had clearly heard the noise, too.

My shoulders were tense and my ears on high alert for the rest of the journey through the forest.

By the time I was coming close to the forest's edge, the sun was rising behind me. It painted the horizon ahead of me a beautiful light orange and then pink.

When the trees thinned, I was shocked at what I saw—I knew there was a clearing here, it showed on the map in my bag, but the expanse of it took my breath away. I could see straight across it, nothing rose above the horizon, just open space. Long ago, I learned what had happened here, but the story hadn't stuck. All I could remember was that this land used to be farmable and no longer was.

The openness made me feel exposed. Even though I could not see anybody ahead of me, it still felt like being out here was not safe. It felt like anyone could see me. I had always lived in the city, so an open field left me vulnerable.

A small strip of blue lined the horizon, growing as the sun rose. I grabbed my map and looked at where I was supposed to be headed versus where I was now going. They weren't far from each other, the Temple Majora just being more north and maybe a day further than where the Sisters lived. They were the ones who were supposed to give me my title after my pilgrimage. I doubted I would be *Adenne the Fair* anymore.

The Sisters lived in an old temple further west than the Temple Majora. I traced my hands along the map between here and there. No one knew why they lived there. They had been around almost as long as the Deities, but their history was not discussed in any of the texts.

The Temple Majora would take me an extra day to get to if I was lucky, but that was the most detail I could get from the map. If things went as planned, I could go to the Sisters afterward. If not, I didn't know where I would go.

Thankfully, it was known that pilgrimages happen in their own time. Some Rulers before me would take a very long time to contemplate the blessing they were given. Some came back quickly. Either way, my prolonged absence wouldn't cause any worry unless they figured out why I was taking so long.

I looked back up at the horizon quickly turning bluer in front of my eyes. It was the beginning of a season full of the hottest days in Polaris, and I could tell the sun would be high enough to cause some severe heat today. I needed to go.

I grabbed Onyx's reins again just as I heard a sound from behind me, the same snapping as before. It was large this time, inhuman.

I pulled up my hood anyway. If it was a person I may

have to flee. My heart hammered again. These last few hours I had done more damage to my heart than the rest of my life combined.

"Temple Majora is north," Ezrah said from behind me.

I took a deep breath as my pounding heart settled. "You are making a bad habit of sneaking up on me."

I would not turn to look at him. I would not take my hood down. His presence would not change anything about my plans.

"You're making a bad habit of not listening to your surroundings."

"You're the one who doesn't seem to be listening. I told you to leave me alone."

He trotted Scout, Sage's horse, up beside me, but I still would not look his way. At least Onyx was happy to see a friend.

Ezrah waited a long time, staring at the horizon before us. I wondered if he knew that staying in silence was one of the many things he did that triggered my irritation. He must do it on purpose.

"You did," he finally said, "but you also said that was how I could *help*. I was not so convinced that was the case."

"Oh, you weren't?"

"No."

"Since when are you interested in what is best for me?"

"Longer than you know," he said, his voice lower than usual. I did not shiver at the sound, but I pulled the cloak closer around me.

"Temple Majora is north, not west."

If this man continued to treat me like I was incompetent, I would push him from his horse.

"I am aware of that."

"Is that why you were facing west?"

"I only stopped because some strange, infuriating man had snuck up behind me."

He had the audacity to laugh. "So we agree you are headed north?"

"Of course I am." I huffed.

"And we agree that was not your original plan?"

I restrained myself from looking his way.

"How much do you love stating the obvious?"

He laughed again. I wasn't trying to be funny. "I do have a point in asking."

"I think we both know well enough I am no longer following the plan." I made a scene of a big sigh, throwing my hands into the air. "Well, get to it then, make your point. I don't have all day."

His voice became gentler. "You are going north now, not west. Now you will be traveling through many small villages full of people who were not expecting to see a Ruler on her voyage. They will not avert their gaze. They will not willingly keep their distance nor show you respect. The people in the villages you cross will only see a young, rich woman traveling alone. They will take advantage of you in every way you can think of. Wearing Sage's cloak instead of your own will not protect you." His voice verged on mocking. I had not thought about that, not that I would admit it. "You are not safe out here alone, and I may not be a Ruler's guard officially, but I am the only one who knows your secret, and I have sworn to keep the Ruler safe."

"I told you I am not a Ruler." I almost said *yet*.

"Yes, you are."

I looked at him then, shocked to hear the words come out of his mouth. When Sage told me he had joined the guard, I almost didn't believe her. Even when I ventured down to where they train and saw him there, I thought it was a lie. Hearing it come from his mouth still made me suspicious. He had stayed far away from me for two whole years, and as soon as he returned, he swore his life for mine. There was no way to make his actions make sense.

"You seem to have had a lot of time to think about this," I said.

"I didn't sleep."

"You can be executed for disrupting a Rulers pilgrimage." My gut twisted again at the thought of him being strapped down in the streets, left to let the sun consume him, starving until the birds picked the flesh off of his bones. His pain for all to see.

"I thought you weren't a Ruler," he joked.

"Ezrah."

He sighed. "It's a risk I'm willing to take."

I shook my head. "That's stupid."

He looked at me so deeply I swore he could see my every fear.

"I don't care," he said.

As much as I did not want him here, risking himself, his warnings made my heart race. They could easily be true, and I could go out there only to get myself in more trouble. I did not think the people of Rhea intended to hurt me, but they did not know who I was. My portrait wasn't hanging in their homes, nor had many ever seen me in person, let alone up close. They may not mean to harm a wandering stranger either, but my presence would come with unwanted attention, especially if I traveled alone. I could not risk anyone else knowing what had happened to me.

I let my facade drop. "Do you really think I would be at risk if I traveled alone?"

There was no smirk or playful tone to his voice. "Yes."

"How do you know?"

He looked back at the horizon. "Experience."

I wanted to convince myself that he was a liar, that he had always been a liar and making trouble was just his nature, especially when it came to me. He did hurt me, and I wouldn't forget that, but before he left, he cared for me in some capacity. It did not matter that I seemed to care for him more.

It's not as if I would trust him enough to let him back into my life or forgive him, but I didn't think he would ever want me dead. What he was describing seemed like it could be a death sentence if I wasn't lucky. So, I believed him. I was not going to be safe out there, and he was the only one who might be able to protect me. Even if he was not far into his training, having a man at my side would be protection enough. It did not matter who that man was. Women had come a long way to earn equal rights in this society, but that did not mean that men would show a woman the same respect they would another man.

I also hated the idea of having to do this alone, even if he was the only alternative. If this plan worked, and I became Ruler after all, I could protect him from the consequences of breaking tradition.

Not saying anything, I set my eyes to the north and squeezed Onyx to get moving. He followed.

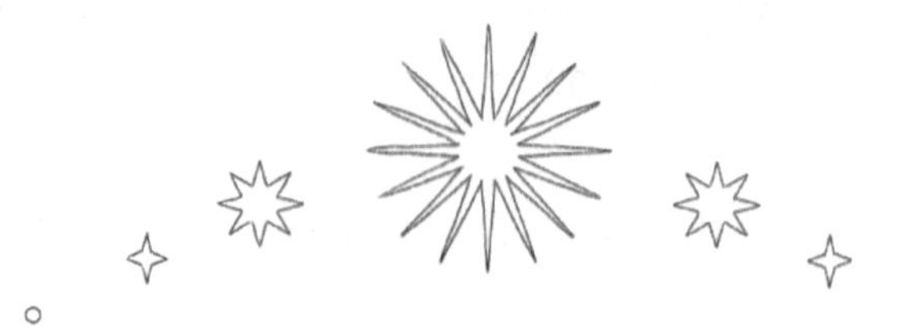

11

A World I Did Not Know

We did not make conversation. My mind swirled around my blessing or lack thereof, and I did not want to talk about that. I was tired of thinking about it, it made my head pound.

I considered asking him about his time out here. It only seemed natural, given our projected route. Two whole years he spent alone. Did he go this path, through the villages he warned me about? What kept him out here for so long?

But I did not want to talk about that either. The mystery of his time away acted like padding over the ache in my heart. I figured as long as I didn't know why he had left for so long; it couldn't hurt me. It was ignorance, but it was the safer option for me. That was the plan I had devised; keep as much distance as possible between us.

Which made all of this feel like a bad idea. I could feel his presence like heat. Every time he glanced at me, I felt like I was burning, my cheeks going red. He looked my way a lot.

"It's going to be a hot day," I said, finally. Then I turned my face away so he couldn't see my outward cringe.

The weather? I led with the *weather*.

"They're all hot days in Rhea."

The Light shows itself in the flickering flames in a home's hearth and in the sun's rays that grow green crops and light the way. Heat reminds us that The Light is always here.

The awkward silence continued, but it was better than small talk. Small talk with him felt wrong. Especially when there were so many significant conversations that never happened between us. I was also pretty sure small talk was useless with someone you have seen naked, or that broke your stupid, fragile heart into a million pieces. I swallowed the lump in my throat and urged the flush to leave my face as I reminded myself why the silence was better.

This was going to be a long trip. It would be difficult not to say anything, the same way it would be challenging to keep my mind from wondering how he felt about being back outside Polaris. Did this make him wish he'd never left or wish he'd never returned? That would fall under the category of a significant conversation.

Being out here with him did not align with my plan to keep my distance, not that any of my plans seemed to work out lately.

Hours passed as the sun beat down, my cloak heating under the bright rays. Even so, I did not take it off. The cloak gave me anonymity that comforted me more than the heat irritated me, and so I kept it on despite the fact there was no one around. A bead of sweat rolled down the back of my neck.

Minutes passed, and my fingers drummed against the saddle. I was growing irritated and itchy.

Ezrah rode Sage's horse.

I did not know how he knew that one was hers. He was nowhere to be found when we learned how to ride them. He was also not around to learn himself, although he always said he would have wanted to.

"When did you learn?" I asked, my voice rough with disuse already.

"Learn what?"

I gestured to his horse.

"To ride?" He asked.

I nodded.

"While I was away."

And I found the end of the conversation quicker than it started.

I didn't want to know more, so I didn't push the discussion further, even though I had a sinking suspicion that he wanted me to. Whether that was because he hated the silence as much as I did or because he wanted me to know more about the past two years was not clear. Instead, I nodded and let us fall back into a silence that was growing increasingly more present.

I hid my slight grin at the thought of this silence making him uncomfortable.

As we rode forward, I swore I heard him inhale as if he was going to speak before deciding not to. He did not know how to be around me anymore, which widened my grin. There had to be some consequence to his actions, to his leaving. Sage had welcomed him back, as she should, but I would not. I wanted him to feel regret, and in this awful silence, I thought he did.

The sun grew high, and the open land showed no signs of changing. Dirt pounded below our feet—a stark contrast from the lush forests surrounding Polaris.

"I always knew the land was dry here," I said finally, unable to help myself. I heard him exhale in relief. "It shows so on the map. I did not realize how far it went."

Ezrah nodded. "It made a big difference to the families that lived here at the time, they lost all of their farmable lands. Now they fight for space up north."

"What happened here, again?" I asked, then immediately felt ridiculous. That was the kind of history I was supposed to know. Ezrah looked at me with an eyebrow raised. "I forget." I blushed. "I am allowed to forget things, and I haven't studied those texts in years."

One side of his mouth tipped up teasingly, making me want to punch him in the gut.

"No one really knows what happened, it was a long time ago. All they know is that a Ruler had angered the Deities at some point, likely a lack of donation at a ceremony, so Justus lit the crop on fire." His eyes clouded over like the distant pain remained generations after. I wondered who told him this. "It was ablaze for days. They assumed the Deities energy seeped into the ground when it finally stopped. They couldn't farm this land, but they tried for years."

I felt his words settle deep in my gut, weighing me down. The story sounded familiar, but something in Ezrah's tone made it sound personal. The people who had lived here had their whole lives taken from them for something beyond their control. I now understood the clouding of his eyes and why his tone had changed. The ground beneath Onyx seemed tainted by this new knowledge. Still, it didn't make sense.

"The Deities took fertile ground away when they were displeased with how little was donated? That is… counterproductive. It doesn't make sense. There must be more to the story."

Ezrah eyed me for a minute, not saying anything. I felt a sweat pool where my hands gripped the reins. Finally, he shrugged. "There could be." He didn't believe that. "That was the story I was told. Sometimes the Deities act without reason."

His words were as dangerous as they were unexpected. The boy I knew did not speak this way about the Deities. He was the most devout child I knew, raised in the palace Temple by two Devoted. He followed The Light without any hesitation. Had things happened differently, he likely would have become Devoted himself. This doubt he had now made it clear this was not the same man. It was an uneasy reminder that I did not know this stranger who rode beside me.

"There is always a reason for what they do," I said.

When I looked at him, I could see the argument in his eyes, like he wanted to challenge me, but couldn't. I knew what he was thinking.

If there was a reason for everything the Deities do, why are we here?

He was wise enough not to say anything. I was wise enough to drop the topic.

When the sun was at high noon, we decided to eat. We did not have much time, but when Ezrah spotted water up ahead, we dismounted and walked the horses toward it. It was a rest stop intended for merchants traveling to the city. Bales of hay for the horses sat near the water. My great-grandfather had created these stops during his time ruling. I was unsure if it was due to what he learned in his blessing or if it was a request from those who live outside the city wall.

The horses needed a break just as much as I needed to stretch my legs. While they drank, I grabbed the bread and dried meat from my bag and handed some to Ezrah.

The first few bites rolled around like stones in my stomach, and I did not finish the small loaf in my hands.

If Ezrah noticed, he chose not to mention it, which was another significant change from the boy I knew. That boy was never contemplative about what he said. The words would come out of his mouth before he realized he was talking. This man was more calculating in his choices.

Usually, I had no issue eating and would have devoured the bread, but something else had changed. The last full meal I had was days before the party. Food didn't sit well anymore, and that wasn't healthy. I hoped it would change.

I tucked what I had not eaten back into my bag, and we

mounted the horses. I ran my hand up and down Onyx's neck as if to say: *sorry, girl, time to get back to it.* The break had been long enough, I thought. I had never ridden her this far out before, but I would keep an eye on her to ensure she didn't seem too tired. It was the best I could do.

Finally, the horizon before us broke with the first sign of life. In the distance, I could see fields of green popping up, sectioned into pieces by taller trees.

I didn't realize how much I craved seeing green again. The landscape before was full of death, this was full of life.

When we got closer, I noticed that the row of trees that separated one type of crop from another had a small dirt path beside it. There were track marks left from previous carts traveling in the shade of these trees. We took that path, our two horses crowding the narrow space. I could sense relief from the horses being in the shade, and it mirrored my own. I let the cloak fall back, exposing myself again. The air hit me like a cool breeze despite the lack of wind.

We were not on this path long before we saw someone headed toward us with a horse and cart. Ezrah led us to the side of the road, tucking me in behind him.

"Keep your eyes down," he said, and I heard the tightness in his voice.

"It is just a merchant," I argued.

"Eyes. Down." He practically growled.

I looked at him instead and saw how tight he held his jaw and the way his dark eyes almost glowed in a dangerous warning. The way he tilted his body and kept me in his shadow was protective. It was almost feral.

I looked down at the sleekness of Onyx's coat as the man

passed us.

As he trotted away, I saw reels of brightly colored fabric sticking out of his cart. We had a few mills and factories operating outside Polaris that many of the people of Rhea worked at. He must have been transporting some of the goods.

A merchant, just as I expected.

Over the cart, I could feel the older man's eyes on me, and I looked at him on instinct. I knew it was not wise, but I was not raised to keep my head down or hide who I was. This was all new to me.

Ezrah exhaled as he watched the merchant's retreating form.

"I told you to keep your eyes down," he told me. His eyes still glowed in that dangerous, intriguing way.

"You think that man meant us harm? He had to be 75 years old, Ezrah."

"Harm doesn't have to be physical."

I let out a gasp of air that resembled a laugh. "And how else would he harm us?"

"He could have recognized you."

My heart jumped to my throat, knowing he was right.

"He didn't," I swallowed despite my mouth being dry.

"You're sure?" He asked, knowing his point was getting through.

"Yes."

Exasperated, he shook his head. "It's better to be cautious."

"Of old merchants?"

"Of everybody," he said.

The intensity of his glare made me swallow deeply. I did

not know the area beyond Polaris as he did. That much was clear, but I refused to fear everyone we would see. They were *my* people.

Well, they may become my people one day.

I looked at the man retreating, then at the sky above him. Gray clouds were in the distance, likely over the top of Polaris, a bad sign. As if on cue, a cold wind blew at us.

"We better get going," he said, noting the same sky I had as he urged Scout forward.

As we moved, I finally let us fall into conversation.

I asked him about the row of trees, and he explained they divide the farms from one another. Ezrah said farmers could be territorial.

I asked about what crops were growing.

"Wheat to the right, likely barley to the left."

"It is still early in the season, then?"

He nodded. "They plant while the weather is not overly hot. The crops will grow over the hottest months."

I nodded along. "By The Light's generosity," I said.

"By the work of the farmers."

"Of course. Our farmers feed our city. I am grateful for their work." I looked over the endless fields of short crops and thought of how large the piles of dried wheat and barley were at the blessing, and those were only the piles I saw. "The crops at the blessing must have been last year's crops, then?"

His tone got darker now. "Yes. Most of last year's crop was dried and preserved for the blessing."

"Most?"

He nodded.

I looked around me and thought of how many crops must

have lined the streets beyond what I saw. It was supposed to please the Deities, to ensure a good blessing. My stomach clenched together.

"And when will this crop be harvested?"

Ezrah was factual and cold. "The same as every year, once the weather turns cold." He acted like he was explaining this to someone who would never fully grasp the situation rather than someone who was desperately trying to. He made me read between the lines of his thinly veiled information.

"That is still a long way away. What will the people eat until then?"

His gaze stayed on the road in front of him. "The people of Polaris will be fine."

"And the others? What of the ones not in the city?"

Ezrah still didn't look at me. Instead, he looked up at the sky as if he was looking for a way out of this. "Hopefully," he said tightly, "they will have enough to survive until then."

Hopefully.

All for a blessing that didn't happen. A lot was given up to ensure I could take care of these people. The thought of stretching food long enough to survive made my already-clenching stomach twist. People would suffer, and because of me, the suffering would have no purpose.

"Surely they would have kept enough," I said softly, mostly to convince myself.

Ezrah sighed. He was at the end of giving his responses gently. "Give too little, and you can be reprimanded for withholding a donation. Give too much, and your family starves."

My hands clenched the reins. That did not seem right.

But surely a generous donation would bring good fortune to these people. They would benefit from their generosity if they survived.

Or if they had a Ruler to ensure good fortune.

Guilt weighed down my shoulders, slumping my back involuntarily.

"I was never taught that," I whispered. That was never discussed with me, by my mother or in the texts. It was possible she didn't know. When I returned, I would tell her.

He shook his head. "It is not taught past the walls of Polaris. I didn't know either before I left. Things aren't … they aren't good out here a lot of the time. But it is the way it is." His coldness melted into something sad.

"Because of the Deities," I supplied.

"Because of the Rulers," he said. My gaze cut to his, but he was already looking at me. "The Deities may have made the rule, but the Rulers enforce it." His gaze softened with sympathy. "At least that is how the people out here see it."

"That's what they think?"

Ezrah shrugged, but I could still see the tenseness in his shoulders. "The people out here are angry, Adenne. At the Ruler and The Light. I would imagine it is hard to be devote if you see your family starving."

My back straightened. "It is not as if my mother and father know this is happening. When they do, I am sure they will find a solution."

I found myself defending a statement I was not sure was the truth. While I was certain my parents would do whatever they could for the people, I also knew the risk of offending the Deities was great. I only had to think of the barren fields behind us to be sure.

When Ezrah didn't speak again, I tried to convince him. "If I get to rule," my voice caught. *If.* "I will find a solution."

"You will rule."

I looked at the man beside me again, how the jawline that used to be soft cut across the side of his face now, how his cheekbones were more pronounced. It was not a face I recognized, nor was the confidence.

The air was trapped in my lungs.

"How can you be so sure of something you know nothing about?" I asked in a single breath.

He shrugged, nothing a big concern to him. "How can you be so uncertain about something you know everything about?"

I shook my head, but he didn't see it. "I don't know everything about this, clearly."

"You know everything the texts offer you. You know every book in that library."

The thought of the library made my stomach twist again. By now, it was a gigantic knot inside of me. "The library I ruined."

He looked at me then and just stared. I wanted to shrink away under his gaze. I hadn't realized the heat I felt from him when we left Polaris had faded until it was back. It was so intense it stung.

Clearing his throat, he looked forward again. "It wasn't that bad."

I thought of the maimed pile of books on the floor. "How can you be sure of that, too?"

He reached one hand up to rub the back of his neck. "I

went back to check before I talked to Sage. I wanted to cover your tracks."

"You spoke with Sage?"

"To tell her I was leaving. I didn't tell her why, though."

How would that sound to a sister who just had her brother return after so long away?

"And she was okay with that?"

He looked at me. "I made it clear I would return in a few days."

I nodded and thought again of the library. I felt guilty when I thought of the books, but I never once thought that they would be a sign of something wrong. "Thank you."

He didn't accept my thanks.

We came to a spot where the trees broke into four different family fields. There was a small stream here and we dismounted the horses to let them drink again.

My legs ached as soon as my feet hit the ground. This aching feeling would only increase the further we traveled, and the thought of that alone was agonizing.

Rain sounded in the distance, and I internally groaned. Ezrah looked to where the storm was coming from and turned quickly. He came before me and pulled the hood of Sage's cape around me. The gesture was sweet, and I started to flush until he said, "Keep your eyes down this time."

I looked back at the rain only to see the same merchant as before coming swiftly toward us.

My heart skipped in my chest. Him returning was not a good sign.

He pulled to a stop before us, and Ezrah stepped in front of me. This time I took his advice.

"Hi there," the man said, his tone friendly.

Ezrah crossed his arms in front of him. "Can we help you?"

The man laughed, but it had a hollowness to it. "I was going to ask you the same thing," he said. When Ezrah didn't return his faked good nature, he continued, "I saw you two on the road earlier and thought to myself, 'What are two young people doing traveling alone?' I wanted to ensure you weren't lost." He emphasized the last word in a way that made me shiver. I resisted the urge to pull the cloak around me tighter.

"We're not lost," Ezrah said after a long pause.

I could feel the man's glare on me. I stepped closer to Ezrah and found comfort hiding in his shadow. I placed my hand on the small of his back.

"I suppose you're not."

The man did not take his eyes off me. It would not be wise to raise my gaze to his, despite wanting to. I was taught to meet the gaze of men like this, men that thought they could intimidate a woman.

"We will be on our way now," Ezrah said, quickly turning to help me onto Onyx. I did not need the help, but I accepted it anyway.

"Of course," the man said from behind me. "I hope you have a safe journey."

Ezrah didn't return the sentiment.

We did not speak as the man retreated behind us, but one question kept playing in my head.

If I was alone, what would that man have done? I could still feel his eyes on me, like he could see through my weak disguise of someone else's cloak.

I shivered at the thought.

I was full of questions, but I made myself stay silent until I knew we were far enough away from the merchant. The sun was setting, and the fields were empty when I finally spoke.

"Do you think he recognized me?"

My voice startled Ezrah out of some intense thoughts.

"I… I don't know. Honestly, I don't. I hope not, but that was…"

"Odd?" I supplied.

"To say the least."

I could almost hear his brain working hard, trying to decipher just how much trouble we were in. Still, I couldn't stop myself from asking more questions.

"Do you think it was weird that he left so suddenly? That he didn't ask us more questions."

Ezrah's answer was more immediate than I expected. "Yes."

My throat felt tight. If the man recognized me and then proceeded towards Polaris so suddenly, he could be going to tell someone he saw the Ruler, off her pilgrimage path, with someone else and with dark brown eyes. He could have seen enough to expose me.

"So what do we do?" I asked.

Ezrah rubbed his hand down his face, stress seeping off him in a tangible way.

"I am going to diverge our path only a little. I know a clearing just west of here where we can camp for the night. Tomorrow we will just be more vigilant." He sighed. "That's all we can do."

The confidence that usually irritated me was comforting,

and I was grateful to be out here with someone with solutions. Ezrah kept me from spiraling out of control.

"Okay," I said.

We said very little else as the sun fell in the sky and the dark of night came. Thankfully, the threatening rain stayed behind us. The moon was almost full, illuminating the small patch of ground in the clearing that Ezrah had mentioned. We were among sparse trees, far enough away from any main road that would expose us.

Suspended between distant fields, we had enough room to set up camp and enough distance to feel somewhat secluded.

This was where we would rest for the evening, although I doubted sleep would come to me. No one was around, but I felt a million eyes on me.

12

Breaking Tradition

T hat was one of the coldest, most annoying nights of my life for two reasons.

One, Ezrah neglected to bring his own tent. He did not acknowledge this fact, and neither did I.

Two, the tent I had brought with me was made for one person, so it was difficult to keep my distance from him. Still, I persevered.

My body hugged the thin canvas of one side of the tent, the wind pushing the fabric into me. The sound of the gusts was deafening as they ripped across the open field. It penetrated the tent and blew into my bones. My whole body felt the chill. Rhea was often unbearably hot during the day, but the nights were dangerously cold. I tugged Sage's cloak closer to me, and for the first time, I wished I had taken the emerald cloak I was expected to wear. It was much thicker and larger, and I knew I would have been sleeping soundly under it instead of tossing and turning as shivers raked my body.

Ezrah, on the other hand, had no trouble sleeping. His big body was shoved against the opposite side of the tent. One arm stretched up to rest under his head. He did not look cold. The man radiated heat. If I rolled closer, I would feel it rolling off him in waves.

Instead of shivering like me, he looked relaxed as he slept. His profile was barely visible in the darkness, but even with the pale moonlight, I could tell his features had softened. His jawline wasn't as pronounced and it was lined with the short beard he had had since the day he returned to Polaris. His brow didn't have that furrowed expression that it often had these days. In his sleep, he looked younger, like he was the boy I knew and not the man that existed now. As I laid there and looked at his profile, his chest slowly rising up and down, I could almost pretend this was a different time, that we were different people.

As children, Ezrah and I would rest beside each other. On more than one occasion, we had gone out to our waterfall and stayed too late, eventually falling asleep on the nearby rocks. Once, he had told me the bugs would glow if we waited up long enough at night.

"I've read about them, Addie," he had said.

I remembered being adamant in my reply. "You were reading fiction, Ezrah. They can't be *real*."

"*They are*," he had insisted.

We went out there and stayed awake as long as possible, waiting to see the glowing bugs. Instead, we fell asleep beside each other, Ezrah with his arm bent behind his head and me tucked into his side.

That night I dreamt of waking up and being surrounded

by glowing spots that encircled us as we laid there, the light creating a beautiful pattern while the waterfall roared in the distance.

I wished we could return to being those people, but dreaming about the blissful ignorance of my youth would not stop the reality of my present.

When I finally did manage to fall asleep, I was assaulted with an image that was new but also strangely familiar.

I run towards the wall that protects the north side of Polaris, tripping on my skirt. Blood pounding, I know I'm not running towards something but away from someone. I trip on my last step, my hands catching my fall against the wall. Heat cascades up my legs as flames engulf the light pink fabric. Before I can reach to put it out, large wings flap in front of me. A woman lands, scaled black wings tucked behind her back. Long, sleek ebony hair goes almost to her waist and her almond shaped eye winks at me.

She glows. Not golden light like I expected but a deep, almost blue hue radiates from her pale skin. Before I can say something, she holds one finger in front of her mouth, silencing me.

I woke with a start in the same canvas tent, still shivering. The heat from the flames had completely faded, but the sight of that strange face had not. I tried to bring it into focus, forcing myself to remember the details even through my fog of sleep. I could picture only pieces of her.

Sleep found me again more suddenly than it has in years. I rested deeply for the few hours left of the night and woke to Ezrah leaving through the fabric doors in the morning. The tent was filled with dampness and a swampy heat that I was unaccustomed to at home. Sweat stuck to my skin. It coated my scalp under my fingers as I tried to tame my hair which was unruly after that restless night. My arms felt weak as I moved them, and even sitting, I could feel the muscles between my legs aching from a full day of riding.

The sun outside the tent was bright, and I lifted my hand to cover my eyes. Ezrah had walked the horses across a small field where there was water. I could see him bend to fill up the canteen from my pack.

When he came back, he looked incredibly well-rested. His eyes didn't have the dark circles under them that mine surely had.

In fact, he looked… nice. A full day on the road suited him more than it damaged him. Every part of me felt sore from the journey, but he seemed more alive than he had in the month since his return.

He smiled at me as he got closer, his white teeth contrasting with the darker complexion of his skin. It was distracting.

When I didn't return the smile, his hand rubbed nervously against his chest—also distracting.

I needed sleep.

He handed me the canteen. "Did you sleep well?"

I knew that the sight of me made it clear that I didn't. I had done a lousy job taming my hair, and it fell around me in knots. I felt drained and dehydrated. I most certainly looked unbecoming. And I was exhausted.

The blurring image of that glowing woman swam through my mind. "No," I said simply, then took a sip.

He bit his lip to hold back his amusement at my morning

temperament. My mind must be foggy with sleep because I was very distracted by his mouth.

It warmed parts of me that hadn't felt this way about him in years. It had been a while since I had felt this way at all.

It was the lack of sleep or my body trying to distract me from the fear I woke up with.

I anxiously gulped more water, then returned it to his outstretched hand. He took a drink from it, too.

It seemed he didn't bring his own canteen, the same way he didn't bring his own tent.

He put the cap on like the thought of sharing the container was no concern to him at all. But he wasn't distracted by mouths and what sharing could imply. He likely had no reason to see anything wrong with it.

Not that I was truly distracted. I was just… sleep-deprived.

Before he could turn back to me, I walked to the water and splashed some on my face. The coldness woke me up and took away the swelling behind my eyes. I repeated the motion a few more times, hoping my mind would work properly instead of in this distracting and confusing way. Then, I took the leather tie from my hair that hung loosely at the back and tried to re-tie it at the top of my head. I had very little experience doing my own hair. When the bun quickly slipped out, I tried to braid it down the middle, but my fingers were fumbling through the task, making more knots than progress.

Ezrah came up beside me.

"Here," he said, gesturing to my head.

"What?"

"Let me—" His outstretched hand waved around in the

air as he reached towards me.

"Let you what?"

"Let me—"

"Braid my hair?"

He nodded.

My answer was quick. "No."

Not after last night, not after my wandering thoughts. No way.

He didn't give me much of an option as he came behind me and wedged the tufts of hair away from my hands. "Don't be ridiculous, Addie. I'm not going to sit here and watch you struggle. You don't know what you're doing—we could be here for hours."

"And you know what you're doing?"

His fingers separated my hair into three different parts. "Yes."

Now that he was behind me, a smile he couldn't see pulled at my lips. "I didn't know you knew how to braid hair."

He was quiet and contemplative as his fingers worked to untangle the mess I had made. "I've done it for Sage a few times."

I shivered as his fingers lightly tugged at my scalp. "Really?"

I could tell in his voice that his mind was elsewhere. "She couldn't reach the ones at the back of her head. Our mother would sometimes do them for her, but she was busy often. Sage taught me."

My stomach twisted into itself. "Oh."

His voice twisted into something brighter, trying to lift the weight from this conversation. "I got quite good at it. This is going to be much better than whatever knot you were about to create."

"I know how to braid my hair." Just not well.

He laughed. "I don't think you've ever had to braid your own hair, Addie."

That was true, but I wouldn't admit it. "Right, well. Thank goodness I have you then."

His hands were at the base of my skull and he gently tugged my hair there, tilting my head back to look him in the eye. The tingling started at my head and worked its way down as I felt his breath on my lips.

"What did you just say?" he asked.

"Nothing," I whispered.

"I think you just admitted you are grateful I am here."

He didn't let go, and I ignored the way I couldn't seem to breathe. "Not in so many words." I argued.

His grip loosened. "No, you always were careful of your words, Addie."

I looked forward to the small river. "And you always knew what I was saying, anyway," I whispered, almost to myself.

My cheeks blushed. His fingers worked their way to the ends of my hair, brushing my neck and back as he went, leaving shivers in their wake. My heart pounded, and I worried he was close enough to hear it.

"You're all done." Ezrah took the braid and laid it over my shoulder.

He walked over to the tent and began packing up as I stood by the small river, composing myself. I splashed more cold water on my face and willed my mind not to think of Ezra's fingers at the base of my skull, blazing dresses or scaled wings. I took deep breaths until I felt slightly calmer.

"Thank you," I said as I walked up to the packed horses and played with the ends of my braid.

"You're welcome," he replied, reaching up to rub the back of his neck without turning around.

I could feel his eyes on me as I mounted Onyx. Now that I was more awake, I could feel an awful tension in the air. One that my distracted mind and out-of-control, tingling body created. It would have been better to ignore the past, but unfortunately, my past rode right beside me all day long. If I said something, I could likely make this more comfortable for both of us.

With my foot in the stirrup, I said, "I haven't slept well these last few days."

He looked shocked, although I was unsure if it was mocking or genuine. "You used to sleep like the dead."

I nodded. "I used to. In the last two years, that's changed."

The double meaning was unintentional. I was trying to be polite, but still, I hoped he understood what my words meant.

The nightmares started just after he made love to me and then left without a fucking word.

I pulled the hood of my cloak up. He didn't say anything back to me, letting me deal with the mix of guilt and satisfaction all on my own.

We rode in that silence, passing fields of different crops. The sun was now stuck behind gray clouds. It seemed like it wanted to escape them, but the clouds were persistent in their coverage. Humidity hung in the air like a promise of rain. The lack of The Light on this journey was not a message lost on me.

Slowly, I saw more people in the fields we passed—women and men bent over, their backs arched. They tended to their fields, ensuring the crops they grew were suitable for the Deities and The Light, even if that meant they would not have enough to keep for themselves.

The thought made me sick again. I watched the curved backs as we passed, imagined the ache they must feel, and wondered if they were hungry.

One man was closer to the edge of the field that we passed. I saw his tanned skin from years of working under the sun. Even from my horse, I could see that the skin of his face was dry and peeling. Despite the clouds today, sweat still dripped down his brow.

When he bent over, I swore I could see the bumps of his spine through his thin shirt.

He was the only person who did not pay attention to us. Every other person in the fields looked up as we passed, their eyes tracking our movements. Ezrah's back stiffened with every set of eyes. He kept his gaze forward, but I sensed the tension rolling from him. He did not wear the hood of his cloak, fully exposing himself to their stares.

I wondered again if he had been here before and if he knew these people. I realized that it was unlikely and that the lands around Polaris were wide, but his knowledge of this place seemed vast.

Still, I wouldn't ask him. I pictured him here instead, tending to the field. His back twisted over just like the others. His stomach empty. The thought made mine knot. Still, he must have been happy out here. He stayed.

He must have been miserable before if he was happy enough to stay out here.

I understand where his misery came from, I saw it daily in Sage. The loss of one parent must be difficult, but to lose both at the same time could destroy you. If he found joy out here, doing whatever he was doing, I could be happy for him.

But then, what had made him come back?

This new man was a mystery to me. I used to know everything about him, but now I journeyed with a stranger.

Did he feel the same way? That I had changed in the last two years? Up until yesterday, I hadn't felt any different.

Now everything in my life was different.

The thought weighed on me less each time I thought about it. It was as if my mind was growing neutral to the fact that my life would not be the one I had expected. I still felt the same guilt of letting people down, the same shame of having to tell them if this all went wrong—those thoughts were the ones that would sink me.

But the actual change? My mind held less concern about that. Instead, my mind seemed to instinctually focus on the nightmare I had the night before. The images played themselves on a loop as I tried to figure out what exactly was wrong with what I saw. My gut knew something was out of place. She had glowed like my mother had described the Deities, but not in the way I expected. She held no light in her, no golden complexion. I saw her long black hair and her form outlined by those wings.

It was the wings my mind clung to. Scaled.

Every depiction I had seen of the Deities had them surrounded in golden feathers.

So, if she was not a Deity, what was she? And why did

she tell me to stay quiet? Was it some kind of message?

Or was I just more exhausted than I knew?

The sun would have been above us if the clouds allowed it. Midday came quickly as we continued north. Eventually, I saw something other than trees and fields in the distance. Buildings pierced the sky along the horizon.

"What is that?" My voice was hoarse.

He looked up. "A village, a small one. It's where some of the families that run these fields live."

"They live together?"

He spoke as if he was lost in a memory that made him uncomfortable. "It's safer that way."

That didn't make any sense. There was no threat to them here. No thieves like in the city, and no wild animals that would be an issue. The pelts of the most dangerous ones decorated the walls of those in the upper society. I had seen them firsthand.

"Safer from what?"

His eyes cut to me. My questions always seemed to shock him, like he expected me to know everything about life out here. Maybe I should, but he was the one who spoke as if he lived it. Only so much could be learned from the texts.

He sighed like he didn't want to explain it. I didn't care, I wanted to learn.

"Some of the landowners out here have more power than they should. It is safer for the smaller farms to band together."

"Power, how? How did they get it?"

"They would have been one of the first families to be given this land, which is why they still own it. Many new farmers don't own the land themselves—"

"Who does?"

I could feel his eyes examining me. "You do. Or the Ruler's family does."

"Oh."

He looked forward again. "The Rulers from long ago didn't want farmers to have too much control, so they started to take back the land. They said it was what they were told to do by the Deities in their blessing. The farmers who had land at the time didn't like that. They wanted the power that they had before. Instead of having a large group of people working under them, they now had less land and worked only with their own families and the ones that stayed with them. Many workers left to pursue their farms."

"It sounds like they have a little power back now, though."

He nodded, probably grateful I was finally following along. "They do, but it took a long time to earn it back. Now they will do anything to keep it and monopolize their power."

"Like what?"

He shrugged the shoulder closest to me. "Reroute water to their own fields, bribe their way to better seeds, better crops. The ones that were best at manipulating their way to the top eventually got horses and Oxen. They could cultivate enough crops that they were the only ones with food to spare."

"You've seen this?" It was out before I could think.

Ezrah nodded. "I spent some time out here working for some of them."

I tried to keep my mind from repainting that picture of him in the fields, of him finding joy in manual labor despite its struggles.

"Did you work for someone with power?"

He paused, and that same cloud came over his eyes. "I worked for someone that would do anything to have it."

I did not push him further, unsure if I wanted to know. The more I learned, the more sympathy I had, and he hadn't done enough to earn that compassion from me.

Soon enough, we came to the road that ran between the buildings. They were tiny houses, all made of wood with thatched roofs. None of them were bigger than my bedroom at the palace.

A few children were in the streets, kicking a ball and chasing each other around. Their playful sounds halted when I came into view. Not a single one was over the age of ten.

They stared at us like the people in the field did, but the children were funny. They didn't have the same distrust in their eyes. Instead, it was pure curiosity.

I could tell by looking at them they were likely not from the same families. There was a boy with dark hair, whose skin mirrored Ezrah's. Beside him was a girl. I would put her around eight years old. She held a younger girl in her arms, but I didn't see any family resemblance between the two.

Even though I was far away, I could see that every one of them was too thin.

"Where are their parents?" I asked, that sick, twisting

feeling coming back to me.

How did I not know that this is how my people lived?

Not my people. They were not my people. The twisting inside of me made me want to buckle over.

"Working in the fields," Ezrah said. "We likely passed them."

"They are here alone all day?"

"They don't have a choice."

One kid was braver than the rest. He came closer to Onyx and smiled at me. I could see his collar bones sticking out unnaturally from the top of his ripped tunic. Even his neck looked thin. I smiled back at him, looking at this frail child, defenseless against the life that he was born into. Only when my eyes moved down his body did I notice his arm was deformed at the end. His fingers curled into themselves, rigid at his side.

I stopped the horse. "Don't," Ezrah said from behind me. I ignored him.

I may never rule these people or get a chance to help them. The weight of that finally came back to me, and I felt ill. Bile rose in my throat, and I swallowed it, feeling it burn.

This may be my only chance to help them.

Swinging my legs, I dismounted Onyx before Ezrah could offer more protests. I reached into my saddlebag, brushing my fingers along Onyx's side to calm her as the children moved closer to us.

All our food was wrapped in a piece of white cloth. Bread, cheese, dried meat, and some apples. It was barely enough to keep the two of us and the horses fed. I took out two small loaves of bread and some dried meat for us and put it back into the bag.

Then I turned with the rest of it in my hand. The child had already stepped closer to me. I could feel the crowd's gaze, but it wasn't on me. It was on what was in my hand. I bent to his level, my eyes meeting his. Despite his circumstance, they had all of the kindness and innocence a child is expected to have.

This was not a solution to his problem, but it was a start.

I held the food to him, and he wordlessly took it from me.

Then he ran down the street, the children following him. I watched their forms retreat behind their houses, scattering like scared animals.

Once we were alone, Ezrah hesitated for a long time before he cleared his throat and said, "That was kind, and I understand why you did it. I want to make that clear before I say this." I did not like the tone his voice had taken. "That food will do them little good. It would do a lot more good if it got you to the Temple Majora."

"And we will get there." I would not let him taint this moment for me. "We can find more food. They cannot." I looked at him. His eyes told me he didn't believe me.

Would it really be difficult for us to find more?

Did I care?

My voice was practically a whisper. "You cannot expect me to watch them starve."

I felt tears rise as he looked at me. I watched his expression soften as one of his hands rose to grasp the back of his neck. His hard resolve had faded away. It was not wise of me to give away our food, nor was it fair to give away his, but these children had never known fairness, and this may be the only chance I have to give it to them.

My only chance to help them.

"Okay," he said, finally.

I mounted Onyx again, and we continued north.

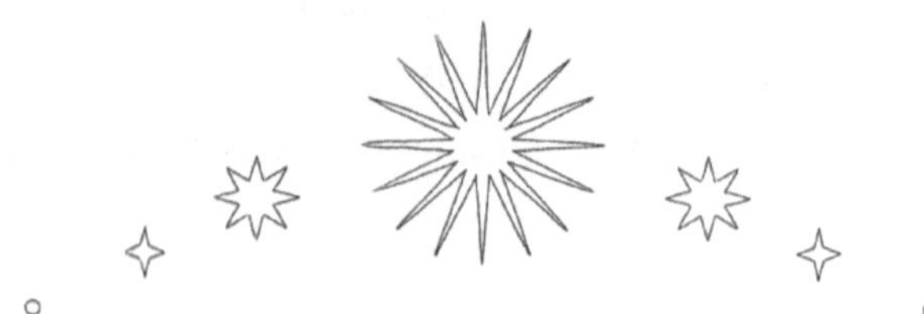

13

In The Hands of The Predator

By dusk, another village could be seen in the distance.

This one was bigger than the last, both in the size of the houses and the number of people. As we passed the farmers working in the fields, that look of uncertainty remained in their eyes.

The closer we got, the more tension rolled off of Ezrah. I could feel it increase with every passing glare. It rolled off of him the same way heat and confidence did. I could always sense these reactions from him.

I knew that the Deities had a way with energy. It was how they could control things like the weather and ruin fields so large that the land was not farmable decades later. It was one of the only things past Rulers had talked about in their blessing: the energy radiating in the room. The Light itself was a type of energy, and the Deities had a piece of it.

I wanted to understand why there was so much tension in his shoulders. "You've been here." It was not a question.

He nodded.

I waited. He did not say more.

I had no idea how to respond.

I used to know how his mind worked. I could almost read it, pull out the bad and make it better. Now I came up blank.

He pulled Scout to a stop just on the outskirts of the village, on the edge of a field growing low green crops. I pulled on Onyx's reins and rested my hand on her neck as she whinnied.

"We're stopping?"

He got off of his horse. "I am going to go get us some more food."

He came up beside me. Ezrah ran his hand along Onyx, who began flickering her tail. She must feel his energy, too. Then he reached into my bags and pulled out the small satchel of coins someone had packed for me.

"Is that wise?" He cut a look at me. "I mean, will they even have anything to sell?"

I watched his brow slowly unravel as he let out a big sigh. "If anyone will, it's these people." He put his hand on my knee. "I will be fine, Addie."

My heart jumped. "Of course."

I didn't believe his words, but I swallowed the worry. The tension in his shoulders gave him away. Something here concerned him.

I was on high alert as he walked away. Thank The Light, I was close enough to watch him enter the village. It did not take long for a man to approach him. More accurately, the man stopped him in his tracks. He was tall and thin. His shaggy black hair contrasted his skin which was still pale despite working out in the sun. The only exception was the bright shade of pink on the man's shoulders.

A crowd gathered behind the man, watching their interaction. Not a single one of them looked happy. Tension hung in the air now so thick I could choke on it. It made my lungs rise and fall quickly.

After a long moment, the man turned and walked into the biggest building on the left side of the street. I breathed a sigh of relief while mentally scolding myself for not asking more questions about his time away. If I had known more about why he was out here, I could have prepared better for whatever this was. I could have helped. Instead, I watched from the sidelines, having no idea what situation Ezrah had thrown us into.

He wasn't the one who threw us into this, I reminded myself. I was the one who gave up our food. His reluctance was starting to make sense.

The tall man with dark hair returned, followed by the largest man I had ever seen.

This man made Ezrah look small, which was a feat. He towered a head over him and must have been twice as wide. His body was pure corded muscle. The large man had dark hair like the other one, but his was cropped short. Instead of contrasting with his skin, this man's complexion had turned dark, evidence of the years spent working in the fields.

The crowd gathered closer around the three of them. I didn't breathe as I watched them exchange words. My gut twisted in a way that was becoming familiar. Ezrah's arms were crossed in front of his chest, and his stance relaxed. I would have thought he was calm if I hadn't known him so well.

The crowd was leaning forward like they were waiting for one of them to start a fight. Ezrah may have filled out, but there was no way he would win a fight against this man. I wanted to jump off my horse, but I would be no help intruding on a fight I knew nothing about. I needed to know what I was getting myself into before I could get us out of it.

The large man stepped closer, and I almost closed my eyes. He reached out and put his hand on Ezrah's shoulder, clasping it.

The crowd relaxed, less intrigued when no fists were thrown. Ezrah still did not relax.

I heard shifting around me. When I followed the sound, I saw he was not the only one that had attracted a crowd. People came in from the fields and swarmed around me. They stared openly, like I was on display. The looks they threw at me made the hair on my arms rise.

I looked back to where the men stood just in time to see the large one looking right at me. I saw him nod in my direction. Then I watched as Ezrah shook his head no.

The people came closer to me. I was now far away from the person who was meant to keep me safe, surrounded by the kind of people he warned me about. On top of that, the man who was in power had noticed me and was clearly talking about me. My hands collected sweat where I clutched the reins, and I could feel any power I may have had in this situation slipping away.

I slid down from Onyx, the reins still tight in my hands, and the crowd parted as I walked slowly toward the two men.

I could feel every single eye on me. When I looked up, I saw that Ezrah had turned to look, too, but his eyes were warning me. He didn't want me involved.

Then he shouldn't have brought me here.

That was likely unfair. On more than one level, us being here was not his fault.

Still, I didn't care as I walked toward him. I would not be left to the side while the people in power discussed me.

When I got close enough, I saw the large man's face crack into a grin that didn't meet his eyes. It looked like smiling was not an expression he was used to. The closer I got, the more I could see the wrinkles that lined his face, how they looked thin and dry like the land we first rode on when we left Polaris.

I stood beside Ezrah, Onyx's reins still clutched in my hand. She huffed like she didn't like the attention.

I let the man speak first. "Look what we have here." He looked at us. "You've brought a friend this time, Ezrah." He reached for my hand.

Ezrah spoke before I could get a chance. "My partner, Addie."

I held my face impassive by sheer luck as my skin crawled.

Partner.

He could have had any other excuse. He could have let me talk. Instead, he makes me his future wife.

I wanted to fucking hit him. Again.

My right hand clutched the reins harder.

The grin hadn't left the man's face. He took my hand between the two of his, clutching it. "Pleasure," he said.

I nodded. "And you are?"

He raised one eyebrow. This man was not used to a woman who skipped pleasantries. "Cedric."

I could feel the townspeople crowding, waiting to see what would happen. My small hand was still between his large ones, but my gaze held his. I would not be the one to look away first. Men like this were the kind that I would deal with for the rest of my life. My mother prepared me for them.

Women of power could not back down.

Ezrah cut in. "We're just cutting through. I thought I would stop in and make sure you knew."

Make sure he knew?

Cedric finally looked away from me and pulled his hands back. "I was told you were nearby."

Ezrah looked like he expected as much. I, however, did not.

I watched them silently stare at each other, just like me and the stranger, Cedric, had. Ezrah was more patient than I was.

"We need food," I said, ending their staring and bringing both of their attention back to me. "We have the coin and we would like to trade with you."

The grin spread wider, making the dry lines look like cuts across his skin. "Would you?"

"We will take whatever you can spare and pay you well."

He looked back at Ezrah. "I never expected you back here, let alone asking for favors."

Ezrah shrugged with more conviction than he felt. "It's not me who's asking."

Cedric looked at us again. It was difficult not to feel defenseless under his towering form. He stretched the silence out, knowing the power he held over us. He looked down at us like a predator at its prey, like he wanted to play.

I would never be a man's prey.

But Cedric didn't know that. He saw me as an accessory to Ezrah, not demure, but still just a woman. He knew nothing of my power, and I hoped he didn't give me a reason to show him the extent of it.

"I will do you one better," he said to Ezrah but was looking at me, "you will eat with us tonight. I can send you with food in the morning."

"That won't be necessary." Ezrah was quick.

"Nonsense," he said back. "You have never been one to turn down a free meal, Ezrah."

Double meaning that I did not understand laced his words. I knew I was at fault for not asking more about Ezrah's time out here. That would have been an asset, and I am comfortable enough with my defects to know that the lack of inquiry was my fault. Still, I mentally cursed the weak leverage I had. If Ezrah was walking us into this predator's trap, he should have warned me. Situations were much harder to control when I was trying to find my footing.

"That is incredibly generous. We would be honored." I felt Ezrah's stare come from my side, but I didn't mind it. I was keeping my eye on our predator.

Cedric laughed, as the tension from the people around us dissipated. They didn't move from their spot, and Cedric gestured for one of them to come forward and take the horses from us. I did not like being left without our transportation out of this place.

"Your soon-to-be wife is much more sensible than you are, boy. Jonah," he gestured to the first man that Ezrah had spoken with, "show them inside. I will be there in a second."

Jonah came around him and walked us to the biggest house in the village. Ezrah grasped my elbow as I tried to move ahead of him. When I met his eyes, he looked at me like I had done something incredibly wrong. I wanted to tell him that if this was so wrong, it was not a mistake of mine. He led us here, and I would lead us out.

We followed behind Jonah straight into the belly of the beast.

14

His Partner

I could smell the food cooking as soon as I walked through the short wooden door. My stomach rumbled, and I was hopeful that I might actually be hungry. It had been so long since my body would let me eat anything of substance. This twisting feeling at the sight of food was new and unhealthy, especially for someone on a long journey.

There were already people inside the building. The same signs of hard labor showed on all of them. If their skin wasn't pink, it was dry and cracked. Every back was hunched. They paid the price to work the fields that had kept me fed my entire life. It was clear in how they walked and grunted as they sat. One of the men was older, his hair already gray. The fingers he used to hold the cup in his hands curled in on themselves unnaturally. They looked nearly useless like they were bent permanently and wouldn't straighten. Amber, my mother's lady's maid, had the same weak grip. I caught myself staring and had to pull my eyes away from him.

This house had to be at least double the size of any others on the street. People filled the room, sitting on wooden stools that encircled a long center table. The right side of the house was blocked off by hanging pieces of fabric, which I assumed led to the bedrooms. On the left was the kitchen, with a small counter holding the required shrine to The Light. A couple of candles were lit, and a small food offering that was being swarmed with flies sat in a golden dish. A makeshift stone oven sat beside it. The only woman in the room besides myself sat near it, stirring whatever was in the pot above the flame while the men rested.

I told myself it was likely this way because the men tended the field, and she took care of the home while they did so, not that she was cooking because she was a woman. But her skin showed the same dark tone from hours under the sun, and her shoulders held that same hunched shape.

One person noticed us, and suddenly voices quieted and everyone in the room looked our way. They stared as Jonah walked us around the table, but not at me. Every person in the room had their eyes on Ezrah. I saw one man nudge the other, getting his attention. I kept my chin level, looking at Jonah's back as he led us around.

Jonah pulled out the two stools we were to sit on and waited for us to do so before going to his seat on the other side. It was clear he was a right-hand man to Cedric, although I couldn't fathom why. Jonah didn't hold the same stern demeanor that the others did. He lacked the power. There was very little family resemblance between the two beyond their hair color.

No one in the room talked, not a single voice. I wanted so badly to be able to ask Ezrah some questions, starting with why the fuck he had brought us here, but this was not the place. When I got him alone, I would struggle not to strangle him.

Even the toughest-looking man in here jumped when the door slammed open. Cedric broke the silence and the stares.

"We have guests tonight."

Cedric nodded to the woman who began to bring bowls around the table for the men. Not a single one moved to help or even leaned out of the way as she served their supper over their shoulders.

A younger man leaned back in his chair, almost making her trip with the bowl she carried.

I moved to help her, but Ezrah's hand grabbed my wrist under the table. Instantly, I felt his warmth. I cut him a look, and his eyes pleaded for me to go along with him. I stayed seated, even though no woman should be shouldered with this archaic burden alone. When she brought a bowl to me, I leaned far out of her way. I tried to meet her eyes, but she had already moved on.

Cedric was the first to get his food. He sat directly across from me and glowered at me as he slurped the broth from his bowl.

"It was kind of you to invite us in," I said. Silence here was wasted.

He grinned. "I'm known for my kindness." I heard some of the men chuckle lightly. "Aren't I, Ezrah?"

I felt his hand grip me slightly tighter under the table. "People talk of your kindness all the way to Polaris."

No one was laughing now. Cedric's tone had lowered into something darker, and it seemed much more in his nature. "I was kind to you once, boy. You seem to forget that." His large head tilted to the side. "Has he ever told you the details of his time away from the capital city? Addie, was it?"

Cedric was the kind of man that knew how to twist people, to manipulate them into a position that would force them to compromise in his favor. Despite his brawn, he could do that with words alone—He was sneaky, which was a special kind of dangerous.

Luckily, he was exactly the kind of man I was taught to handle.

I laughed, and it even sounded genuine to me. "Addie, short for Adeline." Addie was far too close to my actual name, which would cause problems. "Only the stories that were appropriate for a lady to hear."

That got a laugh from a few of the men, and Cedric leaned back in his chair.

I took the first spoonful of the stew in front of me. The broth was light, but it was filled with dried beans and herbs. The flavor was impactful and unique. At the palace, my meals were more separated. Meats, cheeses, and grains were all served at different times. Compared to that, this lacked flavor. I did not think it would keep me full for long, but I had learned to be grateful for anything I could get out here.

My stomach rumbled, asking for more, and I hoped no one had heard it.

"So, where are the two of you heading?" Cedric asked.

Ezrah answered quickly, "Temple Majora."

I sat up straighter. He should have lied.

"You didn't get what you wanted last time you were there?" Cedric asked him.

Ezrah had been there?

Cedric tilted his head, inspecting Ezrah as he waited for a response. When he started to grin, I could tell Cedric thought he had found a weak spot, something he could use against us.

"He did," I said, my voice held a conviction I didn't feel. "He told me of his time here, and I begged him to take me. They say you can feel the presence of The Light so clearly."

Jonah snorted, and my eyes cut to him. He looked at me like I was a silly little girl. He didn't believe in the full power of The Light. Did he know what happened to people like him, how they suffered, and how they died? I had heard their pleas for help from the plaza firsthand.

They were not burned in The Light like the others were after their death—they had no such honor. Instead, they were tied to the same pyre and left there for The Light to have. They wasted away and were fed on by birds and mice. Grown men begged for mercy. It was cruel but necessary to ensure The Light and its Deities were kind to us. In my circles, a snort such as that would be enough to condemn his fate.

I didn't tell him any of this. Instead, I turned back to Cedric. "I wish to pay my respects, and I wish for The Light to bless our marriage."

Ezrah's thumb moved up and down my wrist. I was momentarily distracted. I had not realized his hand still rested there, and if this was his attempt to comfort me for having to speak of any kind of blessing, I did not need it. If his hand rested there for another reason, I did not want it.

I did not want it at all.

Cedric changed the conversation, thankfully.

"Were you there for the blessing?"

He must have felt my hand clench into a fist, because

Ezrah spoke for me. "We left just before it started. You?"

Cedric nodded along. I did not know how much of this he believed. "I couldn't go, unfortunately. There was too much to do here. My crops made it there just fine, though."

Now Jonah spoke, "A waste of food." More people nodded along with him. Now, knowing how some suffered out here, I couldn't wholly disagree. "All to honor a Ruler that will just take more from us. To keep the wealthy fed and keep us right where we are. I would like to teach that bitch a lesson."

Ezrah's hand moved to my knee and squeezed. My mouth was open. I was ready to fight. This man knew nothing about me or how these things worked, yet he would speak this way.

The people I was supposed to Rule did not respect me. They openly opposed me. Ezrah squeezed hard, and I looked at him.

His eyes were pleading again. This dinner was not a place to start a fight. It was a place to survive. It was safest to keep it that way.

I forced a few steady breaths in and out, like my grandmother would have told me to do if she were here.

Cedric nodded his head for Jonah to leave. Jonah didn't hesitate, but the door slammed behind him as he stormed out.

"So you must be the girl."

My hand hung in mid-air, my spoon still full of stew. "I'm sorry?"

Cedric laughed, and the room stirred. "The girl that our Ezrah had spoken of when he was last here."

I did not know what to say to that. Ezrah, or at least the Ezrah I had known, did not have a girl.

Other than me.

And he had me so limply, passively. Physically, we had been together, but it didn't go further for him. If it had, he would not have thrown me away so easily. He wouldn't have left.

Every eye in the room was on him, including my own, and I was grateful I would not have to respond to that question.

Ezrah's eyes were looking down into his stew. "She is."

My heart hammered. I set down my spoon.

Cedric's eyes turned to me. "And you must've been so happy when he returned to you."

I could see his demeanor changing, like he knew he had us trapped. He had stalked us into a corner, and now he would devour us. I knew I could not lie. Partial truths were much more convincing, and I would need to be persuasive to get us out of this disaster.

"I was so grateful that he was safe."

I felt Ezrah's eyes bore into the side of my head. My cheeks reddened, and his thumb moved up and down my thigh. I had to resist the urge to squirm in my seat.

"Grateful enough to fall into his arms. Isn't that sweet?" The men at the table around us either groaned or laughed.

"I didn't make it that easy for him."

"No?"

I likely should have left it alone, but I was on a roll now. "After what he did? After he left me? No. He is lucky I even spoke to him when he returned, that I even looked him in the eye."

Cedric's brows raised. "You sound upset."

"No," Ezrah tried to interject.

"Of course I was. I still am," I said. "Wounds like the

ones he gave me only heal with time, if they do at all."

Cedric's head tilted. "And yet you love him enough to marry him?"

I felt a blush rise up my chest and neck, all the way to my hairline.

Fuck.

"I—" I swallowed the lump in my throat. "I can be both. I can be angry while still …"

There was no sound in the room. Ezrah's hand gripped my thigh, and I turned to look at him. When I did, I could see emotion welling in his eyes, dampness catching around the bottom. It was the last thing I expected to see from him.

But I supposed it was callous of me to assume these words would not have some kind of effect on him like they did on me.

I was sure that every person in the room watched us, but I could not take my eyes off him. I wanted him to see how badly he had hurt me. As I spoke these thinly veiled truths, I was finally able to lower my shields and show him the damage he had done.

He leaned forward slightly, and, as much as I wished they did, none of my instincts told me to lean back. If anything, I leaned into him in a frustratingly natural way.

He tilted his head up just a bit and lightly placed a kiss on my forehead.

How could the lightest touch of his lips cause my heart to flip like that?

"Now, isn't that sweet? Lovers working through their problems. But that was hardly a kiss, Ezrah. Kiss her like you mean it. Kiss her like you love her."

My mind was still whirling too quickly for panic to set in.

The hand on my thigh pulled me to face him more as his other one went to my neck. Before I could think to look away, Ezrah tilted my head and brought his lips to mine.

15

It Made it Worth It

All I had to do was reach my hand out, and I could strangle him, but with Ezrah's lips on mine, I didn't trust myself to move.

If I moved my hand to reach around his neck and snuff the life out of him, I might end up holding him to me instead.

Which I definitely did not want to fucking do.

But his mouth was like fire on mine. Heat invaded my veins and every part of me. My thighs parted on instinct, and I felt his thumb stroke up and down again.

He kissed me like he had spent the last two years waiting for this, like there wasn't an audience here. When his teeth caught on my bottom lip it was easy to pretend we were alone. I quietly gasped into his mouth, and he moved to take full advantage of that before hesitating.

When he finally pulled away, he kept his eyes on the ground as our foreheads rested together, too ashamed to look at me. I felt ashamed, too, but mine was because of the way heat settled between my legs, how I didn't push away from him, and the fact that I wanted him to look at me. But he didn't.

I could kill him.

Leaning back with a jerk, he fell forward for a slight second before righting himself. My lips still tingled as I tried to ignore the way my heart jumped when he pulled his hand away from my thigh.

I was trying to ignore a whole lot of feelings.

They were not natural ones. They were formed from the wanton years spent at his side. They were residual like my body did not know that we felt differently about him now. The need to reach back for him was animal, not emotional. The need to put his lips back on mine was not my own.

For the rest of the dinner I was silent, my thoughts too jumbled to hear what everyone else was saying. I vaguely thought I heard Cedric joke about the kiss, but if Ezrah replied, I did not hear it.

Everyone was likely wondering why I seemed so shaken. I should have played these mixed-up emotions off stronger and wiser. If I were his—if he and I were together, a kiss would not shake me. I could speak up and play into this ruse, but instead of reassuring them, my lips remained sealed. At least that kept me from saying another ridiculous thing. Instead, I tried to use all my energy to keep my mind from wandering to places and memories that would take me far from here.

Because it was not lost on me that Cedric knew exactly who I was, not my actual name or role, but my relationship with Ezrah. Cedric had asked him about me. Which means Ezrah had told him. About me. About us.

This meant when Ezrah and I finally gave in to our feelings, and then he promptly left me without so much as a reason or a goodbye, he still spoke of me. Even when he left me behind, he took stories of me with him.

I wanted to know a whole lot more about that.

At the end of the tense, confusing dinner, Ezrah responded when Cedric tried to insist we stay. His answer was a firm no. Cedric relented begrudgingly, mentioning something about having food brought out to us in the morning. I heard all of this through the tunnel that my ears were in.

It was not until we walked away from the small village with Ezrah holding the reins of the horses. I wished I felt calmer as the open fields surrounded me, but the more time I spent out here the heavier the weight on my shoulders became.

Trying not to focus on the way my lips still tingled, I moved to the next most concerning thing.

"Ezrah," I started, "When you said people were angry was that what you meant? They spoke about me as if—"

"He shouldn't have said that."

"I'm not concerned about name calling. I am concerned about their anger."

Ezrah released a sigh. "Me, too."

"So this is who you meant when you said people are angry?"

He looked at me then as we walked and I could tell he didn't want to tell me anything. I wouldn't waste my breath explaining that I didn't need to be coddled any more than he would try to get out of answering my questions.

"It's not just them. Everyone out here is angry to some degree. Outside that wall things are not good. They blame your family."

I wondered if what he heard while he was out here was part of the reason he returned to join the guard. I shivered at the thought.

"Hopefully, I will be able to fix things when I am back."

"Yeah, hopefully. But Adenne," he pulled the horses to a stop, "I'm not only concerned about people knowing who you are because of tradition." He took a deep breath and I saw his hands clench the reins. "If these people knew there was a Ruler out here with so little protection…"

"They would hurt me." Not a question, a statement. The danger went beyond breaking tradition or my lack of blessing. The concerns of the people out here were much bigger, and they were angry at me.

"They want change so bad I fear they would do anything to get it." Silence stretched between as my stomach rolled around, nausea making that stew feel like it wanted revenge. Ezra's face softened. "I will not let them hurt you."

I held back the tears in my eyes. Never in all of our childhood years did I imagine he would be my protector physically. I would have never pictured us in these roles. Not knowing what to say, I nodded and asked the next least intrusive question.

"How do you know Cedric?"

"I met him not long after I left."

"So why did it seem like every person in there assumed he was going to crush you under his gigantic feet?"

He cracked a smile, full of mischief, and I felt the tension ebb away.

"I did some work for him for a while. In exchange, he

fed and housed me. The terms of my time there were not discussed first. The miscommunication complicated things."

We were coming up to a path of trees at the end of this field. Ezrah looked behind us to gauge how far from the village we had gone. When it was clear that the houses only spots in the darkness, barely visible. He tied the reins of both horses to a tree.

"Cedric expected me to work the entire season for him. I figured it was a day-to-day thing. When I told him I was leaving, he said I was taking advantage of him, claiming I was taking his food and kindness but skipping out on the hard part of the season."

"But you left anyway?"

He unhooked the packs from the horses and walked us through the few trees that were there. "He didn't like that, obviously. Cedric sent people after me to make it clear I was not allowed on his land again until I paid him what I owed." He started setting up our tent in a clearing between the fields, beyond the trees, to give us some privacy. "I told his people I didn't owe him shit, which I didn't. Cedric wrote the terms that favored him once he knew I was leaving."

"He is a powerful man."

"He is."

I approached the other side to secure the tent to the ground. "And you thought it best to walk straight into his lands now?"

I heard his voice come from the other side of the tent. "Did I think it best? No. But likely everyone we walked past today works for Cedric, whether they are farming his fields or not. They all know who I am. Cedric knew we were near before we got to the village, and it was better to face him head-on." He came around the front of the tent with the rest of the bags and threw them inside. "And we were out of food."

"Which explains why you were hesitant to give it away. I'm sorry."

He shrugged. "It's done now. I had to go into that village whether we had food or not." He looked at me now as we stood facing each other. "And you were right. Those kids needed it more."

Heat rose in my cheeks. Of course I was right. If any other person had admitted they thought so, too, I would have rolled my eyes, but the praise from Ezrah sprung a different reaction in me.

I was getting tired of the reactions he was triggering.

"Well, I'm sorry we were in that situation either way."

He stood only a few feet in front of me. "Addie?"

I raised an eyebrow at him. "Ezrah?"

A suppressed smile tugged at the corner of his mouth. "Why aren't you asking me the questions you really want to ask? Or better yet, why aren't you laying me out for what happened back there?"

Suddenly, the exhaustion from the day hit me. There was far too much pretending, and I couldn't do it anymore.

"Honestly? I'm trying really hard to avoid thinking about what happened back there."

He shifted his weight between his feet. "Why?"

"Because if I do there is a good chance I do something irrational like hit you in the face or…" My eyes drifted down to his lips.

He stepped closer. "Or what?"

Blood pounded in my ears. "I don't know, Ezrah," I whispered. "And all this not knowing is scaring the shit out of me, so I would rather avoid thinking about it."

As if I could avoid thinking about it. My lips still tingled at the memory.

Even if Ezrah had spoken of me after he left me, that did not make our situation any different. It did not even mean he spoke of me fondly.

There was no good ending to this line of thinking. I knew that from all the hours I had wasted years ago. He knew as well as I did our roles in this life. I was a Ruler, he was just a guard, and I was set to marry someone else. I may not have seen those lines drawn so clearly two years ago. I didn't think he had, either.

And now? I was not a Ruler. Not yet, at the very least.

The lines were even more blurry to me now.

Still, all of this was wrong. If my head kept spinning back and forth on this, I would be sick.

The sun had left the sky, leaving the moon to highlight his outline. The shadow of hair around his jawline was growing. It followed the same angles on the rest of his face, maturing him. It was hard to look away from.

He had always been attractive, but in our time apart, he had grown handsome. I wondered if he knew it, even if he never acted as he did.

He nodded, always giving me space to process things in my own time. "Okay," he said. "Ask me something else."

"He said you went to Temple Majora before." I crossed my arms around my waist. "Did you go for your parents?"

It is said that where The Light originated, you could feel

intense energy. Some even said you could feel people who had passed. Ezrah's parents had trained there, as all of the Devoted had. It would make sense for him to go there.

He nodded.

"And could you feel them there?"

I could see tears welling in his eyes. "It was the most I have felt them since they died."

Tears welled up in me too. "Good. I'm glad. It makes it worth it."

"What worth it?"

He leaned towards me, his hands clenching at his sides. Mine dropped to my sides, and no breath was left in me. I am not sure how the words made it out.

"You leaving."

A tear fell. As it trailed down my cheek, I tried to turn away and hide it from him.

Then his hand came up, his fingers tangled in the side of my hair. I felt his thumb wipe down the track of that tear.

He was right in front of me, towering over me. When I tilted my head to meet his eyes I could feel how close our lips were. His hand moved down my neck, his thumb on my jawline. It reminded me so much of our nights long ago, and made me want to reach up to him.

I broke the silence. "If you found something… if leaving helped you heal at all, then I'm glad."

And I was. If his leaving is truly what he needed to heal the hole left behind by his parent's passing, it was worth it, even at my own sacrifice. I would give anything to lessen his pain.

"That's not why I left," he said, and my heart twisted. "It wasn't the only reason."

I could only focus on his words enough to know they made no sense.

"What?"

His thumb moved back and forth along my jawline. I tried to meet his eye, but that was not where he was looking.

He was looking directly at my lips.

I felt them part, I saw his pupils dilate.

My back arched instinctively, putting us closer together.

He was going to kiss me. Again. Ezrah was going to kiss me again. And I wanted him to despite him leaving me, hurting me. I wanted to go back to that time two years ago when everything made sense.

That's what his lips felt like on mine, I realized. He made sense to me.

"I left because." His throat worked. "I was losing control over something, and I couldn't let that happen."

He stepped back from me.

My body was shocked. It was cold from the lack of him. I pulled my lips closed. My chest still heaved like it couldn't find air.

I was going to let him kiss me. Again.

He wasn't going to.

Fuck.

"What does that mean?" I gasped.

He shook his head at me. "I can't…"

Anger rose in me. "You can't what?"

"I can't say more. I'm not going to, Addie."

My jaw clenched as I nodded. "Of course, you won't. You keep toying with me however you want, and I will just forever lack a fucking explanation."

His hands clenched into fists at his sides, opening and closing as he fought with himself. "I have told you what I can, all that I can." His voice broke. "Can't that be enough for you?"

I couldn't fight his words. He sounded desperate, like if I asked him to tell me more it would kill him. He asked me if that was enough, begging for mercy.

"No," I said.

And walked into the tent to give him what little mercy I could offer.

Curled up on my side, I did everything I could to will myself to sleep despite the hollow ache in my chest.

I was awake hours later when I heard him come in after me. Laying with my head facing the canvas, I felt him pause, looking at me. Then he turned to his side of the tent.

I woke immediately refreshed. Every part of my body was more relaxed than the day before. The sun streamed through the tent's canvas, but I didn't care. I was warm, and for the first time in days, my eyes didn't ache. Relaxing back into the ground, I decided I could stay here forever.

The ground beneath my cheek slowly rose and fell.

I stayed utterly still, but then it happened again. The ground was rising and falling. It wasn't as hard as it had been when I went to sleep, and it was much warmer.

The ground felt a lot like Ezrah's chest.

My brain came out of its morning fog as I laid there. If I listened closely, I could hear the slow sounds of his breath in tandem with the rising and falling. I could even feel his heart beating under my hand.

Not an inch of me wanted to move.

Or all of me did.

This was the man that two days ago I wanted nothing to do with. It was also the man that, two years ago, I would have done anything to wake up beside.

He had made my heart into a wall and then destroyed it brick by brick. He built me up, only to tear me back down.

I wanted to stay here and wanted to move.

That blurring line was so incredibly frustrating. I did not know what I wanted.

But it was early in the morning, the sun had just risen, and I had this moment to myself while he slept. A moment to just lay there and just *be*. I could relax without worrying about blurring lines or what I wanted and what I should not.

His chest moved in such a soothing rhythm I let my breaths come and go at the same time. That similar woodsy scent surrounded me. I let myself lie here and enjoy that I was in his arms as he slept. He never had to know how I stayed here and let myself feel him.

I could feel him, even with my eyes closed. I felt every part of our bodies that touched. His heat radiated through my skin, and I could feel it in my bones. My head was on his chest, as was my hand. The front of me was pushed up against the side of him, except for my leg, which was wrapped tightly around his. It was a position that I didn't understand how two people could get into while they slept.

I let the heat run through me, and enjoyed this quiet moment. It would be a secret that I kept for myself. A younger me imagined doing this, and now I was giving myself the pleasure of living it, just for a bit longer, while he slept.

If he was sleeping.

He hadn't moved since I had woken up, so I assumed he was. It was reasonable that he was asleep. Yet, my breathing was just as slow as his.

If he were awake, he would pull away, surely.

I was awake, and I still hadn't.

Not wanting to break this moment but needing to know, I slowly opened one eye. I could see the underside of his jaw, where hair now grew. The angle prevented me from seeing most of his face, but what I could see looked softer than it did when he was awake, the lines less defined.

My guts twisted, telling me this was a bad idea. I took one last look at him, felt his breath one last time, then began to slowly pull away.

He pulled me right back to him. His hand was wrapped tightly around the curve of my waist, pushing me against him. The softest part of me pushed in. I couldn't breathe.

His breath had grown unsteady, too. I thought he must be awake, but when I looked up I could see his eyes were still closed, lashes fanned out against his cheeks.

Still, he was not unaffected by this. I could feel that against me.

My whole body felt hot, and my blood pumped furiously through my veins. My breaths had come out of rhythm with his short inhales and shamelessly shaky exhales.

On instinct, my hips slowly rocked forward, seeking traction. I bit my lip and tried to force my hips to keep still. I needed to stop this, to move.

Or to wake him.

The hand on my waist moved over my hip and down to my thigh. I let out a quiet sigh when I felt it move from the outside of my leg to the inside. It came so close to where I needed him.

Still, he slept. I thought he did. My attention was focused on how tightly I was wrapped around him.

I wanted this, even if I shouldn't.

My hand moved to his wrist. It could have been to stop him or to move him forward.

His fingers stilled at my contact. I felt his breathing go shallow. I knew he looked at how tightly I was wrapped along his leg and where his hand was.

For the slightest second, I considered just letting go.

If I let go of his wrist, would he continue what he started? The very thought of it filled me with heat. I felt myself aching and resisted the urge to push my hips forward again.

But if I moved, he may also pull away from me. This could have all been a dream to him. He may not want the reality of it.

Although I could still feel his wanting pressing against me.

Slowly, his fingers moved. They had no real direction. The movement was so small. They rubbed the inside of my thigh back and forth. I pushed closer to his hand, urging him on.

At the same time, I glanced at him. He watched me, his eyes heated. He had the same expression of shock and something else on his face that mirrored mine. I knew then that he wanted this as much as I did.

I don't think he would have stopped it.

So, I had to.

I pulled myself off him, moving swiftly as if it would lessen the pain of it. Sitting up and bending my knees, I looked at the tent's opening so I wouldn't have to see his expression.

I didn't want to know if it was disappointment or relief.

"The sun is up. We should be going."

My voice sounded strained. I could feel his eyes burning into my back. My cheeks heated. It was best if he didn't say anything about what just happened, but if he did, I would have to devise a good excuse for why I was rubbing against his leg while he slept. I could feel my face turn crimson at the thought.

"I'll go get the horses," he said.

I tried to overlook the fact that his voice sounded even rougher than mine.

It felt like it took hours for him to move out of the tent. I kept my eyes forward, away from him, until he was entirely gone. Then my head collapsed in my hands.

That was stupid, but it was thrilling. My blood still raced.

I had convinced myself that I despised this man. I did, in some ways. He had left me, and he still would not explain why.

But I wanted him just as badly as I did back then.

My plans were in shambles. I had no idea why I wasn't blessed. I may not be able to do the one thing I have lived my whole life expecting to do. Now was not the time for distractions. That was exactly what I had become, distracted. I needed to focus on the real reason I was out here; finding answers.

Every part of me wanted to follow him out of this tent.

I groaned and tried to force my mind not to run through the implications of what that meant. My hands squeezed my head, trying to force my thoughts back in. It didn't work.

I heard footsteps outside the canvas, and my heart pounded. I watched a large shadow come toward the tent. I had no idea what I was going to say to him if anything at all. He may pretend like it didn't happen, and then I would have to as well. The task felt impossible.

"Ezrah, I—" A hand reached into the tent, roughly grabbed my ankle, then dragged me through the canvas.

16

<hr>

Weaponized Words

I was on my feet. There was the cold bite of a knife at my throat. The metal pressed into my skin as I sucked in air. I didn't know who held me or why, but I could tell he was not much taller than me. The smell of sweat and must filled my nostrils, and I could feel his dampness pressing into my back. I did recognize the other person who walked past me and into the tent.

Jonah.

I kicked out against the man holding me, and his hand on my stomach tightened, holding me closer to him. I felt like I couldn't breathe.

"You're a dumb bitch getting involved with a man like that," his hot breath was in my ear, "but Ezrah is going to pay us what he owes."

I looked toward the group of trees in the distance where Ezrah had tied up the horses the night before. They were on the other side, out of sight. There was a chance they hadn't found him yet.

That would also mean there was a chance Ezrah didn't know they were here.

If he came back here, he would be in trouble. If he did not, I was. This man may not tower over me, but he was strong. I could tell by the thick forearm that held me captive. Even if I knew how to fight, I could not overpower him. My heart pounded.

A Ruler was never taught how to fight.

There was never a need, with the Ruler's guard always there. Safety was never an issue. An attack on a Ruler was an attack on The Light. The punishment was far too severe. My parents had never been attacked.

But that was inside Polaris. Beyond that wall, people were angry.

I forced myself to take slow, even shallow breaths to avoid getting caught by the blade held at my throat. Breathe in. Breathe out. Repeat. Repeat. Repeat.

I could do this. If I had a logical mind, I could get out of this.

These men were angry, but not at me. They did not know who I was. As far as they knew, I was just Ezrah's partner, not a Ruler. That could help me. I was collateral damage to them.

Or they might take less care knowing I was not someone of significance.

I slowed my breath, calming the panic rising in me. I kept my eyes on those trees, looking for any sign that Ezrah was there. Or even better, that he wasn't.

Clouds were rolling in over the trees. Soon enough, they

would block out the sun. I heard one horse whine and felt my heart drop. I struggled again, and my skin stung as the knife bit further into my throat. Something trickled down to my collarbone and I smelled rust. Blood.

An involuntary sound came out of me. The one holding me leaned his mouth so close that his lips grazed me as he spoke. "Don't you worry. Ezrah is just learning an important lesson."

"Fuck you," I spat back.

He laughed. He actually laughed. "Maybe you need to learn one, too."

My stomach revolted like it was trying to leave my body. I did not make this mess, but I was in it now.

But we also wouldn't have been out here if it weren't for me. We wouldn't have needed food if it weren't for me. Maybe my lack of judgment was just as to blame as Ezrah's.

The man's hand moved lower on my stomach, his fingers spreading wide. "I had heard the new Ruler was attractive, didn't believe it, though." I stopped moving. He laughed again. "Now that I have seen it myself, I would have to agree."

Acid rose in my throat. It coated my entire insides.

I was wrong. They knew exactly who I was. They had known the whole time.

I thought of what Jonah had said the night before. They were unhappy, and their anger had everything to do with me. Now I was alone in a field with a knife to my throat.

When the man's hand moved lower, I tried to squirm away. My throat stung, and I could feel liquid dripping down my chest.

"Fuck you," I repeated.

He chuckled again. "You're a nasty little thing, aren't

you?" He pulled me even tighter, his fingers now touching the top of my thigh. "I'll tell you what, I've got an idea. Since you and your family continue to take and take and take," he spat a little every time he said the word and his groping hand moved quickly, gripping the length of my hair, tugging my head backward, "I think I'll take something from you in exchange."

I could see his eyes from this angle. They held no mercy. Ezrah had said these men would not hesitate to take everything from a woman who traveled alone. I hadn't wanted to think too deeply about what that could mean. Now I stared it in the face.

He fisted my hair harder, forcing my head backward to look at him. He was distracted, and the movement pulled the blade away from my throat. I used the extra room I had to elbow him in the gut.

But it was a feeble attempt, and the man tugged harder on my hair until I felt my scalp burn. He tossed me beside the tent. The impact caused sparks of pain to shoot up my arms.

"You're lucky I like it when they fight me."

He lurched toward me at the same time I scrambled to get away. I was his prey. He was my predator. My heart hammered. He let me crawl away from him like a wounded animal while he stood over me and watched. He laughed. I crawled in the direction opposite the tent and Ezrah. In trying to escape, I would be even more alone. Hot tears burned tracks down my face, and I heard my body's desperate gasps.

There was a loud thump.

To my left, Ezrah had knocked the man to the ground. He grabbed the back of the man's shirt and turned him over. His fist landed squarely on the man's jaw. I sat there motionless, shocked.

Ezrah fought with none of the precision that I had seen the Ruler's guard train with. He had the man pinned under him, and his fists raised and lowered in savage way. It was not something I ever expected to see from him. Bile coated my throat again.

He looked at me over his shoulder, and his eyes still held the softness I knew. They contrasted the panic in his voice. "Adenne," his words were rough, "run."

My mind finally registered the quickly darkening shade around his eye and the trail of blood falling from his lip.

Lower, more blood was soaking him, and I had no idea if it was his or someone else's. He needed help.

Ezrah shook his head. "Go!"

I went.

I ran toward the horses, pain pulling at my throat. My chest heaved in and out.

Help. I needed to find a way to help. Ezrah could be hurt. He *was* hurt, and I had no idea how to help him. I looked over my shoulder just in time to see Jonah leaving the tent.

Jonah.

I'd forgotten he was there. Ezrah could take down one of them, but he couldn't take two at a time.

I was not a fighter, but there was a knife in my saddle bag in case of emergencies. It was small, but if I could get it to Ezrah, maybe he could use it. It could help.

Or I could bring him the horses. If he could overpower the two men, even for a second, we may be able to get away.

Or... fuck. I didn't *know*. I didn't know what to do.

The trees were close now, and I could see Onyx and Scout. Relief came over me at the sight of the two horses unharmed. They may be our only way out.

Just beyond the first few trees I heard something running through the clearing. Cedric was riding his horse directly toward the men. I squinted my eyes, trying to see what was going on. All I could make out was one man flat on the ground and the other standing over him. It was impossible to tell which man was which. Not that it would have mattered if Ezrah was on the ground or standing, with Cedric coming, he was in trouble.

It took me a split second to turn and grab the knife, but at this point, I was confident I wouldn't need it.

I was useless with a knife; ruling, and negotiating were my strengths. My weapons were my words, that is where I held my power, and now there was another person with authority here.

I had a fighting chance.

Cedric cleared the open field much faster than I could, but still, I ran as fast as my feet could carry me. My throat burned, and the back of my head pounded. Overhead, dark clouds blocked the sun, a storm rolling in across the fields.

When I got close enough, I could better assess the situation. It was not good. Ezrah was on the ground beside the man who had held me. Jonah stood at Ezrah's head, and Cedric was lowered to one knee with a knife to his throat. My heart hit the dirt.

"I wouldn't do that."

I put the knife I was holding behind my back. It was unlikely Cedric saw me as a threat, but there was no point in making myself a target. I waited there, hoping my presence was enough to grab his attention.

"Why?"

I had a card to play. The man who attacked me had given it to me. He made it clear they knew exactly who I was, and they had likely known this entire time. It was unlikely Cedric knew about the loose lips of his men, or he wouldn't have wasted all this time playing along.

I needed the knife off of Ezrah's neck to focus. Hopefully, I hadn't shown my hand too early. "You know the punishment for harming a Ruler's guard." Ezrah's gaze tried to cut to mine. When Cedric didn't move, I continued, "You know who I am, Cedric, so you must know why he is with me."

Cedric laughed. "He is no guard, and you are no Ruler."

"Is that so?"

He didn't say anything.

"If you hurt him, the rest of the guard will follow."

He leaned into Ezrah. "We have a score to settle."

I could not let him get the knife any closer to Ezrah's neck. The reasoning wasn't helping, so I changed tactics.

"Are his debts worth your life? I thought you were wiser than that, Cedric."

My mother taught me that a man's ego was always more important to him than the task at hand. If reason didn't grab their attention, an insult would.

He leaned back, slowly away from Ezrah. Then the huge man turned and faced me. I was now a more significant threat than the man on the ground. Good.

Ezrah went to get up, but Jonah swiftly kicked him back, and I tried not to wince at the hollow thud he made. Ezrah didn't fight back, meaning he was in worse shape than I thought. I had to act quickly.

Cedric squared his shoulders. "You say the guards will

come if I hurt him, but it's clear they have no idea where you are."

I tilted my head. "Do they not?"

"You're here, which is way off the path leading you to the Sisters. You are with another person, and you let other people look at you. Your eyes aren't golden. I don't know why, won't pretend to, but you're no Ruler. You aren't expected to be here."

The truth in his words stung. I wanted to shut my eyes and hide the fact that they were still dark. Instead, I looked at him as if I expected him to continue.

My mother always said it was not wise to lie in a negotiation. They were too easy to get caught up in. Lies could lead the way to failure.

But when backed into a corner, sometimes it's the only way out.

I let out a harsh laugh and tilted my head to the side. "I'm sorry," I said, "I thought you would have figured it out long before now. My original judgment of you was far from what you are." I looked at him from head to toe. There was more confidence in my words than I felt. "I am on the way to my blessing now."

His mind was going in circles, trying to understand the meaning of my words.

I continued, "You can't believe the blessing actually happens in Polaris." Jonah was looking at me too, and Ezrah's head was tilted to the side at an awkward angle. I had to look away from him and stay on the task at hand. Otherwise, I would only worry about the speed at which his eye was swelling.

I looked at Cedric and changed my tone to the one I usually reserved for children. "The ceremony was there, I walked the street, and people brought their donations, but the Deities never come to Polaris. That is all a show for the people. The Deities only appear where The Light first came."

Jonah spoke, "The Temple Majora."

I nodded.

Cedric was shaking his head. "That doesn't make any sense."

I kept confidence in my tone. "Doesn't it? Why else would tradition say no one can look at me for my whole pilgrimage? What other purpose would that serve than to hide the fact that my eyes had not changed? Why else would I be headed north with a guard? Use your logic, Cedric."

His cheeks reddened. Making such a large man feel small made me resonate with power.

I waited for him to say anything, to dispute my claim. He stayed silent. I looked at Jonah, and he wouldn't meet my eyes. For the first time, my lack of blessing being completely unprecedented was a good thing; it made this lie easier to sell. The odds severely tipped in my favor, but it was time to take this home.

"I am to rule Rhea. I will spread the will of The Light to my people, and I will do so with the Deities' blessing." The words made my heart fucking ache. "Which means you have made some awful choices here." I stepped toward him, looking up to meet his eyes. "But you have options."

"Options?"

"Three that I can think of." Both my hands clutched the knife behind my back. "You could kill Ezrah and let me continue. That would mean that I would send the guards here as soon as I returned home." I leaned into him. "I value him too much to forget an act like that. You would die at my command.”

“I could kill you both,” he suggested. Anger made his face turn red. He looked like he might explode with the pressure to hold it back.

“You could,” I nodded, all too unconcerned with the probability that he could choose that option, “and I think you’d like that, but the guards know I am here. If I didn’t return from my pilgrimage, that would cause alarm. They will never stop looking for me. Every field in the area will be turned upside down. When they find out it was you? You will face the same punishment that one does when they speak against The Light. Your entire village will. The entire plaza in front of the palace will be filled with the bodies of the people you love. My parents are not forgiving people, Cedric. I would assume they will let you die last. That way, you would fully understand the results of your actions.”

His jaw worked back and forth. This large man was backed into a corner of my creation. I could only hope he feared my family’s power more than he hated it.

“The third?” He asked, and I tilted my head at his question. “You said there was a third?”

“I would have assumed you would have figured that out by now.” I stepped closer to him, and from there I could see the sweat dripping down his neck. Gray clouds rolled overhead, and thunder sounded in the distance.

My voice was low and powerful. “You can leave us here. Walk back to your village and pretend you never saw us pass through. Forget any debts that you think this man,” I gestured my chin towards Ezrah, “owes you. You can hope that by the time I return home, I will find mercy for this misunderstanding."

I stared him down until I saw his brows furrowed in anger. He knew he had lost. Then I watched him reassess me, realizing I was not what he expected.

I got to watch his eyes slowly close, accepting his fate.

Cedric was a man who thought he held all of the power, but I stripped him down. I took a threatening, controlling man and brought him to his knees, just like I watched my mother do time and time again. Just like I was trained to do.

I may not get to rule, but it was not because I was incapable. I held all this strength inside of me, and I would find my chance to use it.

He looked behind him, where Jonah still had his foot on Ezrah's chest. It only took a quick look to see that Ezrah had grown pale. I looked at where the blood was on his shirt and tried to tell myself the spot hadn't grown.

Cedric shook his head at Jonah then turned to me. He bent his head down to meet my eyes. "Until we meet again." A chill ran up my spine. They both moved then. Cedric walked past me while Jonah grabbed the other man and pulled him upright. I was shocked he could stand at all. They strolled ahead, presumably towards horses they had stashed somewhere.

Cedric pulled himself onto his horse. He looked at me one last time, smiled, then trotted away.

17

Healing Wounds

I dropped to Ezrah's side as soon as they left. He was leaning back on bent elbows, which only slightly calmed my nerves. His skin didn't have that deep tone I knew. It was paler. My stomach clenched.

I wanted to help him.

I wanted to get Cedric back here and bring him to his knees.

I told him he might get my mercy, but now, looking at Ezrah, I could make no such promise.

It only took me seconds to assess what had happened to him. Blood trickled down one side of his face from a split eyebrow. His lip was already starting to swell on one side, and his eye was turning an awful shade of purple. Bruises were starting to cover his knuckles as well.

The most concerning was the amount of blood that coated his shirt. I was hoping it was someone else's, but with how pale Ezrah was becoming, I knew it wasn't.

Fuck.

I hovered my hands over his body, unable to decide where to start. The longer I looked, the more they shook. Rage filled me, starting in my chest and working its way outwards until my hands shook.

"Where are you hurt?" I asked him, my voice cracking. It was a ridiculous question; I could see where he was hurt. It was everywhere. When I looked at his hands, I could still hear the cracking of their impact on the man that held me. I could still see how that man had bled.

"You were supposed to run," he said.

I met his eyes, a shade of brown slightly lighter than mine. He looked more blessed than I did.

"What hurts the most?"

"Why didn't you run, Addie?"

My hands still shook. I watched them instead of him. "I need you to tell me where it hurts," my head was shaking, too, "so I can help you."

His bruised hand came up and grabbed both of mine. Ezrah blurred in front of me, and it took me a moment to realize it was because tears were clouding my vision.

"I'm okay," he said, always so confident.

"No, you're not," I said. I felt tears run down my cheek. I would have wiped them away if he weren't holding my hands still.

"I am. Are you okay?" He pulled my hands down so they rested against the side of his chest with no blood. I could feel him breathing in and out, and it soothed me. I focused on my breathing, struggling to match the even cadence of his chest.

"Adenne," he said, "did they hurt you?"

I looked at him again. His piercing eyes hadn't left mine. One could easily get lost in them.

"No," I lied. The back of my head throbbed from where I had hit the ground, and my neck stung, but it was nothing compared to what he must have felt.

Suddenly, he sat up. He grunted at the effort, and we were almost nose to nose. I could feel that steady breath against my mouth now. I wanted to take it inside of me, breathe it into my lungs, and see what comfort it would give me.

"Don't lie to me."

"I'm not."

His hand left mine and came up to my cheek.

"I will come back here, and they won't have a chance at the mercy you promised them."

How did his words mirror my exact thoughts from earlier?

His hand moved to my chin.

Was he going to kiss me?

His thumb moved back and forth, grazing my bottom lip.

Was I going to let him?

I held his stare as our breaths mixed. If he kissed me now, I would let him. Many things were uncertain, and my body begged for the one thing he could give me that would be true. This was true. He was here, and he was safe. He was *okay*. There was need in his eyes as he stared back at me. His hand moved to my neck, away from the cut.

I knew he felt this as much as I did.

He leaned back, and immediately I missed his closeness. Ezrah was looking at my blood on his fingers. I saw his chest rise and fall sharply, and I knew he was holding back his rage.

"We can't stay here. It isn't safe."

It took me a full ten seconds to answer. "But you're hurt."

He looked away from me and up to the gray sky.

"I am not as bad as I look." He gave a half smile that lacked conviction. "We need to go. Once we are further away, we can patch each other up."

"That's a bad idea," I said.

"It's worse to stay here. Can you get the horses?"

I looked him over again, not even remotely convinced this was a good idea. "Okay," I said.

When I got to the trees, I was relieved to see both horses were still there. In my earlier rush, I couldn't say for certain if I had loosened their ties before running back to Ezrah. Onyx was uneasy when she saw me. Her tail flicked back and forth anxiously, and she backed away as I approached. I murmured to her and stepped slowly closer. Once I was within reach, I grabbed the harness around her head and pulled her face down so her eyes could meet mine. I took a second to rest my head against hers. She huffed out against me.

After one more moment, I untied her from the tree, then Scout. The horses' presence comforted me, but if I stood there a moment longer, I would have become stuck. I would think about what happened and what that man said to me. What he was about to do to me.

I could not sink into that. I needed Ezrah to believe I was fine.

I was fine.

The sooner I returned with the horses, the sooner I could

get him somewhere safer.

He was standing by the time I reached him. I did not want to think of the effort it must have taken, but based on his rapidly paling color, it was not an easy feat.

He grimaced when he looked at me. "I may need you to pack the tent."

I started right away because I could tell he hated asking. He must be in a lot more pain than he was admitting to. My stomach rolled at his unspoken admission. When he pulled himself up onto Scout, I tried to ignore the loud roar of pain that came out of him. Instead, I focused on my task, giving him the same dignity I would have desired if the roles were reversed.

Once astride Onyx, I let him set the pace, and we rode as quickly as possible without the horses jostling us too much. My head was still throbbing at the base of my skull. If the surrounding scenery was moving any quicker, the pain would escalate.

Fields passed us, and I watched the crops change from one type I could not name to another. The clouds above us were rapidly growing darker, filling with rain. Pressure filled the air in a way that felt tangible. It made my head feel heavier.

All the while, Ezrah stayed silent. I let him, not wanting to make anything worse—I had done enough of that.

If I hadn't given away the food to those children, we would not have had to stop at Cedric's village. If I hadn't interrupted the conversation when Ezrah had first walked into the village, we would have never been invited inside. If I hadn't let Ezrah leave the tent this morning, things would not have gotten that bad.

Worst of all, if I had been blessed, we would have never

been out here. I was at the center of every problem, and now the people I cared about were getting hurt. All because of me.

Guilt grew like a disease inside of me. Inch by inch, it infected my body, eating me from the inside out. I could feel it consume my guts to the point my stomach contracted.

That was all I could feel when I looked at Ezrah, his face drawn in pain. He bounced up and down as we made our way forward. Every once in a while, his brows pulled tight, and he let out a small gasp.

He was in pain, and that was another guilt I would shoulder.

Thunder cracked above us, but the clouds held the rain at bay for the moment; whether this was because of the Deities, I could not say.

A small cluster of trees was ahead, just beyond where the nearest crop ended.

"Here," I finally said. Ezrah stirred like he struggled to remember I was riding beside him. "I want to look you over."

He nodded, not fighting the idea or telling me he was fine. My stomach turned again.

The thunder rolled overhead.

When we reached the cover of trees, it was easier to forget the gray clouds. The canopy of green leaves was dense for this early in the season and it sheltered us well.

A small stream also separated the fields from each other, crossing the path we were taking. Despite its shallowness, the water ran clear and looked clean.

I dismounted first, and Ezrah quickly followed with a grunt before I could come to his side to assist. He swayed, and I grabbed his elbow, guiding him closer to the stream. I brought him down to the base of a larger tree and leaned his back against it. "Wait here," I warned him.

I brought both horses to the stream and let them drink.

When I looked back, he was watching me, his eyes tracking my steps around Onyx. I grabbed the small medical kit someone had packed for me and returned to him. I crouched before him, meeting his eyes for only a moment—any longer and I might become lost there.

Instead, I focused on opening the kit. These bottles were mostly unfamiliar to me. The only time I had seen something like this before was when I had hurt myself as a child. I often got scraped knees and twisted ankles from playing in places I shouldn't.

That had been a long time ago. Still, I would do what I could. Some of the bottles were labeled.

My hands hesitated over the kit when Ezrah spoke, "I'm sorry," he said, "for getting you into this."

I didn't look at him. I read the labels instead. "You didn't get me into this."

"I did," He insisted. I took comfort from the strength in his voice. Maybe he wasn't as hurt as I had thought.

I sighed. "You did not." I found the bottle I was looking for, a liquid meant to clean skin. "We would not be here if it were not for me."

He paused, I could feel his eyes on me, yet I still would not meet them. "This isn't your fault, Adenne."

I busied myself opening the cap and putting a small amount of liquid on the cloth from the kit. It was kind of him to say, but I was not an oblivious child anymore. I could recognize the faults in my actions and the boldness with which I made mistakes—the last few days had been littered with them.

He reached out, his touch startling me as he grabbed my wrist. His gaze was so intense I wanted to look away.

"It's not, Addie. None of what has happened is your fault."

I pulled my hand back and added more liquid to the cloth. "You cannot know that."

"I don't have a clue why this is happening. I do not know the ways of The Light like you or my parents did. Maybe if they were here, they would have answers." He sounded broken at the thought, like it hadn't been the first time it crossed his mind. "But I do know you. I have known you forever, for longer than I can remember. You have followed The Light every day since I've known you. There is no one more deserving of a blessing, Addie."

My chest collapsed inward. No air was left in me. When I worked up the nerve to look back at him, his eyes almost killed me.

I could see in his gaze how certain he was of me, but that certainty came from the assumption that I was the same person he had known.

When he had known me, I walked in The Light. I was not certain he would feel the same if he knew what his years away were like, how I could not find The Light, no matter how long I introspected or how hard I tried.

"Whose blood is it?" I asked. Instead of an appropriate response, I gestured to the stain on the front of his shirt.

I tried not to take notice of his pause. "The outspoken one from dinner. The one who called you—" His mouth curled into a smile on the one side, "I don't feel remotely bad about what I did."

"Will he—"

I would not say it. Instead, I let him. "Die?"

No matter his reaction, I told myself I would not judge his actions. How could I when they were done to protect me? If he were to be my guard one day, I should be grateful for any length he would go to keep me safe.

Still, the mere concept of him doing that contrasted so deeply with the boy I knew.

I held my face in what I hoped was a neutral expression.

"No," he said, and his face softened. "When I left him, he was hidden away in trees but still breathing."

Some men took pleasure hurting others. The one that held a knife to me was that kind of man. So was Cedric. They took pleasure in having power over another, even if the source of that power caused another person pain. Ezrah spoke without that satisfaction, and I took comfort in knowing that, even if his time out here had changed some things, it had not changed that.

I took the damp cloth and wiped the dirt and blood away from his brow. "I didn't know he was there."

"He tried to sneak up on me by the horses. I heard him in the trees and went to investigate."

My leg pressed into his as I leaned in to continue wiping the blood from his face. The cloth was quickly becoming filthy, and I folded it carefully to make it last as long as possible.

"What happened?" My voice was quiet.

He let out a sigh. "I saw him before he saw me. I had the jump on him. I knocked him down hard enough he wouldn't be getting back up. Then he said some… inappropriate things—"

"About me."

He didn't verify that. "I made him stop. He pulled a knife—"

My eyes narrowed. "A knife?"

He shook his head. "It wasn't an issue. I took care of it."

"Did you not have yours?"

His jaw clenched. "It was in the tent."

"Ezrah."

"I took care of it, Adenne. I'm fine."

My head shook as my heart pounded. That could have gone a lot worse.

He winced as he reached over to the kit and pulled out the same liquid and fresh cloth, soaking it.

"What are you doing?"

Ezrah gestured for me to come closer and I complied. He lightly swiped at the cut on my neck and I winced.

He pulled back. "You okay?"

I nodded and he continued.

"I hate seeing you hurt," he whispered.

"I'm okay."

He shook his head. "What I saw happening when I was running towards you was not okay. You don't have to pretend it was nothing. Not with me"

I opened my mouth to protest but nothing came out. Instead, tears welled in my eyes.

Ezrah set down the cloth and lightly placed his hand on my cheek, forcing my gaze to his.

"I'm not going to let them hurt you again. I won't let anyone hurt you, I promise." I held his stare for a moment, watching those colors in his eyes swirl. With no words to offer him, I gave a small nod and he let go.

Not wanting to think too deeply on what that promise would mean, I reached my hand down to rest it where the blood was on the side of his chest. It was still wet.

Ezrah hissed out a breath at my touch. When I looked at him, his eyes were pulled tightly shut.

I pulled my hand back and lifted his shirt. A long open gash of skin curved around his side, and blood still seeped from it. When his chest rose, I could see the skin pull open. The base of my skull pounded again.

"Were you not going to tell me?" The question left through gritted teeth in the same manner his gasp did.

"It's not as bad as it looks."

That was not an answer to my question.

If he weren't hurt, I would have fucking hit him.

"You're a stubborn prick."

He laughed and then winced. "You can't call me names, Addie. I'm hurt."

Ignoring him, I twisted at my waist to pull out a different bottle I had seen earlier. I knew this one was for open wounds, but nothing about how it should be applied. I reached for a thinner white cloth and folded it in my hands.

Why send me out here with a medical kit without knowledge of its contents?

"For fuck's sake, Ezrah." I turned back to him, straddling him to get close enough to inspect it. "You don't know how serious it is." I gingerly put my fingertips above the wound, pulling his shirt upward to expose it fully. When his teeth clenched again, I traced the skin even more lightly. "It *hurts* you, Ezrah. Why didn't you say anything?"

"I told you," his eyes watched as my hand moved against

his bare skin, "it's not that bad. Besides," I felt his leg shift under where I straddled him now, "I am thoroughly distracted from any pain at the moment."

His leg moved upwards, creating pressure between mine. It made me acutely aware of how close we had become. My hand was against his bare chest, his leg fully pressed against me. I could feel his breath on mine like I had before. His hand grabbed the back of my thigh.

The contact reminded me of those few moments before Jonah had arrived. The way I pressed against him in the tent, how he pulled me back to him when I tried to move away. I wasn't sure what he wanted then, but the longer he held me here, the more certain I became.

"I like it when you curse," he said. My cheeks flushed.

If it weren't for my hand being so close to where he bled, I would have gotten very lost in… whatever this was.

Against my body's instinct, I leaned back slightly. Having space brought me clarity.

"You won't be distracted long." I ignored how raspy my voice sounded. "I have to clean it, and I imagine it will hurt badly."

He looked at the cloth in my hand. "Yes, it will."

When I moved my hand closer, he stopped me. "I would imagine," he said, "that you have not done this before?"

"Fixed a gaping hole in a man's chest? No, that was not part of my training."

He sighed. "It's not a gaping hole, it's just a cut, and you're not going to fix it, just clean it. I'll get stitched at the Temple Majora."

"It's a bad idea to wait."

"Giving you a needle and thread would be worse." He smiled at me through the pain.

I did not return the gesture. "Ezrah—"

"If you don't know what you're doing, you could make it worse, Addie. This isn't a great solution, but it's the best option. You'll pack the wound here, and I will get it properly tended at the Temple."

My heart jumped. "When will we get there?"

"By nightfall, I think. We are not far off now."

That sinking feeling in my chest came back, emptying me. I filled back up with fear.

So close to getting my answers. My last chance. I still had no idea what I would do once I arrived.

"Okay," I whispered.

"You'll need to soak more of the gauze."

"Gauze?"

"The white stuff."

I had no idea how he could be so gentle even while bleeding before me. As a silent kind of thanks, I did not fight his instructions.

"Now," he said, "you are going to clean just the edges of the wound…"

"Okay."

"Then push what you can of the gauze inside of it."

"I—what?"

I looked at the slice, how the skin opened and closed when he breathed.

"Admittedly," he whispered, "It may have been a deeper cut than I originally thought," I could kill him, "but that should slow down the bleeding long enough to get us to the Temple."

"Should?"

"I'll be fine, Addie."

"I'm getting tired of you repeating that."

The corner of his mouth tilted upwards. "I'm getting tired of you doubting me."

His confidence usually irritated me. It could drive me insane, but right now it centered me. I took a deep breath. "Okay," I said and shifted forward.

His hands stopped mine. "First, I need something to bite down on. Something thick, leather would be best."

I was unwilling to get up and leave him; if I did, I would lose my nerve. I looked him up and down, my gaze settling on the strap of leather that held up his pants.

Gently, I turned and put the gauze back into the clean medical kit. When I turned around, my hands met the metal clasp of the strap and pulled it open.

His leg shifted again.

"Now that," his voice was raspy, "is distracting."

I looked at his eyes and picked a shade of brown to watch as I pulled on one side of the leather, the strap coming off around his body. When it came loose, he let out a stream of air.

I would not let myself get distracted, not by the fact that his pupils were so big they were taking over the color I had been watching or by the fact that his pants hung loosely around his hips now. One less obstacle between us.

Heat rushed through me, redness creeping up my neck and face.

I did not look down. I kept searching for that color in his eyes as my hands folded the leather over itself. I handed it over to him.

Before he put it between his teeth he said, "Whatever you do, don't stop. It will hurt more if you do."

I swallowed even though my mouth was dry, and nodded.

He bit down as I grabbed the soaked gauze.

When my hands came back to him, I did not stop. Not even when he screamed.

18

Expectations

It was not easy to get Ezrah back onto his horse. The sound he made when he pulled himself up echoed against the few trees that surrounded us. I offered him help, holding my two hands clasped together at his foot level so he could step on them to further boost himself. We used to do that as children when we were trying to climb a new rock or tree; one of us would boost the other, then the other would turn back around and pull them up.

He shook his head no, refusing my help, and I stood awkwardly bent over for a moment. Blood rushed to my face as I straightened. It was likely for the best. I was not sure I could bear his weight now anyway. We were no longer children.

Once he was on his horse, I looked back at him. "You okay?"

"Yeah," he said. I wasn't convinced.

His shoulders folded in on themselves, and his eyelids

were heavy like he had not slept. I understood that, though. This day felt so long, and it was not even halfway through. I couldn't imagine being in that amount of pain on top of everything else.

I had done what he asked and didn't hesitate, pushing the gauze firmly into his thin, deep gash. By the time I pushed all that we had into the wound, the dripping had stopped. I wiped up the blood around it and watched to ensure it didn't restart. Still, I kept a close eye on him to ensure he didn't take a turn for the worse.

We rode as quickly as we could. The rain clouds had begun to let loose their drops just as we turned out back on the shallow stream. I knew getting him to help was best, and the Devoted at Temple Majora would be the closest option. As much as I wanted to get there quickly, I did not want the ride to hurt him more than it already had.

The wound was deep. His screams echoed in my ears when I pushed the gauze into it. Yet, he had said nothing, going the whole way to the stream telling me he was fine.

That meant one of two things.

One, that he was trying hard not to worry me. I am unsure if I should be thankful for the consideration or angry for how he always tried to keep me sheltered.

Two, he had faced much worse things while he was alone out here.

Those stories were the ones I wish I could shelter myself from. If I didn't know, I wouldn't have to worry or care, and I did not want to care.

As I looked at him, though, the way he still tried to hold his shoulders high despite the weak way his hands gripped the reins, I decided that trying not to care may be a wasted effort. I cared, and it would be easier to accept that than to suppress it. I let out a long, quiet breath.

He cared about me, too, and he had proven that in a way beyond words. He didn't have to say anything.

He protected me. He bled for me.

And I did not know how to thank him properly.

"You were never much of a fighter when we were young," I said. He gave me one of those quick laughs, like he could recount several memories that would make that true. Ones of trying to save birds with broken wings and crying when he couldn't. "What happened?"

I saw his expression shift from wistful to strained. "When you're out here traveling alone, you learn how to defend yourself quickly."

My voice was quieter now. "Did you do that often?"

"Defend myself?"

I nodded, and I could feel him watching me. "Not much at first. From the time I left to the time I worked for Cedric, things went smoothly. Afterwards, though..." he shrugged, "strangers would try to take advantage, take my food, money. Things like that. I learned how to make sure they didn't."

"How?"

He hesitated, then said, "Trial and error."

My stomach rolled over itself. I looked at the darkening purples around his eye socket and wondered how many times he had gotten bruised like that before he learned.

"I was shocked at first when Sage told me you had joined the Ruler's guard." Something fluttered in my stomach and I kept my eyes on the horizon to hide what my face would clearly give away. It was the same feeling I had when Sage first told me.

"Now it makes more sense."

He gave me that laugh again. "You weren't the only one who was shocked. Sage didn't believe me when I first told her. She laughed for a minute straight."

My heart ached a little, wishing she was here and I could hear her laugh. "If only she could see you now."

His laugh was labored, like it was a chore in his state. Still, I held onto the sound like they were a dessert I had stolen from dinner. "She would probably laugh at this, too, then tell me I need more training."

I grinned. "That sounds like her." And it did. Sage and Ezrah had always acted like they had one mind despite being born years apart. When they were very young, people assumed they were twins. It wasn't until Ezrah shot up in height that people could distinguish between older and younger.

She was right, though. Ezrah had not made it far into his training before I had pulled him away. Even if he had learned to fight out here, he still didn't know a lot. I did not want to see him get hurt like that again.

I did not want to cause it, either.

"Train me," I said.

"Train you to what?"

"To fight."

His eyes cut to mine then, his brows raised, and he winced at the movement. "You want to learn how to fight?"

I wished he did not sound like the idea of me fighting was impossible. "Yes. Well, no." I was doing an awful job explaining myself. "I want to learn how to *avoid* fighting. How to defend myself."

He laughed again, and I did not want to keep that one. It

was condescending and irritating. "I think you did a pretty good job defending yourself. You talked Cedric out of what he was doing. That is far more impressive than throwing a good punch." I did not blush at the thought of him thinking I was *impressive*. The heat in my cheeks was unrelated. "Besides," he continued, "you won't need to fight. You'll have the whole Ruler's guard."

"I might not."

"You will."

Stubbornness was not his most endearing trait.

"Still, if you had not been there—"

"I am going to be there."

"But if you weren't. Things would have gotten a lot worse, Ezrah." I felt his eyes on me, but I looked forward still. "He would have…" I cleared my throat, "it would have gotten worse. I do not want to get into a situation where no one is around to stop things from happening." When I met his eyes, they were sad. "I may not ever need it. Hopefully, I won't, but I would like to know."

The heat continued to crawl up my face as I watched his hands. His grip tightened on the reins for a long while, his knuckles going white. Eventually, they relaxed.

"Your parents won't be happy about it."

"They don't need to know. Besides, it won't be the first time we have snuck off alone together."

Words were sometimes just like vomit: thick, escaping unexpectedly, and impossible to shove back in once they were out in the world. The heat in my face was relentless, and my hands mirrored his, knuckles going white around the reins.

"You'd lie to them?"

"Ezrah," my laugh lacked humor, "that is all I have done

in the past few days. I'm an expert in it now."

He gave me another laugh to add to my collection. "Okay, I will teach you. Defense only. The fighting will be left to me. You will not be the first Ruler racing into battle."

"There has never been a Ruler with a battle to race into. Although, knowing my luck, I would be the first."

His smile tilted up on the side that faced me. "And aren't you so lucky?"

We rode without stopping for most of the day. The crops we passed changed in color and size. Thankfully, there were no more villages. The few people we saw in the fields paid us no mind. I felt my shoulders relax, knowing not many eyes were on me.

It was a rare feeling for me, even before this journey. Solitude was a commodity that I had to manipulate my way to get. I was never alone, but there was no doubt most days, I was lonely.

When I went back to Polaris, no matter how I returned, eyes would be on me again. Expectations in every glance, judgments in every glare. I wondered what color they would see looking back at them: gold or brown.

If they were brown, how long would people bother paying me any mind? At first, I was sure to garner their attention. Gossip would spread quickly, and people who did not know me would make assumptions about what happened. Solitude would be impossible to find for a long while.

But afterward, when the dust settled, would they bother to care about me? If I wasn't their Ruler, would they remember me at all?

Would it be the worst thing in the world if they didn't?

How would they write me into the texts?

An embarrassing mark on Rhea's pristine history. The Ruler who was not blessed.

I thought of the feeling I had when the heavy air filled my lungs in my special place behind the palace, how the croaking from the animals and the water crashing were the only sounds for miles. How my muscles relaxed, and my head finally cleared. No eyes found me there.

Maybe it wouldn't be so bad to be left alone.

I had no idea what I would do with myself if I didn't rule. I was not trained for an alternative path, but there was no doubt that a new path may lead me to alternatives worth considering.

My eyes cut to Ezrah, and I traced the line of his jaw until they settled on his lips. There were specific alternatives I had not considered for a long time.

Still, I was in this place of not knowing. There was no sense in making plans when I had no idea what our visit to the Temple Majora would bring.

I *could* rule, and things may still go according to my plan. The people of Rhea may be none the wiser of this minor mishap.

My hands were shaking with the need to finally have answers, and for all of this to be over.

In the sky above us the clouds were much grayer with no sun to be found. An unnaturally cold breeze pushed through me, making me shiver.

"Do you think we will make it by tonight?"

He looked up too, his eyes squinting like he was trying to see through the clouds. Then he glanced around like he could find a landmark he would recognize in these fields that were all the same to me.

"Hard to say for sure, but we might. Are you nervous?"

Ezrah was paler now, his eyelids drooped heavily over his eyes and his shoulders hung with exhaustion.

"I'll be less nervous when we get you some help."

His eyes were on me again. "Have you thought about what you will do once we get there?" he asked.

I nodded. "At first, I thought I would go to the library and see what I could find. I imagine there is more information there than at home. But that won't be an option."

"No?"

"As soon as we ride up to the doors, they will know who I am. They may not expect me, but once they see these—" I gestured to my eyes. "—they will know something is wrong. It is better to ask for help right away. Hopefully, the Highest Devoted will have an answer for me."

If anyone would, it would be him. The Highest Devoted oversaw the training of all the Devoted below him. He orchestrated the Temple's role in all ceremonies, be it a solstice or a blessing. Not only that, but he is the only one living who has communicated with the Deities besides my mother. If The Light or the Deities have something to say, it will be through him. He is the most likely person to know what I did wrong.

"He will." He sounded so sure again. "You will get your answers, Addie."

Sweat pooled in my palms. "We do not know that for certain."

"You may not, but I do." His face softened, his features becoming much more familiar. "You're going to get what you deserve. This is it—ruling is it. It's all you've ever wanted. If I'm wrong and we don't find answers here, I'll be with you until you get one. I will make sure you get what you want."

My stomach flipped over itself, and my heart squeezed together like it was trying to protect itself. My hands clutched the reins tighter. "Don't make a promise you don't intend to keep."

"I intend to keep my promise. I'm not leaving."

My heart unraveled and doubled in size, pressing against my chest, wanting out. He would be with me. He promised that.

For two years, I was certain I would never see him again. For the first while, that absolutely broke me. He was my best friend, the one person I always relied on. He helped me escape from the part of my life that had trapped me. Even as children, he understood what I needed. I relied on him entirely and without hesitation. As we grew up, our lives seemed to fuse together. We were not separate beings. My life was so deeply intertwined with him, and I would have done anything to become closer.

He was mine, and I never thought I would have to live without him. When he kissed me, I was confident that was true. When we went further, we were making a promise to each other. Despite coming from different worlds and how unwise and complicated a relationship would be, we chose each other. Those few weeks we spent together had been the happiest of my life.

When he left, everything changed. It was difficult, but I learned how to be on my own. To trust myself. To hold myself up. I was ripped apart, half of who I used to be. The pain I felt when I lost him was something I refused to go through again. Instead, I learned to function on my own.

I opened myself up to other people, to Sage, but never like I had with him. No one would ever replace him for me, and

I wouldn't let them if they tried. It was not a risk worth taking. Instead, I learned how to be alone, thinking I would always be that way.

And I was angry at what he had done to me, how he had left me there. I didn't understand. Not then and not now. He still has not told me why he left.

While he was gone, I made my assumptions about his choice. He was grieving, so deeply hurt when his parents passed. That alone would be enough to make someone need to escape.

In all the time I spent trying to understand his actions, I never thought I would hear him say he still wanted to be with me, promising he wouldn't leave me. There was a part of me stopping me from wholly believing it. Instinct was still trying to protect me from his words, claiming they weren't true.

But a bigger, more hopeful part of me wanted to believe him. He would be there until I got my answers and got what I wanted.

I thought of what he just said, that all I had ever wanted was to become Ruler.

Was that true?

"No." The word came out of me unexpectedly and hung in the air and I explained myself before he misunderstood. "No, ruling was not something I always wanted. It was always what I was expected to do." I cleared my throat. "There is a big difference. I am not sure it was something I ever *wanted*."

I did not know where the feeling had come from, but I knew it was true as soon as I spoke it out loud. The breath I let out was so heavy it made me dizzy. My shoulders felt lighter. How long had I been holding that weight?

Slowly, I looked at him. His eyes were assessing me. He

was trying to understand what I was saying. I wanted to explain myself further, but I did not think I could form the words. Not when I watched as his pupils grew large and his bottom lip fell open slightly.

His eyes didn't leave my face. I flushed red again, but I didn't look away from him this time or try to hide it. I held his gaze, hoping he could understand what I meant even if I didn't fully understand it myself.

"Maybe," he said, his voice rough, "if you don't get what you expected." He paused again. My heart wanted out of my body so badly it hurt. It strained against my chest towards him. Always toward him. "You could have what you wanted."

"Yes." My voice sounded rawer than I had ever heard it.

The look he gave me was open and honest. He knew exactly what I meant. We wanted the same thing.

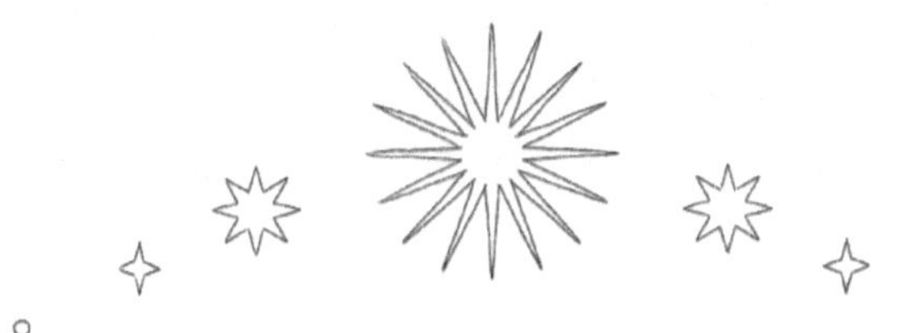

19

Better to Know

The closer we got to the Temple Majora, the faster my heart pumped. The place where I would find the answers.

The Temple was still out of our view, but the panic growing inside of me told me how close we were. I pretended it was because my body could feel The Light radiating off of the Temple walls. I had read about the feeling countless times. The Light had first come to Rhea here. The ground we walked on was the beginning of everything.

With The Light came life. Plants grew, animals were born, and humans eventually followed. But The Light was not finished until it created the Deities out of its own power.

The texts say that the Deities were created to control humans. Before them we were full of darkness and needed to be saved. They provided structure to keep all of Rhea on the right path by assigning roles to those within the city of Polaris and beyond. My ancestor took the place of Ruler and led the people based on the guidance given to them at their blessing ceremony. We thank them for this protection by celebrating The Light; burning our donations, introspecting and following the wishes of the Deities.

The Deities are a salvation for the weak and a gift to the needy. The Light has given them to us and so we give all we have in return.

The Light created them to help, so I could only hope they would help me.

The feeling around the Temple was always *euphoric,* like the weight that hung on people's shoulders and minds was lifted. I had read that any person who came here was forever changed by it.

"Do you feel it?" Ezrah asked with awe in his voice.

"Yes," I lied.

I didn't feel anything beyond my own fear.

Instead, I felt my body trying to shrink away from it. Not The Light itself, I still sought that, but I was shrinking away from the idea that this place would give me any answer, good or bad. If Ezrah was right, this place was where I would learn why I wasn't blessed and if there was anything I could do to repair the damage. It was here that I would figure out if I were to be a Ruler or if my life was about to become full of unexpected circumstances; whether or not I would get to do what was expected of me.

If I even wanted that, anymore. The conversation with Ezrah still ran through my head as the horses brought us closer.

There was a difference between what I wanted and was expected to do. For years I believed them to be the same, that I wanted to do what was expected of me.

But now? Did I want to rule, or was that the only option? Always the expectation.

And if I couldn't, rule? Would that change anything?

Would I want something different if I had more options?

Or was all of this worrying and change of heart due to the fact that I was scared shitless of what lay beyond those Temple doors?

I felt myself teetering again on this precipice.

That was the tricky part about being in this position. There was no way to know the result of the decision. I was on the edge of a cliff and had no idea what I was allowed to do about it. I did not know my options.

It was all too much.

I was so fucking tired of this feeling.

My fists clenched, my shoulders hunched over, and I could not loosen either. My stomach had twisted itself up, groaning through the latter part of the day from the lack of food. My body was retreating from whatever was about to happen.

I wanted to know.

I did not want to know.

I didn't know.

My thoughts circled that way. Every rotation making me feel sicker. Even though the clouds were still gray and blocking the sun, I knew the day was growing late. I could feel it in the soreness of my legs and the way Onyx seemed to drag her feet. We were getting close.

The fields that had once surrounded us ended. The ground was dry here like it was just outside of the palace, the land cracking apart in tiny cliffs of its own, creating patterns that spread as far as I could see.

"It looks like home," Ezrah said, but the ground did not feel as dormant as it did outside of Polaris, it was filled with something… else. Something *other*. My skin tingled, starting at my fingertips. The feeling worked through me until it ran down my spine, making me shiver. It continued until I felt it everywhere. I could not tell if the feeling was relaxing or causing my body to clench tighter.

Maybe my body would finally loosen once this was over.

The clouds above us finally parted, and the sun broke through them in glorious ribbons. It streaked across the sky as if leading us forward. I breathed deeply, and with every inhale, I pretended to pull those rays of sunshine into me. I tried to fill myself with them.

Maybe The Light was sending me a sign. It was here.

Perhaps this would go better than I expected.

Suddenly, Temple Majora appeared on the horizon in a golden flash. It was so bright I had to look away. Yellow still glowed behind my eyelids as I blinked away the glare.

"We're here," Ezrah said.

Looking back, I took my time to blink it into focus. A beam of sunlight glowed directly on the Temple, reflecting its golden walls back to us. There were still gray clouds in the sky, but they circled the Temple like they wouldn't risk coming any closer. Even though the sun was low in the sky, it still had the power to turn the Temple Majora into a beacon of The Light.

I had always known it would be an impressive sight, but I never expected it to shine this brightly, even from a distance. It looked like the sun had crashed onto the ground or that The

Light could be standing on the horizon's edge.

My back straightened.

Ezrah was grinning widely at me. "Ready?" He asked.

"No," I said, only half-joking.

"Yes, you are. You have been ready for an answer since the night you left home."

"I want an answer," I said, "I just…"

I did not have to explain myself. He knew what I meant.

"Better to know, though, right?"

When I knew I could make a plan. Anything was better than the suspended state I was living in now.

"Better to know," I agreed.

With that, Ezrah led us forward. Our pace quickened as we approached, and the closer we got, the larger I realized the Temple was.

The building was of mammoth proportions. No structure in Polaris could even come close to it. Golden spires came out of the roof, large and round at the base before tapering upward. Its spires went so high that if the clouds dared to come any closer, they would break through them. If I squinted, I could see each spire was made out of individual golden tiles. The light winked off of them and back to us.

"It's…"

"Yeah," Ezrah said.

At its front, there were towering doors made of solid gold. They had to be taller than the palace itself, and they beamed at us like we were being summoned to go through them. From a distance, I could see a slight split between them—the doors were slightly ajar. A tall wall encompassed the building, obscuring parts of it from our view and creating a singular entrance and exit. Even though the walls were made of sleek white marble, The Light favored them just as well. The marble gleamed in the sun. The rest of what we could see of the building above the wall was white as well, but golden decorations covered the walls in beautiful, indistinguishable patterns.

I could not take my eyes off its reflection. I let them burn until they watered. Now that we were past the clouds, the sun came and heated my skin under the cloak. I nudged it back to expose myself to The Light, and heat coursed through my veins.

The words people had written about this place could never do it justice.

For the first time in days, my bones felt steady. My back sat straighter, and my heart was no longer fighting me—there was no twisting or racing. After so long not feeling it, I could not tell if it was The Light making me feel this way. I hoped it was.

I felt full. I felt light.

Peace. I think I felt at peace.

I wondered if this was what Ezrah felt when he first came here. Did this feeling come to him even in his grief?

I had never lost someone like he had, but I could imagine this place would be healing for that kind of pain.

It was only after my eyes stopped burning that I saw how many Devoted waited outside those large golden doors.

They had blended into the white marble wall, but now I could see that they stood in two lines on either side of the entry in their long white cloaks. They all had their hood up and their eyes pointed downward, and looked identical, standing there like marble statues, waiting for something.

Were they waiting for me?

My hands clenched. They would not know I was coming. How could they have? No one would expect me to be coming to the Temple Majora. It was so far off my path. If someone had seen us on the road, they would not have been able to get word here this quickly. They could not be waiting outside for me.

And yet they stood there, stoic in their composure, when I arrived.

My heart racing, we continued forward until they surrounded us on either side. Still, they did not move.

Straight ahead of us was a man. He was short in stature, probably just coming up to my chin, but he held the same authority as a man much larger would. The cloak he wore differed from the rest, white with gold edging and no hood. He was bald on the top with gray hair circling the sides—the hair stopped just a little too far into his face, making his eyes seem too far apart.

He was the only one who looked at me as we approached.

I knew this man only from his reputation. My parents had met him, and I supposed I had too, but I was too young to remember. Mother said he was a powerful man, integral to how our nation ran. He was the only one closer to The Light than the Ruler's family. Other than the Deities, he was the closest one in Rhea.

His power went beyond being close to The Light. He led all of the Devoted to follow the same way as their teacher and their guide. He ran all Temples, along with any ceremonies, and ensured The Light and the Deities got their donations. He kept them happy.

To say the Highest Devoted was integral was almost an

understatement.

And he was looking right at me like he was expecting me.

I heard Ezrah say something beside me, but he was quickly interrupted.

"Finally," the Highest Devoted said, "you have made it." His voice rang out across the crowd smoothly. His tone could calm an entire room of angry men with one syllable. Even among these tall walls, it did not echo.

Onyx took us to the edge of where the path to the marble stairs began.

"You were expecting me?" I said. My voice did not waver, even if my grip did.

"Of course."

When I glanced at Ezrah, he was observing the man.

It was inappropriate to ask questions of anyone in the Temple, even if I was a Ruler. Or almost a Ruler. How could one question someone so close to The Light?

I asked him anyway. "How?"

He watched me for a long moment before letting out one singular burst of air that almost resembled a laugh. "Our visitor told us of your arrival."

My heart dropped from my chest to the ground.

"Visitor?"

It was clear I was pushing my luck with my questions because this time, he did not laugh. His eyes turned from inviting to piercing.

"Come," he said. Then he turned on his heel, expecting me to follow.

I looked at Ezrah again and his fading color. "Wait," I

said, testing the patience of a man that did not seem to have much to spare.

He did not even fully turn to me. His body only half-faced me, the eyebrow I could see was raised.

"My friend." I hesitated, the word *friend* not sounding as foreign as it should have. "He needs help. He's hurt."

"Addie," Ezrah muttered to my side. He, too, could sense the test I was putting the Highest Devoted through and did not think it was wise.

The eyebrow lowered, and the Highest Devoted just nodded his head. The two closest Devoted came forward and held Ezrah's horse as he got down. One held him steady while the other began guiding his horse away.

"I'll find you after," he said to me. "Good luck."

"You too," I said meekly.

I watched him being led away for too long, but my eyes were stuck on the way he was limping, leaning to one side. I hoped The Light was kind to him and that Ezrah was right when he told me it wasn't a bad wound.

Looking away, I saw a Devoted by my side as well. With their eyes down, I could not tell if it was a woman or a man, but their hand was already grabbing Onyx's harness, ready to lead her away.

I jumped down, pulling my cloak straight around my shoulders. Onyx was walking swiftly away, leaving my side, and I was alone in this new place, surrounded by strangers who wouldn't look at me.

Ahead, the Highest Devoted was still turned only halfway toward me, watching me intently.

I walked up the few stairs toward him, my steps echoing

against the marble floor. When I was within reach, he stepped away, leading me forward into the Temple.

The walls inside the hallway were white, too, reaching far above my head. They held the same golden detailing as the exterior, but up close I was able to better see the details.

Elegant patterns made of suns and stars depicted The Light in its many forms. The stars seemed to swirl together on the wall, glittering as they moved. It was as if they were desperate to tell me a story, screaming to show me the history these walls held. As I looked at them, tears welled in my eyes that I could not explain. They were beautiful.

This place was comforting and warm. Still, as I looked at the golden patterns, I was reminded of the dress I had worn only days before. How the beading glowed like these walls did, and how, when Sage placed the cloak over my shoulders, I felt the same warmth.

Those moments were the last ones I had before my world changed.

I wanted to return to them, where my family would be with me. When my mother and my father told me how proud they were of me.

I wanted to go further back to when Ezrah had still been with me, and no tragedy had found us yet. Back to the times spent within Temple walls much shorter than these. The marble was a little darker, and the hallways a little less wide. Where waterfalls were mere steps away. Those memories gave me comfort that no Temple ever could because they held certainty.

What I walked into now held no certainty at all. The beautiful walls around me seemed to be leaning forward above my head, caging me in. Somehow, despite my body sensing the comforting energy of this place, my mind told me I did not belong.

I had yet to learn who this visitor was, how they knew I was here, or if being blessed was still an option.

The Highest Devoted seemed to know I was coming, and he was not shocked by my brown eyes or that Ezrah was with me. He knew I was not blessed, but did he know why?

Nothing about what I was walking toward was certain. Still, I followed his steps as he led me further into the Temple. Hallways branched off the path we were walking, constantly asking me to go left or right, but we stayed straight.

My heart raced, and I wanted badly to ask who this visitor was again, but I had tested the Highest Devoted's patience enough. If I asked another question, I was not sure he would answer it.

He stopped finally in front of two more large doors. I could see the details painted onto them that depicted when The Light first came. I had seen pictures of these exact doors in the texts, but I never knew I would see them in person. I could look at this art for hours, taking in every detail.

The Highest Devoted opened them for me. When he stepped to the side, he lowered his head, like the others had when I first approached the Temple.

I walked past him, past the beautiful doors, and into the Temple's main room. The energy here was tactile, all-consuming and definitely not *human*.

Then the doors shut loudly behind me.

20

Answers Found

I looked to the left, where the white walls met a skylight above my head. The sunlight crept through and lit the gold detailing in a beautiful glow.

Then I looked to the right, where the same gold detailing was cast in shadow, giving me a sinking feeling.

There was no sound in this room, no echo coming from my feet. Even the sound of my breath was muted. I stopped walking near the middle of the room and waited, dread filling me. The whole thing was so similar to my blessing.

A man *flew* down from the high roof and landed in front of me, golden wings tucking in behind him.

I blinked once, trying to bring him into focus and make sure he was real.

He had to have been the tallest person I had ever seen. His skin was tanned like he had been basking in the sun. A bare, defined torso with lines so sharp, if I touched them, they might cut me. He was made of pure angles, right down to how his cheekbones cut sharply, dividing his face into two neat halves.

I blinked again, trying to get my eyes to focus. The man seemed to be in a haze.

Not a haze, a glow.

The man was *glowing*.

He was not a man.

My knees connected with the marble. I felt the impact go into my hips and back. Even still, I held myself upright, and my eyes fell to the floor.

My heart pounded, blood pumping into my ears.

Fuck. A Deity.

He was here.

Tears pushed their way into my downcast eyes as relief loosened the tension in my shoulders.

Answers.

I was about to get *answers*.

I looked at the thin gray lines that spread across the white marble-like lighting strokes and waited, my chest heaving up and down.

I expected to come to the Temple Majora and have to beg for help. I hoped to get answers but never fully expected to receive any.

And now answers were standing right in front of me. He was waiting for me.

And he wasn't saying anything.

My chest rose and fell heavily as I waited in silence.

Very few people met the Deities, so there was little written on the etiquette of it, but it did not take a brilliant mind to assume that I should not address him first.

Still, the silence stretched in a way that consumed me, eating away at my skin and making me grow hot.

"I—"

"We do not have time for that," he interrupted, his words ringing out against the marble walls.

My heart pounded so loudly that I was sure he could hear it.

Why was he *here*?

My head tilted up as my eyes scanned him, this Deity, standing before me.

In the same way little was known about the etiquette of meeting a Deity, little was known about what they looked like. All that existed were artists' best guesses. They could capture their bodies and some basic features, but never the details of their faces.

Still, I knew who stood before me. I recognized him from his copper hair. A few wisps were loose around his face, streaking across his sun-kissed skin like flames. Every inch of him was hard, like there was too little skin stretched over his enormous frame.

This was Justus, the first made.

For someone claiming they didn't have time, he was not rushing to explain why he was here. Instead, he stared at me. His gaze started as impassive, like I could be anybody. Then, slowly, his impassiveness faded into something that made me squirm.

He was disgusted by me.

I looked away again. "I am sorry, I—"

"We do not have time for that, either."

He did not shout, but his words echoed all the same. When they came off the walls and back to me, I felt them split me open and fill me with shame.

I sat on my knees before him and did not know what to do.

"You are not blessed," he said. His words gripped my heart in his giant fist and squeezed. My cheeks reddened, and I felt that familiar heat creep up to my hairline.

Bile coated my throat.

He said it like he was stating a fact, without the cadence of blame. Still, it was a fact that both of us knew well, and I did not need reminding.

Silence fell again, and I knew if that kept happening, the urge to scream would grow.

"But you don't know why," he finished his thought.

It was not a question, but I answered. "No, I do not. That is why I am here."

He spoke like someone that had all the time in the world.

"I am here to explain why."

Answers.

My lungs tried to expand to gasp in air, but I suppressed them, trying to stay as impassive as he was. I clasped my shaking hands and pushed them into my legs. Relief was only moments away.

And yet, my heart twisted in a way I was beginning to grow accustomed to.

I wanted to know, to have answers. Not only that—I needed it. My body craved it.

But I was not ready to sit in front of Justus and The Light and have them tell me what I did wrong and why I was not deserving.

I thought I was ready for that but I was wrong. The truths

of the mistakes I had made were safe inside my head where I could control them. Once someone else acknowledged them, said them out loud to me, and blamed me, those mistakes would finally destroy me.

I was not ready for that. Every muscle in my body told me to run.

But I stayed there, on my aching knees with my hands pressed into my thighs, and I prepared to be destroyed.

"There has been a disagreement among the Deities."

About me, they disagreed about me.

"We are on the cusp of war."

My eyes cut up to his. "War?" The word escaped me before I could stop it. His eyes narrowed. He was not impressed with the human in front of him.

"With each other. The Deities are at war with each other."

Had what I had done been so wrong?

"War over what?" I asked, digging myself further into his disgrace.

He sighed. "War over how *people* should be controlled."

He said *people* with the same disgust he looked at me with. I wanted to shrink into the ground, melt into the marble, and become one with it. He wasn't making any sense, and I needed him to make sense. I needed any of this to make sense. "Controlled?"

"Ruled," he said, irritated. "We disagreed with how you all should be ruled."

They didn't want me to rule. This war was my fault.

So quietly, I wasn't sure I even said it aloud, I whispered, "So this is about me."

"You have been foretold to us for a long time."

"Foretold?"

Something in the air *cracked* and it took me a moment to realize that it came from him. I looked back at the floor, tracing the gray lightning in the marble as I waited for him to chastise me. His tolerance was growing thin. I stayed there, eyes low, while that awful silence stretched again. Somehow, the lack of noise was deafening. That is, until it gave way to a ringing in my ears, as if my body was trying to fill the silence with something.

"I am sorry. I am just trying to understand." I paused, still waiting to be reprimanded. When nothing happened, I looked up at him. "Is this why I was not blessed?"

He took two steps closer to me. His footfalls made no sound as if he was walking on air.

"This is why you *cannot* be blessed." At my empty stare, he continued, "All three of us are needed to bless you. One has been swayed by darkness and veered from the path of The Light. Manumit does not want to see you in power, and because we need all of us to bless you, we cannot do the ceremony until his threat of divergence is dealt with."

Manumit.

I felt dizzy from all this knowledge. None of it made any sense. I fought to control my mind and understand what Justus was trying to tell me. He was so vague I had to comb through his words to find any kind of meaning.

The Deities were powerful in different ways. Justus controlled light in a tangible way, fires, sun, lightning, and heat. Hebera embodied life and growth. Manumit was full of enlightenment, inner knowledge. They all were so closely linked to The Light that I didn't understand how any of them could be swayed away from it, or why they would.

Unless it was about how I was somehow foretold. Did Manumit know what this… prophecy about me was? Was that why he would turn against the others? Would my time as Ruler be that bad?

Asking questions was not a good idea, but I still lacked answers.

"What did I do wrong?"

"This is much bigger than you."

I swallowed. Justus did not like to be questioned, but I did not like that I traveled across Rhea to find answers to deal with cryptic warnings of war. He could hurt me, he could kill me, really, but I was through with the unknown.

"So why now?"

His jaw clenched. "Because not all are strong enough to resist a prophesied future."

"Who prophesied this? What does the prophecy say?"

In all the texts I have read, I had never heard of the future being decided by prophecy. And yet this Deity…

He stared at me, his brow furrowed. His eyes swirled like there was a fire in them. I watched his hands make and release fists three times before I realized he would not answer me.

I tried another question.

"This war, what will it mean for the people? For me?"

"That is out of your control."

It seemed a lot of things were.

"Will people be harmed?"

I saw his jaw tighten again. "That is out of your control," he repeated.

My heart stopped. I couldn't breathe as reality settled in

and made my hands shake.

A war.

Fuck.

"What am I to do?"

His eyes were slits as he stared down at me. My mother's eyes were like molten gold, but Justus' were like flames. I could see swirling red through his narrowed eyelids. It was hard to keep contact, so I looked away.

"What you were born to do."

"What?"

"Rule," he said simply.

I almost laughed, doubled over on myself and laughed in the middle of the Temple. Then, I realized he was serious. He was telling me to do the exact thing he just told me I couldn't.

"I-I do not understand."

"Is that not what you have trained to do?"

"It is."

"Then I do not see a problem."

His tone implied that this was a simple problem and a low level of concern to him, that this war was merely annoying. It suggested that taking my life and completely turning it inside out was not a concern of his. He spoke as if he didn't care, which was the opposite of what I had been taught about the Deities. When The Light made the three of them, it did so with the intention that they would take care of us. Yet, the first one made was standing before me, telling me there was a war, and acting as if he would rather be anywhere else.

He may not see a problem with his suggestion, but there were plenty. The people would not accept a Ruler who was not blessed, nor should they. How could they trust me when The

Light would not, even if the reason for that was not my fault, as Justus had suggested?

If I went back home and told them I was not blessed, they would know I had left here and lied to them. My parents would know I left rather than seek their help, and for the first time, I wondered if that would hurt them.

And if I go back and tell them that the Deities are at war? They would think I was crazy.

"It will not work." I paused, waiting for him to ask me why. He stood there with his arms crossed, his golden skin flexing. "They will not let me become Ruler if I am not blessed."

"Who are *they*?"

"The people, my parents. I cannot rule if I am not blessed."

I looked down at my hands again and how they hung limply in my lap. These answers were not what I expected. I wanted a simple conclusion. This was just creating a mess that I did not know how to clean up.

Justus took a long time to answer, and I did not have to look up to know that his brows were furrowed as he looked down at me in that same inferior way. His wings flicked as if he were irritated.

"That is your problem, not mine."

My eyes cut upward at that. "What?" I asked.

"I am not here to interfere with the struggles of humans. I am here to explain, not fix this for you."

"But it is a problem of your creation," I said, my voice raising. I was through with kindness and timidness. It had gotten me nowhere. Even if this man, this *Deity*, could kill me, I would no longer be quiet, nor would I be patient.

It did not look like he would, either. His eyes lit up, and the glow under his skin looked like it caught on fire, flickering and growing.

"Be careful," he warned.

I was done being careful.

"You have come here and given me answers with no solutions. Now you wish for me to pretend this is not your problem?"

A bright light emitted from him, blinding me. I looked away, squeezing my eyes shut as I heard him scream, "I am not here to fix your problems! You are the Ruler and so you shall rule!"

Lightning cracked overhead, created by his rage. The air in the room felt changed, like there was energy around us. It buzzed, making my heart pound as anger rose in me.

"Tell me how!" I shouted.

I felt tingles dance across my skin, like lightning was branding me. I wanted to lean into it just as much as I wanted it to disappear. I wondered if this was what it was like to feel The Light in its truest form.

"You insubordinate little thing. I should kill you and put an end to this."

Sweat dripped down the nap of my neck as the room grew hot. I was dizzy and I thought I was crying but my skin was too numb to know for sure. "I just want your guidance," I begged in a whisper as I looked down to my shaking hands.

His voice was eerily quiet compared to the energy that buzzed around us. "You will continue this pilgrimage. You will seek out the Sisters and get your title. When you arrive back in

Polaris, you will find a way to rule your people with a fist of iron. If you do not, I will strip you of everything you are."

The lighting cracked again overhead. I felt my skin charge. Tiny bolts of lightning danced against me and grew hotter until they burned. I wanted to itch them off. I needed them off. Panic set in at this invasive feeling, this energy I could not escape. I rubbed my hand up my arm, but it was no use.

I could not feel my hands or my arms. Every part of my body was buzzing and numb. I felt alive and dead. I couldn't breathe, and yet my chest lifted and fell rapidly. I was trying to understand what he said to me, but the words wouldn't register like my brain refused to accept them.

Thunder cracked at the same time as lightning flashed, and my head filled with pressure. It felt as if my skull was shrinking, compressing my brain. Instinctually, my hands came up to either side of my head and squeezed as if applying more pressure would somehow fix this.

I could hear cracking that sounded too close to be the storm outside.

In front of me, the light that Justus was emitting was growing brighter than before. Even when I closed my eyes it was still there, as persistent as the lightning on my skin or the pressure in my head. Colors danced behind my eyelids as the light grew, creating patterns of yellows and oranges. I pressed my palms into my eyes, trying to stop myself from opening them to see what those colors looked like without any barriers. Despite the pain, I wanted to see what a Deity really looked like. I wanted to see The Light.

Suddenly, it was dark. Silence hung in the room like an old friend, this time much more welcome company than it was before. There was no lightning on my skin or pressure in my head. No colors danced behind my eyelids.

I knew what to expect when I opened my eyes. I just wanted to deny it.

When I finally peeled them open, the space that Justus had occupied was gone.

Once again, I was alone in a Temple.

21

More Questions

I didn't know where I was going, but my feet carried me out of the room, through the tall doors, and into the hallway. The decorated walls didn't have the same shine they had before.

My arms circled my waist, my hands clutching their opposite sides like I was trying to squeeze myself in tighter. I wasn't sure if I was trying to merely hold myself together or to squeeze tight enough that I would disappear. Either way, I missed the corset, the way it held me upright because now my back hunched over in a way that made it immediately ache.

I had just seen a Deity.

That statement played on repeat in my head. It was not what I expected when I came here. I expected to scour libraries and beg the Devoted to help, to try to get them to believe that I was their Ruler. I had hoped for answers, but I never expected to meet a Deity.

Not that Justus had provided me answers.

I had met a Deity, and I was still not Blessed.

The thought halted my steps for a moment. It made the space behind my eyes sting like I had been holding them open for too long. I did not expect to meet a Deity and come out the other side unchanged.

To say I was completely unchanged was unfair. I was different. I knew more now. I just was not certain this change was for the better.

It was all… confusing. It was too much back and forth for my brain to comprehend. I was only ever given half of what I wanted, just bits and pieces of what I needed. Like someone was dangling my desires just outside of my reach, and I could do nothing to grasp them.

That was what Justus had left me with; no clear plan, just enough information to confuse me. It was no wonder why my head ached. My vision was so blurry I could no longer define the lines that made the pictures in the hallways. The swirling stars and suns were just blurs of gold, and did not shine like before. I did not know if that resulted from overcast skies or something… else.

My body ached almost as much as my head did. It begged me to lie down and sleep, and I craved my bed, with its four posters and plush sheets. I craved being home. I craved what my life was like before all of this. I wanted that back. All the while, I was avoiding thinking about the biggest problem.

I met with a Deity, and he told me he was at war.

My mind couldn't fully comprehend it. It almost seemed like a joke, although I doubted the Deities did that. How could I have not noticed the beginnings of a war? What signs had I overlooked?

The skies had grown gray and stormier through our journey, that much was true, but the weather hadn't been extreme in any way. There were no droughts, no high winds, or impossibly heavy rains. The storms seemed normal, even if I knew they might have come from the Deity's energy.

But even if I had missed the sign that the storms had brought with them, I had known something was wrong. When I was not blessed I had felt this *shift*, like the world was changing around me and I was the catalyst. I never expected to be right.

I came all this way to find out what exactly had happened, what I had caused. I never expected the answer to be a war.

It was right in front of my face this entire time. I assumed that it was something I did wrong, but this was apparently much bigger than me. I wasn't the cause of this war, but I was foretold to play a part in it. The Deities were at war because Manumit no longer agreed with the others, and somehow it involved me.

Yet, I was the smallest part of a bigger picture, one with The Light and Deities and war. My lack of blessing now felt so little in comparison.

"We're going to be at *fucking war*," I whispered to myself. It echoed off of the empty halls.

What would war look like? For my people? For me? The word was always more of a concept, something that the texts instructed was to be avoided at all costs. My people had never fought, there was not anyone trained to fight beyond the Ruler's guard. The people were starving from all they had given to The Light, and as a reward, they would suffer.

War meant people would suffer.

Even if they didn't fight in it, if the Deities fought over our heads, the energy would not be avoidable. The power The Light gave them would mean destruction.

My feet continued to carry me forward across the marble floors. My vision was blurry, but I could sense I was in a different area. Ahead of me was greenery, tall trees, and plant life that twisted among itself. It looked like it had been here a long time, like the Temple Majora may have been built around it.

These gardens were encompassed by short, white marble fences that created a walking path through a labyrinth. The greenery pushed against the fences, refusing to be contained.

The air here was heavy, and it reminded me of home. I took a deep breath and let the dampness fill my lungs. I wondered how much water would have to be in the air for a person to drown.

Drowning was worth the risk to get this familiar heavy air into my lungs. I craved the familiar so badly. Slowly, my hands released the tension on my hips, easing with each breath. It was not until they fell to my sides that I stepped forward again.

The garden was beautiful. The longer I spent walking among its paths, the more my eyes came back into focus. There were some plants that I recognized from home and some that were completely new. They wrapped around me, spilling onto my path and caressing my arms as I walked past.

What felt like a raindrop fell on my shoulder, then another drop confirmed rain when it fell on my face, running down the side of my nose. I looked up and saw no ceiling above me; dark gray clouds created a ceiling instead. The Temple walls still surrounded me, but instead of a roof above me, it was an open sky, allowing the rain in. I understood now why the air seemed so clear to me.

As more rain dropped, I tilted my face back, letting the water run down my cheeks freely. Cleansing me of the day, of this whole journey. It did not take long for my face to become soaked as the rain fell heavier. Above me, thunder roared and lightning soon followed.

Justus must be upset or angry.

I shivered at the thought of him being angry enough for their energy to create a storm like this, and I hoped that the rain only fell here. If there was lightning in Polaris, they would know something was wrong. If not the people, my parents would. My blessing should have brought a prosperous, joyous time filled with light. It wouldn't have brought storms. They would know.

That was if they hadn't heard rumors already. What happened in Cedric's village would be circulating.

I walked forward as the rain poured down on me, being given the occasional shelter when large leaves hung over my head.

Eventually, I came to a bench, short to the ground and made of marble. Sitting, the sight before me almost made me laugh.

A small waterfall cascaded down large rocks, leading into a pond of green water. It was much smaller than my sanctuary at home, but it brought me a similar peace. I watched the water closely, enjoying how it rushed over some parts of the rock and where it trickled slowly.

My body finally gave in to its exhaustion, the weight pressing down onto my shoulders. All this work and still no solution. No plan and no end to this whole fucked up situation. A situation I was in the middle of, with no escape. Problems that didn't involve me, and yet I would be the one to solve them. I was expected to go back and… rule. To lead through a war that I knew almost nothing about. Still not blessed. Still, with these dark brown eyes, still not getting the one thing I wanted. After all this work.

And still so much further to go. I could have cried as I sat there, the rain making my dirty clothes stick to me. My cloak did nothing to stop the insistent drops.

If there were tears, I let them flow freely.

I did not hear footsteps behind me, not that I ever would with him. Ezrah was far too good at sneaking up on me.

"Leave it to you," he said as he sat, "to find a waterfall, even here."

"I think it found me," I said back, not looking at him yet.

I wondered if my eyes had grown red, or if my skin had the red splotches it always got when I cried.

"You got help?" I asked him, avoiding the topic at hand with one that would bring me much more comfort.

"From the healers," he answered. "It was not as bad as it looked, like I said."

I still did not believe that for a second, not when I had been the one to push gauze into his open wound. It could have been a lot worse. I could have lost him.

I looked him over, starting at the top of his head, where his hair had lost its tightly woven curl, sticking out further now. His skin still hadn't fully returned to its familiar dark hue, but he looked much better than he did before. His one eye still had an array of colors surrounding it, and the skin was swollen. My own skin felt tender just at the sight of his. His earnest eyes watched me inspect him, not interrupting, but letting me confirm his condition for myself.

His shirt was new, the stained one likely discarded. Not forgotten, though, not to me. Every time I blinked and reopened my eyes, I could see the blood again, just for a second.

All this pain, because of me. All that pain and no solutions.

Ezrah sat silently, not pushing or demanding to know. He likely was impatient to find out who the guest was, what they had to tell me, and why I was crying.

But he did not ask. He did not pry. Instead, he gave me time.

I leaned my forehead forward and rested it on his shoulder. Every muscle in my body relaxed and I wasn't sure if it was at the relief of seeing him healed or at sheer exhaustion. He leaned his head to rest against mine and his lips lightly grazed the top of my head and he inhaled deeply. It wasn't a kiss, but it was exactly what I needed. I reached over and grasped his knee, taking a second in this tentative embrace to build some courage.

Straightening, I looked back at where the water trickled slowly. My eyes followed it down the rocks three times. Each time I breathed deeply.

"It was Justus," I said in one breath. Otherwise, I likely would have lost the nerve.

He watched me from the side. "It—what?"

"I—" I looked at him, his uninjured eye wide open. "I just met a Deity."

He stared momentarily like he expected me to tell him I was kidding. When I said nothing, he said, "I—I didn't know what to expect." He shook his head. "But it wasn't that."

I let out a small laugh. "Me neither."

His eyes flicked between mine, checking to see if they were gold and slowly realizing they were not. I saw him register what that might mean before proceeding, knowing now he must tread cautiously.

"And?" he asked. Again giving me the freedom to explain this the way I had to.

"And—shit. This still doesn't even sound real to me, yet. Justus came alone, and he told me," One more deep breath, "the Deities are at war.

Now I gave him a moment to process that. He took his time.

Finally, he asked, "You're not kidding, are you?"

I laughed. "I wish I was."

"War?"

"War."

"What does that mean?"

I could feel my heart sinking, and I wanted to reply honestly, that it could mean pain and death, and that things would likely get a lot worse.

"I don't know," I said instead.

He looked up to the sky, where the clouds were still gray, and it continued to pour. Thunder rolled as if on cue, and he shivered. "Why?"

"That's where it got… confusing. Justus was not a great conversationalist."

He shifted warily like he expected lightning to strike us down. I did not care if it did. When Ezrah looked back at me, his head was shaking.

"He said," I started to explain, "that one of the Deities did not want me to rule. Or anyone to rule? Manumit does not agree with the rest of them. His opinion had been *swayed* or… something."

"Manumit?"

"Yes. I cannot be blessed unless all of them participate. Manumit will not."

"Why?"

I shook my head. "I don't know. He said something about this being foretold. That I was—that they knew I was coming. But I don't know what that means."

This time, Ezrah looked at the water as I watched him. His eyes trailed up and down like mine did, his breath slowing.

"So, what are you going to do?"

It was the exact question I expected, yet the most frustrating to answer. "Justus said I should finish my pilgrimage. Then I should rule."

"Without being blessed."

"Yes."

"And through a *war*?"

"I think so," I said.

Ezrah paused again, and I granted him time. I waited until his brow smoothed before I continued, "He said it like it was simple. That the people will accept that." I scoffed.

"They might." He looked at me. "The people may be open to more change than you think."

I shook my head. "Not this kind of change. Even if they are, my parents won't be."

"They may," he said.

I raised one eyebrow. "They won't."

"Even if there's a war?" He looked up again. "War could change everything."

I looked up, too. The clouds moved quickly across the sky at an ominous pace.

This war could change everything. It would. I could feel it in the winds, how they made these damp clothes stick to my skin.

The Deities were starting a war, in the age of my time.

It was almost as if he could hear my thoughts. "The blessing, then, it's not your fault."

It might not be, but it was still unclear why Manumit had chosen it now. Out of all time, he chose when I was to rise to power for change.

I did not look at him when I said, "We should go. You shouldn't be out in the rain."

He laughed. "I'm not as easy to break as you think. I'm not the same boy you knew."

He was quiet as we stood. His hand came to the small of my back and led me out of the garden. Ezrah knew his way out of this maze of leaves.

○　✧　✴　✧　○

Ezrah informed me that after he visited the healers, they showed him where we would be staying. The hallways turned from the gorgeous, detailed marble into plain stone bricks, the elegance of the front of the Temple gone. I realized we were heading into an area of the building not meant for guests.

These hallways reminded me more of the ones in the lower level of the palace, where the workers lived and Rulers rarely went. I felt my cheeks pull into a smile when I thought of those hallways and the people that filled them, the ones that had grown used to my presence, even if they did not want me to be there.

These halls lacked the usual chaos I would see at home. Silence loomed over us, as if the people living in the doors we passed were told to be quiet. I missed the noise.

"Here," Ezrah said.

Our door was much like the others; small and wooden. It creaked loudly when Ezrah opened it.

This room was smaller than my bathing chambers at home. It had only two small beds on opposite walls with a table between them. An oil lamp sat on top, casting the room in a golden glow.

Despite the size, my body sagged in relief at the sight of a bed—an actual bed, with a pillow and blankets, and a mattress. I ached to lie down and let its warmth consume me. I would not have to sleep on the cold, relentlessly hard ground for at least one night. The room could be half the size that it was, and I would not care, not if it had a bed.

"They apologized," Ezrah said, "for only having one room. They said it was better to keep you secluded, and that the Devoted rooms were scarce."

I was tempted to remind him we had been sharing a room for a few nights, even if the walls were canvas.

Instead, I said, "This is perfect."

He stood behind me, his form looming over mine. A week ago, having him this close would have irritated me and made my skin itchy. Now I caught my body from leaning back into him. Something beyond my comprehension pulled me in.

"I asked them for food," he said, his voice sounding lower than before. "I figured we could both use a meal. It looks like they took care of that for us."

He moved to the bed closest to the door, sitting beside a tray of food in the middle of the bed. The plush mattress bent under his weight as Ezrah relaxed back on one arm and reached for the tray.

It was full of assorted meats and cheeses, and there were figs and olives in a small dish. If it were not for how artfully it was arranged, I would assume that they were just serving us what they had to spare, but it was made with such abundance and care that I knew that was not true. My mouth watered at the sight of it.

I sat on the other side of the bed, my body sinking into the mattress just as he had. "Thank you," I said.

I had not realized how often Ezrah took care of me until he left, but it was always in the little gestures. He would hold doors open for me and sneak extra food away from the table for when we would see each other later that night.

There were many days when I would be studying things Ezrah would never have to know. He could have gone somewhere else and spent his time in a more entertaining way. Instead, more times than not, Ezrah would sit with me while I did what I needed to do. He had been my constant company like he knew I hated being alone.

Time was something of value, I had learned that when I was much older. It was something that few people ever got enough of, yet Ezrah gave me his. He did so willingly, like it was not a sacrifice for him as it would have been for others.

He donated his company to me, and over the years, I had grown to rely on it.

"You aren't eating," he said, pulling my eyes back to his. I hadn't realized my eyes hung low, resting on the food tray, or that I hadn't eaten yet.

I gave him a tight smile, which only increased his suspicious gaze on me. He knew my mind wandered, but he did not pry.

Comfort, companionship, and the ability to have someone to lean against. He had given me that before, and I felt it again now.

It was in the ease of how we sat together, in how my body ached to lean against his. It was the way his eyes could read me, how he knew how to handle me. Everything about this Ezrah was familiar to me, even when, just days ago, I did not recognize the man he had become.

I wanted this. I wanted the way he knew what I needed. I wanted that boy who would sit by me while I did my work even though there were better things to do. That boy sat in front of me now, and every part of me wanted him there.

My heart swelled at the thought. Then, almost instantly, my heart dropped. My swollen heart sat low in my guts and pulsed, warning me against doing this again.

I had felt this all before, the comfort of him. I had let my heart grow, slowly over time, until it took over the rest of my body. My heart led my mind then, pulling me to him. Even though I knew I was living a life where I was unlikely to get what I wanted, my heart made me blind to anything else.

And he wanted that too, then. We both sensed the change between us.

Then, he kissed me. And again, he kissed me. Our stolen moments led to more, and I was certain I had him.

My heart had never felt larger and I gave it to him for safekeeping.

Then, the next day, he walked away with mine. Again, without words, without explanation, he took that part of me and left me empty.

It took me two years to grow a heart again, to replace what he took. The one I had now was crooked, broken, and wrong—it did not function as it used to. I had to learn how to move on without him and without my heart all at once. After endless days of having a hole in my chest, I did it. I healed myself. I functioned on my own. I grew back a heart.

And now, in the dim flickering light of the oil lamp, I felt his comfort again like an old friend. I wanted him, so badly it hurt.

Even though this new heart did not know it, I could not have it. I was not sure I would survive it when he left me again.

That is what he did. He left people. He left me.

He would do it again, and this time I could not give him pieces of me to take.

When my eyes met his, Ezrah was still waiting for me to tell him where my mind went. I took a piece of cheese and chewed it slowly to stall. It scraped down my dry throat as I swallowed.

"You should know," I started softly, ashamed, then let

my voice harden, "that I appreciate you coming with me. Without you, I may not have made it here." I cleared my throat at his narrowing eyes. "But I have my answers now. That is what you came with me to find. Now that that is done, you can go."

I dreaded how my eyes had fallen to my hands, where my fingers twirled around themselves in my lap. Rulers did not shy away from confrontation. Yet, here I was.

I kept my eyes down and waited for him to respond. A part of me wished he wouldn't, and instead, he would just get up and walk out the door, taking his cue. That would be much easier.

The silence stretched like it had no concept of time. It took the air out of the room.

Finally, he spoke, "You're fucking with me, right?"

He said it with a thin veneer of humor that came off as disbelief. It was not what I expected his response to be.

My voice was quiet. "I do not want to keep you here." I pushed my hands into my lap and then looked back at his face, noting how his jaw clenched. He was angry, but anger felt safer somehow. I could handle his anger.

When he didn't respond, I continued, "I can do the next part alone." I stood then, needing space. I walked until I hit the wall on the opposite side. I stared at the bricks rather than turning to face him. I wished the room was bigger.

The gasp of air he let out faintly resembled a laugh. "When are you going to learn, Adenne, that you don't have to do everything alone?"

I kept my back to him and felt my blood boil. I took a deep breath, trying to calm myself, but the words burst out of me anyhow. "Oh, now *you* must be fucking with *me*. I don't have to do this alone? I do all of this shit alone. I'm the only one that will become Ruler, the only one with this fucking pressure. When have I ever had help with that, Ezrah?"

He scoffed. "Right now. I'm here for *you*, to help you."

I heard him stand behind me, and my jaw tightened just as his had. "And I told you, I appreciate that." Calmness was a fickle thing, and I was losing my grip on it. "But I do not need your help."

"I know." His voice was closer now. "That you do not need it, but you have it. I am not going anywhere."

My heart did that thing again, grew larger, and then fell. It took the air out of me.

"How can you keep saying that?" I whispered.

I felt his presence directly behind me, his breath on my neck.

"Saying what?"

"That you won't go anywhere."

"Because I am not, Addie." His voice softened, which made me angry. I did not want softness.

I turned then and lifted my chin to look him in the eye. My voice was a sharp contrast to his. "And how do you expect me to believe that after what you did? After you left me?"

"Addie, I—"

"No, I do not want your apology. I want you to listen. I know why you left. I am not so broken or so hard that I lack understanding. When your parents passed—" I saw his eyes glaze over like the memories were still painful. "—it broke you. I'm so sorry for how it broke you, and I understand why you needed to get away. That you could not stay in that place. I can't blame you for leaving." As I said it, I knew it was true, and I saw just the slightest bit of tension leave his shoulders.

"I do blame you for *how* you left. That's what I could never understand." I stepped back from him, my arms wrapping around my middle, trying to protect myself from the memories I was reliving. "You *fucked* me, Ezrah, and you must have known what I felt for you. You must have known what that would mean for me. Then it kept happening and I thought you wanted me. I stupidly thought that despite everything we were going to try to be together." I was gasping like the air was leaving the room. "Then you *left* me. You were my only friend and you left without saying a word. You left me, you left Sage, you left your *life*, and now you act as if that will be without consequence—as if I could ever believe you when you say you will stay."

Despite my step from him, I felt like I had no room. He towered over me, his chest rising and falling quickly. This would have been much easier if he had left when I told him to.

"I didn't want to leave," he whispered.

I refused to accept that as the truth. "Then why did you?"

His lips drew into a straight line. "For a lot of reasons. It wasn't only you, us."

My naive heart swelled again, refusing to learn its lesson. I contracted the muscles in my chest, trying to keep them at bay.

"You've mentioned that before. Still, you have given me no explanation."

"Because I can't."

I scoffed. "Because you can't?"

He gave one curt nod.

"Then I don't believe you." My voice was raised now. "The same way I do not believe you'll stay."

"I am going to stay." His jaw was clenched.

I shook my head. "I won't let you. Not unless you give me an explanation."

He stepped towards me once, and then again. I lifted my chin to keep my eyes on his face. When he kept coming forward, I was forced backward. My back hit the cold, stone wall. It sent a chill through my skin that was only warmed by the heat his body gave off.

"I left…" His jaw worked as his gaze pierced into me, the browns and golds of his eyes churning. "…because I wanted you. I wanted you, but it was made clear to me, Adenne, that I could never have you."

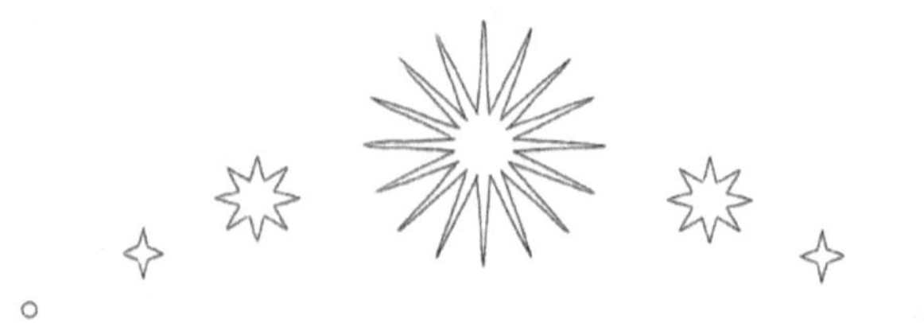

22

Always Yours

There was no air left in the room except Ezrah's breath. I could feel it dancing across my lips.

"I can never have you," he repeated, and I couldn't tell if that was for his benefit or mine.

When I let out a shudder, his gaze dropped to where the air escaped me.

My naïve heart beat rapidly, and my chest felt so weak I was unsure I could contain it. Could he hear it? Feel it?

"You had me," I heard myself saying.

His hand unclenched from where it was at his side and came slowly up to my jaw. He used one finger to trace from the side of my face to my chin. His thumb sat so close to my lips.

"And now? Do I have you now?"

My whole body said yes. I felt myself lean toward him, putting pressure where his hand held my face. His other hand came to my waist, grasping at the fabric there.

I wished my mind would tell me no. I wished he didn't have me and that I could lean back and walk away from him.

But I couldn't. I wouldn't. Despite knowing that I should and knowing what the outcome of this would be, I leaned even further forward.

He had me. He always had.

Our chests brushed against each other just slightly. I felt the air leave him at the contact. I had never seen his pupils so wide, desire filling them. Still, Ezrah did not move closer.

He waited there, suspended. He would not take something that wasn't his.

I was his.

One of my hands came up and clasped the back of his neck, pulling him closer to me. His breath shook out unsteadily against me. I stepped up on the tips of my toes, our bodies melting together. This restraint was hurting him so badly I could feel it.

I brought my lips so close to his that only the thinnest amount of air separated us.

Our lips brushed when I said, "I have always been yours, Ezrah."

He devoured me then like he had been starving for me.

His mouth came down on mine forcefully, and the hand on my chin moved to cup the side of my face, tilting my head further, giving him better access.

I was lost in him. My body arched forward, needing to be as close as I could get to him. I could feel his hand squeeze my waist, then move to the small of my back, bringing me closer. The contact made me gasp, and Ezrah used that opportunity to deepen the kiss.

In the back of my mind, I was worried I would hurt him. His swollen eye and the wound at his side came to mind.

But if this hurt him, he would stop us, and he was far from doing that.

I tilted my head to the side to breathe.

"I have wanted to do this again for longer than you know," he gasped.

Lifting my chin, I looked at him. His eyes were molten shades of gold and bronze. They shifted as he looked at me like he wanted to take all of me.

I would let him take all of me.

"How long?" I asked.

The hand that held my cheek trailed down, and his fingers drew a line down my neck. He stopped at the crook of my neck before tracing down the side of my chest. He watched how my body responded to him. His hand skimmed where I clearly needed them, not giving me the friction I craved. My lungs expanded forward, doing whatever I could for more contact.

His hand went past my waist and then grasped my hip. He lifted and pulled, bringing us together in the most intimate way. I could feel all of him against me.

My body desperately needed him to kiss me again. When I pushed my mouth forward our breaths danced together, and he said, "Too long. I have wanted this for so fucking long."

His lips returned to mine as he used his hand on my hip to lift me further. At this new angle, he pressed one of his legs between mine, adding pressure where I needed it. I arched my back and rolled against his leg.

He pressed into me harder, and I moaned his name.

"Fuck," He muttered against my lips.

I curved my leg around his waist, and he let out a guttural sound.

My hands gripped the wet shirt that clung to his chest. I wanted to take it off but didn't want to pull away from him.

Ezrah must have sensed this because he leaned back slightly. I was quick to pull his shirt over his head.

My hands started on either side of his neck, then made their way downward, exploring his body the same way he had with me.

He was not refined muscle, like some men on the guard. Ezrah carried his strength under softer lines. When my hands moved over his chest, those soft lines shifted as he let out shuddering breaths. His whole body reacted to the way I touched him. It made me feel powerful.

When my hands went lower, his stomach tightened. He pressed in harder with the leg that held me up. I gasped at the same time as him.

I made it to the waistband of his trousers. My fingers started to work their way into them, just hinting at what I could do. And he would let me. Ezrah would let me do whatever I wanted at this moment.

I parted my hands, my fingers trailing to his sides, still at the edge of his trousers. Once I reached his hips, I pulled him closer.

"You," he said, moving his hand from my back to my face, tilting me up to meet him again, "are going to kill me."

Just as his lips returned to mine, I rolled my hips, making him groan. This time I seized the opportunity to deepen the kiss, my tongue meeting his.

Ezrah's hands came to the side of my shirt, where it clung to my body. It was all too tight, with too much fabric. I wanted nothing blocking his skin from mine.

He pulled back slightly, in a question. Instead of answering, I lifted my hands above my head, and he used the opportunity to remove my confining shirt.

Then, I reached behind me and removed the final layer of linen covering my chest.

I was exposed to him. His eyes made my already-hardened peaks almost painful. He raised one finger and trailed it between my breasts, making me gasp.

"You are absolutely beautiful."

His hand moved to the side, drawing his knuckles across me.

"Ezrah."

He touched me, and I couldn't breathe. My chest pressed forward into his hand, wanting more. I could feel myself blushing at the way he watched every reaction my body had to him. "Don't blush like you don't believe me. You're beautiful, Addie."

I met his golden eyes, not an ounce of humor in them.

"Do you not believe me?" he asked as one side of his mouth crept forward in a smirk.

His hand moved and I moaned, distracted instantly to the point I did not register what he asked.

His mouth came to my neck, trailing kisses and scraping his teeth down until he found where my pulse pounded.

"Should I try to convince you?"

Fuck.

"Yes." My answer was rough.

Ezrah lifted me and wrapped my legs around his waist, bringing my chest closer to his mouth. Some sense came back to me, if only for a second.

"You're hurt," I said, pulling back slightly.

He dragged me back to him. "I'm fine. In fact, I don't think I have felt this good in a long time."

"Ezrah—" I tried to pull back again.

His eyes met mine. "If it's hurting me, I'll tell you, okay? Please."

Him saying please almost killed me. I nodded, and he licked my pulse before moving downwards. I was making sounds I did not recognize. I was going to explode.

His mouth over my body and he whispered, "Absolutely beautiful," against me. I loved the way his breath coursed over my skin, and my hands came up to the back of his neck to hold him there. I rolled my hips.

I felt his breath against me when he leaned back and whispered, "Fuck, Addie. If you keep moving against me like that, I'll get distracted. I'm trying to convince you here."

I rolled again, and he growled before bringing his mouth back to me.

Fuck, I wanted this. I wanted him. I did not know how I had gone without this, how I had survived that long. Even after he returned, I avoided him when all the while I could have been feeling this.

At the scrape of his teeth, I moaned, "Ezrah."

He pressed in harder and my legs felt weak, but I needed his lips back on mine. I had to show him how much I needed him.

I tugged on the back of his hair, and his head came to

mine easily.

"Do you believe me?" He asked between breaths.

"Will you keep doing that if I told you no?"

Just as one corner of his mouth tilted upward, I pulled it to mine.

I kissed him passionately, trying to put my feelings into something he could understand. His breaths shuddered against my lips. I wanted him to know what I felt without having to say a word. My teeth grazing his lip gently, pushing us further.

And things turned to chaos.

His hands came under my thighs, and he guided me until I could feel him pressed against my core. I pressed into him, my hips rocking.

Ezrah moaned and pulled back for air. He did not need a break. I knew that in the way his hands still held me tightly to his hardness.

He rocked his hips into me, and I lost all control. Memories of him I had tried to suppress came back. My breaths became shallow. When I said his name, he pushed harder, one of his hands coming to my chest again.

I had needed this too long, and the built-up tension already had me near the edge. The friction was becoming too much. My legs were already shaking as I ground against him.

"Ezrah." I gasped. "I need—"

He let out another curse and pressed impossibly harder, his hips moving faster than I could meet him.

His lips made their way down my neck, starting just under my jaw and moving lower with small bites and licks. My head tilted back against the wall, giving him full access.

He used that access to his advantage, leaving marks on

my neck that I would see tomorrow. I did not care. Nothing mattered beyond how Ezrah was making me feel.

I wanted his trousers off, but there was no time for that. He was shaking just as much as I was.

"Addie," he said against my pulse.

"Fuck." I rocked against him, lost in him. "Don't ever stop this," I said, and I felt his lips hesitate where they were on my neck. "I want this forever."

His hips hesitated in their movement as he looked at me. There was doubt in his eyes. I brought my mouth back to his, and I moved my hips against his length.

"Please," I said against his mouth. That unlocked him, and he pushed into me harder, quicker. I reveled in the feel of him, how even with layers between us, he could undo me.

His hand moved to where I needed him most. Even through the fabric, the pressure was enough.

I found my release. I couldn't feel my legs, and I was pretty sure I screamed either a curse or his name. Ezrah found his release just after me, his mouth gasping against mine.

We didn't even get our pants off. Fuck.

He kept me against him, not lowering my legs from his waist. Ezrah's forehead leaned against mine, our breaths combining.

I had wanted that, needed that, for so long. Longer than I realized, longer than I wanted to admit. Now that I had it, my whole body relaxed. Nothing felt as complicated as it had. Not when I had this.

The one thing that I wanted.

His breath still heaved out of him and eyes cast were downward, where our bodies met. I wanted so badly for him to look at me.

Instead, he lowered me to the ground. My legs felt like they could collapse right out from under me.

"That was—" I began.

"Incredible," he said. "That was fucking incredible."

I placed a hand against his heaving chest, and he winced, but not out of pain from his injuries.

"Addie," he said, his eyes meeting mine now. He looked disappointed, which was the last thing I expected. I felt like my heart was falling. "I'm sorry."

"For what?"

"We—" He shook his head. "I shouldn't have—" He gestured between us and then used that same hand to rub down his face. "I got carried away. That shouldn't have happened."

My head was shaking back and forth. "Don't," I warned as tears sprung to my eyes.

I knew where he was headed with this, and I did not want to hear it. I could not have another thing taken from me.

"I don't get to have you, Addie."

It was like a fist in my chest squeezing my heart, "Why?"

His hands hung helplessly at his sides. He was not far away, but the distance between us felt wide. "It's just the way it is."

"Says who?' I asked. At his sigh, I continued, anger growing inside of me. "No, Ezrah, honestly. Says who? Because a lot of things in my life were happening because *that is the way it is*, because that was the plan, and none of that is true anymore."

"I know."

Anger was the easiest thing to cling to so I grasped it. "So why? Why can't I have this one thing? Why can't we?"

"You know why."

I quickly wiped away a tear that had escaped me. "No, I am not sure I do. I don't know anything."

As more tears fell, I let them, embracing how they burned down my face.

Ezrah stepped forward, his hand gently wiping them away for me. "Addie," he said, sounding resigned, "you will still rule, you'll still marry someone else, you'll still live the life you had planned. It's a life I do not have a part in."

"You don't know that." I shook my head. "We do not know anything about how my future will turn out. Not anymore."

He did not say anything at that, just watched me as my anger resided, sadness taking its place. I felt just as helpless as he did.

After a moment, I asked, "Don't you want this?" My voice was desperate. His eyes fell again. "Don't lie to me," I begged.

Ezrah looked resigned, like the need to fight me on this was leaving him. "I want you." He leaned into me, subconsciously, like he couldn't stop himself. "More than anything. I want this, but you're out of my reach."

"And if I wasn't? If things were different? What if nothing goes to plan?"

His finger traced my cheekbone back and forth. "That is not how I want your life to go. I want you to get what you deserve."

"That doesn't answer my question."

His lips came forward to me, and I thought for a moment his mouth would meet mine. Instead, it tilted upwards, his lips softly coming to my forehead.

"If things don't go as planned, I would want you just as much. More, if that were even possible."

Finally, air came back to me, filling my lungs. His arms circled my waist, pulling me into a hug. My arms were trapped between our bodies, but I did not care.

"I am yours," I said against his chest. Making a promise, even if it was unwise.

"You may not be able to be, Addie. You need to know that."

I pulled back to look at his gentle eyes. There was a chance that whatever would happen next would lead me away from him. Still, my words were true. I was his. I had always been his, even when I could not admit it and even when he had hurt me so deeply. Whatever happened in this war would not change that.

"I know that, but, please, can we not live as if things were the same as before? I am not asking for us to be reckless, or pretend we will get our way. I know we may not. But, can we please live like there is a possibility we might? That we might both get what we want? I don't think—" My words caught in my mouth. "I don't think I can go on otherwise. I can't go on without you by my side, even if that is just for now. I need you for as long as I can have you."

The truth of that absolutely terrified me, but I knew when I said it, I meant it. My independence was stripped from me, and for once, it did not bother me. For all that I had been put through, I was finally willing to give myself sympathy, and right now, sympathy looked like leaning on Ezrah. I would not allow myself to feel guilty for that.

His lips lightly traced mine, sealing the agreement more than words could. A weight lifted off my shoulders.

When he pulled back, he nodded.

"Okay," I said.

His lips tilted up in the corner.

The room felt a million times lighter now.

"They left us fresh clothes," Ezrah said. "They instructed us to leave whatever was dirty outside the door. They will clean it and deliver it back."

I nodded, then looked at our state of undress and the condition of the remaining clothes. "We should change."

When he saw where my eyes had landed on him, he laughed. "We should. That—" He looked down to where my eyes were stuck. "Has never happened before. Not without even—" He was shaking his head.

"Me either," I said.

His eyes moved from his own situation to my state of undress. "You…" He let out a breath. "I think you could do that to me with just a glance. Just words. You have no idea, Addie."

I blushed right to my hairline.

Ezrah went to the pile of clothes at the end of one bed. He tossed me a shirt that looked far too big.

"This is—"

"Just for sleeping," he said. "You will be far more comfortable. Although now I'm unsure." His eyes fell to my chest, and I instantly remembered what his hands had felt like. "I think I would much rather you stay like that."

I almost stepped toward him, taking us to where we both

wanted to go. One step further from where we had just been.

But wisdom overcame me instead. I pulled the shirt over my head.

"What will you wear?" I asked. When my head popped out of the shirt, I saw the end of him pulling on new trousers and leaving his chest bare.

"This will do."

I could not take my eyes away from his hands. "That is more than okay with me," I whispered.

I pulled my trousers off, the shirt coming down long enough on me to act as a kind of dress. Still, I kept myself covered to an extent, wisdom ruining my fun again.

He took my hand and pulled me forward, towards the bed closest to the door. Then Ezrah wandered the room, piling our clothes outside the door and putting the rest of the food, mostly uneaten despite our empty stomachs, on the table beside the bed. All the while, I stood there helpless. A yawn overtook me, and I heard him laugh lightly at the sound of it.

He came up beside me and then pulled back the cover of the one bed. With his hand on my waist, he crawled into it, and I quickly followed. There was no questioning, no hesitating. We both wanted our bodies to be together. The other bed was forgotten as I laid my head on his chest.

I felt him move, reaching over to turn out the oil lamp. When he adjusted back to me, he leaned down and placed a kiss on the top of my head. I have never felt warmer than I did at that moment.

We laid there, surrounded by the possibility that more nights could be like this.

This could also end badly. It could hurt me worse than

anything that had happened to me before.

As I drifted off, I decided that this would be worth it. He was worth it.

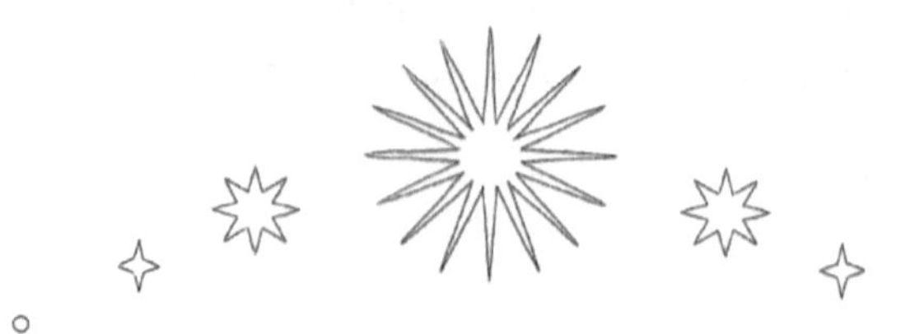

23

We Feel The Same

I woke to the sound of rain pattering on the roof. Rain did not happen in times of prosperity. For many, the sound would be unnerving and concerning, but it brought me comfort.

That, and who I was tangled with when I woke.

My head rested on the unwounded side of his chest with our legs intertwined. How we were connected felt natural, like I was meant to be here with him.

I had a nightmare last night, but I only remembered the same familiar pieces. Dark wings flying above me, clouds blocking out the sun. Books burning. I remembered trying to read a page of paper that blew toward me, but it had turned to ash before I could.

Normally, these nightmares left a stone in my stomach that would stick around all day, but with Ezrah here I felt lighter and with everything that happened my restless mind was not concerned.

His fingers trailed lightly up and down the arm wrapped around his waist. Shivers followed where he touched. With my head resting above his heart, I could feel it beating steadily, slowly. It followed the same rhythm as the rain outside and brought me even more peace. I could feel his chest rise and fall with his light breaths.

I felt stronger with every draw of his fingers and breath he took.

When I thought of what we did last night, I felt… hot.

The way he touched me and the things he said to me left me unraveled. Last night I had been taken apart and put back together.

It was unwise to trust someone else with something so fragile. Yet, I trusted him as much as possible after everything that had happened.

And even if he hurt me again, I would not regret that trust because it gave me this slow morning with quiet breathing and steady hearts.

And it gave me last night.

I wanted more nights like that. I wanted more of him.

It was the way I shuddered that stirred Ezrah into speaking. His words tore me away from the direction my mind was heading.

"We should go," he said. His voice lacked conviction.

Perhaps his mind had taken on a similar train of thought.

When I shifted slightly, the hand that traced up and down my arm stopped and instead came to my waist, holding me still.

I pressed my face to the center of his chest and lightly kissed him there. I felt his breath shudder the same way mine had.

"We should," I agreed. I did not move.

He did not want to go any more than I did. In this room, I could forget everything that was falling apart around me. The war, Justus, how I was still not blessed. I felt steady here, steady and worthy. I did not want to leave.

His fingers were moving again, tracing up and down my lower back. When I arched into him, he shuddered.

His hand traveled again, up the center of my spine until his fingers toyed with the ends of my hair, and I shivered again.

"We're headed to the Sisters?" He asked.

I nodded.

He nodded in return. "They're a day away if we're lucky. The day would have to be long and in perfect conditions, though."

I nodded against his chest, still breathing him in. I was taking in exactly what this felt like, to be utterly consumed by him. I was memorizing this moment for later when I needed it. I wanted my nose to remember the smell of him and my body, the feel of him.

"I wish I had known," I said finally, quietly. My words bounced off the center of his chest, my breath returning to my lips. "I wish I had known for certain that we felt the same before you left. Maybe I could have done something that would have made a difference."

I felt him shift, and his head tilted. Ezrah pressed a light kiss on the top of my head that undid me further.

His voice came out just as quietly. "And we do?"

"We do what?"

"Feel the same."

I tilted my head then, trying to understand why he was shying away from me. His features were the soft ones I knew well, but they contrasted sharply with the growing stubble on his face. His eyes did not meet mine.

I needed him to look at me.

"I thought I made it clear last night," I said. Then I inched the leg I had thrown over his higher, giving me the leverage I hadn't had before to press my hips in slightly. He looked at me then, and his eyes were pure heat, almost molten.

I used my newfound leverage to bring myself forward, up to meet his lips. Our breaths mingled when I said, "Maybe I should make myself clearer."

I kissed him, lighter than either of us wanted. It was a light whisper, as light as his fingers had been on my arms this morning.

I memorized the shape of his lips, how they felt against mine, and what it felt like when his breath came out in small gasps.

"Is this any clearer?" I asked.

His hand moved to the back of my neck, holding me there. "Addie," he groaned.

I rolled my hips into him, and his other hand came to my waist. "Because I can make myself clearer, Ezrah. I can show you how I feel."

My fingers inched down his chest as I rolled against him again. I could feel his breathing quicken.

"Don't," he said.

I pulled my lips back from where they were grazing his. His eyes were dark in the same way they were last night.

"Don't?"

"Don't start something we can't finish. We've got to go, and if you keep doing that," he took my hand and brought it lower so I could feel his hard length through his trousers, "we aren't leaving anytime soon."

Would going to the Sisters be worth walking away from this? My hand moved slightly, and he grimaced.

We had to leave soon, and I had to make a point. I pulled back before we could both get distracted.

"We feel the same, Ezrah. I have always felt this. Even when I should not have, even when I didn't want to. I have always felt this."

He let out a breath, and I fell into him again, deciding to spend one more minute here before facing reality.

I looked at the profile of the man I knew best in my life and yet was still learning so much about. What he told me last night, that he couldn't have me, shook me.

There was truth in it, I was not naïve nor young enough to be blinded by the fact that our lives were very different, and that we had different plans. Even when we were younger, I had known this, but it never stopped me from wanting him.

We both knew that our likelihood of this ever happening was low. The Light did not shine on the possibility of this.

But The Light also did not shine on a possible war.

So now maybe we had a chance. Even if it was slight. I may still have had to rule, but the marriage? Would I be expected to marry someone else after all of this?

Tradition had already been shifted, and, in doing so, tradition had taken so much from me. My blessing, my plan. All I wanted was for the rules of tradition to give me something back.

"I can ask them if you want me to," I said, unaware that his thoughts did not follow mine.

He was confused. "Ask who, what?"

"My parents. I can ask them to make an exception... for us. If you want that."

I desperately wanted to look away from his eyes. The intensity of them made me shiver. He looked at me like he was trying to understand the track my thoughts took, like he wanted to understand the exact way I functioned.

His eyes did not, however, give away anything about what he was thinking. I felt the same insecurity he had earlier and wondered if my suggestion was too big of an ask.

I was compelled to explain myself further. "They cannot expect me to follow tradition now, not after everything."

He let out a sigh. "It won't work," he said finally.

"You don't know that."

He stared up at the ceiling. Something in his voice, in the resignation in his words, told me there was more to what he was saying. Ezrah was leaving words unspoken.

"How are you so sure it won't work?"

"I told you all I could last night."

After everything that had happened, his words were foggy, but I tried to recall exactly what he said.

I wanted you, and it was made clear to me that I could never have you.

It wasn't just clear to him, it was *made* clear to him.

"Who made it clear to you? That you could never have me?"

I couldn't swallow as I waited for a response. His jaw clenched like he was keeping himself from saying something he shouldn't, but I needed to know this.

"Was it my mother?" I asked.

He closed his eyes against my question as if that would keep it away from him.

"Did she say something?" Rage filled me at the thought of my mother intruding on us. Ezrah was all I had back then, and if she took part in his leaving, she would pay for it.

"No," was all he said, but I could tell the word pained him.

"Who, then?" My voice was direct, tactful. The same voice I would have used to rule. It contrasted sharply against the soft rain.

Ezrah opened his eyes and saw the rage in mine. He brought his hand to my cheek, running his thumb back and forth until my brow smoothed.

Softly, he said, "Your father."

Shock passed through me in a wave. "My father?"

Ezrah sighed deeply again. "Your father made it clear to me that being together was a bad idea. That any games we were playing were foolish, childish acts, and they had to stop. If we went any further, I would only hurt you when you had to marry someone else."

"He said that?" The rain sounded more like walls crumbling now.

"He wasn't wrong, Addie. He was trying to keep you from getting hurt."

"It hurt me a lot more when you left than it ever would have otherwise." Ezrah let out a pained sound. I did not mean to hurt him, but my words were truthful. I would not take them back.

"I know," Ezrah said, "and I'm sorry. But you shouldn't blame your father. He didn't make me leave."

I squinted my eyes at him. "But he told you we had to stop."

"I left on my own accord. He never forced that."

"I don't understand. I want to understand."

"Addie," he sighed, then licked his lips in the way he only did when he was concentrating. "Your father just told me the truth. I couldn't have you, despite how much I wanted you, even then. What I felt didn't matter. I had lost you, in a way. Just days before I had lost almost everything else I had loved in this life. In a week, I'd lost everything. So, I left. It was cowardly, I know that. I was fleeing things that would only chase me. I left Sage, something no good brother would do. And I left you, which I will never forgive myself for. I should not have left, but, fuck, I remember feeling like I didn't have anything to stay for."

I could feel my heart breaking, shattering to pieces inside my chest. My eyes welled at the rawness in his voice.

His voice dropped to a whisper. "I left because it felt easier. I didn't think of what that would mean for anyone else in my life and I'll live with the guilt of that until the end of my days."

What he went through was something I could never even begin to imagine, and that pain stuck with him still.

My shattered heart squeezed, forming again. Then I said something I never thought I would.

"I forgive you, Ezrah, even if you cannot forgive yourself."

"I wasn't asking for your forgiveness."

"But you have it."

He was shaking his head. "I don't deserve it."

I brought my hand to his cheek the same way he did to me, and I stilled him. "Maybe not," I said, "but I don't want to live with guilt or hate or regret, not with you. I want forgiveness. I want you."

Tears welled in his eyes, making mine water, too. He leaned in and kissed me then, pouring everything into it. The kiss was full of gratitude and apology.

The more he kissed me like this, the more I forgave him.

His hand moved to the back of my head, tilting me up to give him better access to my lips. He pushed his body against mine and rolled me underneath him. His weight came next, pushing into me as his lips met mine in reverence.

If we continued like this, we would not make it to the Sisters in two days.

When his legs parted mine, I decided I didn't mind.

I moaned his name against his lips, and he cursed. It made me want to do it again.

Then he slowed his breathing and his hips. I wanted more.

But it was Ezrah's turn to be wise. He tilted his lips away from mine but didn't pull back. His forehead leaned against mine, and I savored his breath.

"Thank you." His voice cracked. "You'll never know— thank you, Addie."

"If you want to thank me, you can keep kissing me like that. That makes me feel very thanked."

He chuckled lightly, and I felt it vibrate against my chest. "You are fucking dangerous."

I smiled at him, and he finally pulled back, leaning off of

me and giving me air that I didn't want.

I was supposed to be sensible.

I was also supposed to be blessed.

Perhaps I was becoming something else entirely.

He moved slowly to the edge of the small bed, and I knew our morning was ending. I didn't want to face what came next, but at least now I felt a little more grounded.

"If they knew what you did for me and what has happened, they might say yes," I said, changing the conversation out of nowhere. He looked at me, his eyes still almost black, and I wondered if I really cared what my parents thought.

But Ezrah did not say anything, which filled me with that creeping insecurity again.

"All I mean…" I looked at my hands as I twisted them in my lap. "…is that I will ask. If this—" I gestured between us. "—is what you want."

He moved forward then and grabbed my hands from my lap. Slowly, he untangled them and pulled them to his lips, kissing the tension out of them.

"I want any piece of you that I can get."

My heart swelled so much it hurt. Those were the words that I had wanted to hear for so long, and he gave them openly and willingly. The weight of hating him, hiding from him, trying to ignore him fell away from me. I was no longer forcing my body to do the opposite of what it wanted. I gave myself permission to be with him and to feel what I felt. With that permission, I finally felt some kind of peace.

"And would you take all of me, if I had that to give?" I asked him.

His lips parted, and I reached out to cup his cheek and

run my finger across his lower lip.

Ezrah answered in the way he kissed me. It was soft, just a light whisper of lips. There was no rush to it. It was the kind of kiss that made me certain more would follow.

When he pulled back, I could not help my smile. It had been so many days since I had genuinely smiled as wide as I did now, and it felt odd. But despite the blessing and the war and the rain coming heavier, I smiled, and Ezrah smiled back.

"We should go," I said.

He nodded. "It is going to be a long day. Even longer since we will be soaked to the bone."

I shrugged. "Maybe the rain will stop, and The Light will shine down on us."

As he stood, I heard him mumble, "It feels like it already has."

24

A Ruler

Our struggle to pull ourselves from bed meant we were behind schedule. We would have to ride quickly if we wanted to reach our halfway point by midday. I could still hear the rain falling against the side of Temple Majora, its persistence making it clear how miserable this ride would be.

Even so, I felt lighter than I did yesterday.

I had gotten to meet with a Deity, and even if he did not offer a straightforward solution or any answers, I knew more now than I did before. It was a step, and I was trying desperately to teach myself that not everything would happen at once. Sometimes, I had to be okay with taking things one step at a time.

What happened with Ezrah was not one step at a time. It was an all-at-once spiral into morning kisses and touches. He helped pull the new tunic over my head as we dressed, his knuckles dragging across my bare waist.

He was taking every chance he could to touch me. When I had pulled my hair back into its tie, he tucked a loose strand behind my ear. His hand went to the small of my back as he moved around me in the tiny room.

It was as if there was a force beyond my comprehension that had been turned back on between us. My body hummed in the awareness of his presence. Every time he came near me, the humming increased, begging for another touch. It was such a stark difference from the days before when I did everything I could to not want him.

It was foolish to believe that this pull was not always there. I had always been his, and he was always mine.

Dressing took longer than it should have, but soon enough, we were both ready to go. Still, neither of us made a move toward the door.

I was so incredibly grateful to be wearing new, clean clothes. Despite being slightly ill-fitting, I could tell that all of it—the tunic, trousers, and undergarments were freshly laundered. The only thing that would have made this better was a bath.

"Are you ready?" He asked.

I wanted to say no.

"Yes," I said, my voice rough.

He put his hand under my chin and slightly tilted my face upwards. The kiss he gave me then was soft, the kind meant to comfort, and it wrapped around me like a warm hug. My skin tingled.

He pulled back before I could push us further, having more control than I did.

"Okay," he said, before turning to open the door. His hand returned to my back and remained as we both made our way forward to face what was coming.

Reality hit me as soon as we left the room.

I would not become the Ruler I always thought I would.

If I did at all; there was a war coming.

Still, when I contemplated *not* ruling, I was not filled with the dread I had grown to expect.

If I did not become Ruler, I could find other joy. The hand still lightly touching the small of my back as we rounded the corners in this twisting hallway assured me of that.

There was also the fact of the war. If I did not rule, it would not be my problem. The issues of war would fall to my parents, and they were as prepared for that as I was. Perhaps even less so since they did not have the warning that I had. There has been no war in recent history, let alone in their lifetime. Neither of us would know what to do.

Which could mean they will not want me to rule, sparing me, or they will push me into it, sparing themselves.

I did not think my parents would sacrifice their only daughter, but I did not think they were built for war.

Not that anyone is truly built for war.

Let alone one between the Deities. Which is something that has never happened before.

I didn't even really know what this war could mean.

We reached the more heavily decorated hallways, with their gold filigree and carvings of The Light and all its forms. I was less in awe than I was before. The stars no longer seemed to shift before my eyes. The pounding of the rain took the magic away from it.

The next wall featured a depiction of all of the Deities together. The three of them were side by side, perfectly framed in the middle of smooth marble. It was one of the only places I had seen in the Temple that was not decorated, which made the Deities stand out in contrast.

They were faceless, the artist having never seen the Deities themselves. Still, I could tell who was who. Hebera stood to the side, her long hair cascading down past her hips. Crops twisted up her legs, healthy vines showing what the power of life could do. Manumit was on the other side, stacks of books acting as pillars around him. Long locs were hanging loose over his shoulder and down his marble torso. Justus was in the middle, a sun depicted behind his head. Twin flames came out of the palms of his outstretched hands.

Even without seeing his face, the figure shown here was welcoming. The carving was not as cold as the man I had met.

I wished I had met the man in the sculpture, I wished his arms were open, and he offered me more guidance. I wished he had blessed me. It was a validation that I had been seeking since I was young. Now, it was so deeply ingrained in me I would have to hurt myself to get it out.

Ezrah had let me walk closer to the carved wall, even though I did not feel myself move. He let me look and take this moment despite the day moving on without us.

"Are you okay?" he asked after a while.

I looked at where the sun depicted Justus' head and could not get his scowl out of my mind. "He's not like this. Every artist has gotten it wrong."

I turned to Ezrah, his calm features contrasting the much harder ones I was trying to pull from my memory. He waited for me to elaborate, but all I could say was, "Sorry, let's go."

The hallways got wider and taller the further we went, and by the time the arched ceilings had begun, creating an echo of our footsteps, we were in the same front foyer we had entered through. The Highest Devoted was here again, standing with only a handful of Devoted. They did not raise their heads to look at us, sticking to tradition as they were trained to do. Their downward-facing hoods and long white robes sent a chill down my spine when they stood this still.

"You have made it. Finally," the Highest Devoted said. I sensed his irritation again.

"We have," I said.

He nodded and held his hands together, fingers intertwined like the bars of a cage.

He had a high position here and was well respected. The Devoted had always run efficiently and well under his time in charge. Still, I did not like the air around him. He looked down at me, I could tell. He held himself in higher esteem than he thought I did. He may have been the Highest Devoted, but I was meant to be a Ruler. How he acted was wrong. I wondered if my parents thought the same of him. Maybe that was why it took until now for me to meet him. I would not be inclined to invite him to the palace any more than I had to.

"Your horses are being brought around. They have been fed and watered and were given time to rest."

He said that as if we should be held accountable for their condition, as if the length of this journey was our fault. The horses were fine. We made sure of that.

I grinned. "That is appreciated, thank you."

He nodded, having gotten the praise he so clearly

wanted.

Then there was a long pause, the horses taking an eternity. "You brought an honored guest to our Temple. I hope you got the answers you have been seeking."

I met his eyes, dark brown with dots of gray floating in them, showing his age. He looked tired, yet keen at the same time, and I wanted to know how much he knew about my meeting with Justus.

I would not give him any more information. There is no reason to give men in a position of power any more leverage, and that was what information was to someone like him.

"I am happy I have brought this honor to the Temple, Highest Devoted."

"Yet," he tilted his head to the side, his crossed hands unmoving, "you must be disappointed to have broken such a long-standing tradition."

I tensed. Tolerance was not a virtue I had in any kind of abundance under normal circumstances. This was anything but normal. My hands shook where I held them tightly in fists at my sides as I contemplated how to respond.

Ezrah spoke from behind me before I had a chance to lose control. "All traditions start somewhere. Perhaps this is a new one."

I felt Ezrah step closer to me, and the tension in my shoulders relaxed.

It took the Highest Devoted a few moments to pull his gaze from mine. He watched me tense and relax, and saw how deeply I breathed. When I finally returned home, I decided to look into exactly how this man got into this position. His eyes cut to Ezrah's, and a slow smile broke across his face. It looked like it pained him.

"Here are the horses," The Highest Devoted said.

Hooves sounded behind us, and the other Devoted parted, still not meeting our eyes. Their white cloaks swayed with the movement.

Seeing Onyx and Scout let me breathe again—I never thought I would feel relief from being back on the road. My thighs still ached, and the rain was still pouring down, but these now felt like small things compared to staying here any longer.

Ezrah went down the steps to take the reins of the horses. I heard him say a quiet "Thank you," to the Devoted that had brought them. The Devoted nodded their heads in return.

I let Ezrah mount Scout first and ignored the sound he made as he did. The healers here helped him, but he was still in pain. We would have to make time to tend to his bandages, and he may need to rest sooner than usual. The extra time that would add to the end of this journey was frustrating, but essential—I did not want to see him in pain again.

And if something happened to him, I could not do this next part alone. I was sensible enough now to know I needed him.

I walked to Onyx's side and ran my hand down her neck.

"I hope you can do what you are meant to, Adenne." The Highest Devoted said from behind us.

I noted how he did not call me *My Ruler*, as he would have had to if things had gone to plan and my eyes were golden.

"With all due respect, Highest Devoted, you have no idea what I am meant to do." I did not know either, but I would not leave here while he thought he was higher than me. "Thank you for your dedicated service to your Ruler. Until we meet again."

I bowed my head and pulled the hood of my cloak up before mounting Onyx. I did not give him a chance to respond before marching Onyx into the pouring rain.

My heart pounded in my chest, and it was not lost on me that I just did what Justus had told me to do. I ruled, in my own small way. I declared myself the Ruler of this land to the Highest Devoted before his people, all while still having these dark eyes. All while still not being blessed. Blood coursed through my veins more powerfully now.

I did not feel like a Ruler, yet at the same time, I felt more in control in those few moments than I had since I walked out the front doors of the palace just days before. As I pressed Onyx to move more quickly, I let myself consider what Ezrah had said to the Highest Devoted may be true. Traditions have to start somewhere. Perhaps I was just a pawn in making a new one.

Not a pawn or a part of some prophecy.

I was given an opportunity to carve my own legacy.

As if on cue, Ezrah trotted beside me, one side of his lips turned up in a smirk.

"Do you know where you are going, my Ruler?" he said, without any tone of mockery or foolishness. He said it like it was sacred.

"To stop a war," I said. Chills ran down my arms before the thunder roared above us. Light flashed brightly, temporarily combating the dark clouds.

"In that case," he nodded west, "lead the way."

He did not walk ahead of me. I urged Onyx forward, fighting the chill of the rain.

I did not look back at the Temple Majora, but somehow, I knew exactly when it faded into the distance behind us.

It did not matter.
I was moving forward.

25

To be Titled

I felt the cold rain as soon as my adrenaline stopped pumping through my veins. Ezrah and I were back to being surrounded by open fields. No one worked in them today. The rain came down in thin drops, creating a heavy mist across the sea of green crops. Trees stood in the distance like people warning us to turn back, lurking in a white mist. The air was eerily still, suspended around us, blurring our way.

And it was cold. Rhea had always been a hot place, unbearable at times. If it did rain, the water was warm, but this was frigid. Every tiny little drop that hit my bare hands felt like the prick of a needle. Those needles were making their way through my cloak now, penetrating the fabric like when a seamstress slipped at a fitting. Except this time there was no way to escape them, and the needles came in the thousands.

I missed the warm bed at the Temple. More than that, I missed my bed at the palace. My mind wandered to a freshly drawn, warm bath, and how that heat would sink into my skin if I got in a minute too early when the water had not cooled down. If anything, the thought made the cold worse.

I was beyond shivering. My skin had resorted to puckering itself into little dots. My jaw chattered, and I could not stop it. Even if I had a hand to hold it shut, I knew I could not stop the insistence with which it moved up and down.

Ezrah and I couldn't talk. Even if I could use my mouth, we would not have been able to hear each other over the sound the rain made. Little drops making such a big impact.

The sound made it hard to think, which was the only benefit. It made it hard for me to wonder what all of this mist and none of the sunlight could mean for me.

Just as I had become certain that this would go on forever, and once the chills hit my bones and they rattled inside of me, our surroundings changed color. The bleak white tone held a hue of yellow ahead of us. Then, the yellow transformed into a brighter gold. Light was breaking through the mist.

There was a gap in the clouds, a bright streak across the dark sky like someone had taken a knife to the clouds and cut them open.

Under normal circumstances, the light would have calmed me, but I still shook when I thought of what was coming. Still, the incoming sun brought the heat with it. It began in my chest. The heat made my heart swell and stilled my shaking, just for a minute.

When the sun was above us, Ezrah stopped beside a tree. He took down the hood of his cloak, and I could see how flushed his dark skin had become. A shiver raked through his body when his eyes met mine, and I wondered how cold he was.

"This is a rest stop. We should give the horses a break, feed them while we can. We can eat something, too."

My stomach grumbled at the thought of it.

"Also, we should change into our old clothes, and get out of these wet ones."

I nodded and dismounted from Onyx. Ezrah had already taken off his cloak and draped it over his arm. I began to work at the clasp on mine. When my frozen fingers wouldn't function as I hoped, Ezrah came to me. His fingers, barely warmer than mine, found my throat and grazed my hands. Effortlessly, he unclasped my cloak and caught it before it hit the ground. Then, Ezrah draped mine over his, grasped my hands in his, and brought them to his mouth. He kissed each palm and blew hot air on them. That was better than any bath. I felt that warmth in more than just my hands.

"It is so fucking cold." My jaw was chattering again.

He laughed. "The sun is out now, though. That's a good sign."

My eyebrows pinched together. "If there is a war, why hasn't The Light done something? The Deities are its creation. Don't you think it would come back to fix this? It is clearly still around us." I gestured up at the sun.

"The Light hasn't manifested itself since the beginning of time. You know this."

"And there hasn't been a war in all of that time either, I just think—" I sighed. "I just don't know."

He leaned into me just slightly "You'll figure it out."

I snorted. "You don't seem nearly as worried as you should be," my voice dropped to a mock whisper, "I have no fucking idea what I am doing."

He laughed again. "You just don't have a plan yet, but that hasn't stopped you. You'll figure it out."

I crossed my arms. "And the war? That doesn't worry you either?"

"I'm trying not to think about it."

"Ezrah."

His lips pulled tight. "It does. But war can mean many things. I don't think we should worry too much until it becomes more… solid. Until we know what it means. People aren't dying yet. No one is fighting—"

"But they're angry."

"Maybe so, but they aren't fighting."

"That we've seen," I argued.

"That we've seen," he agreed. "All we have is more rain than usual and cryptic warnings. That's the only sign of war so far. I'll worry when there is something to worry about."

I thought about what he said. It made good sense, but even still, I couldn't agree. "Okay," I said, "I'm going to start worrying now, to be safe."

"Yeah, that sounds about right," he teased.

I pulled away from him, looking down at his chest before I got too far. No blood had come through his shirt, and his skin, despite being rosy from the cold, did not lack color as it had before.

I placed my hand on his side right above the wound under his shirt. "I want to check on this, too, while we are here."

He nodded, and I kept my hand there for a moment too long, feeling the shallow breaths he was taking.

How we had gone from not touching at all to being so utterly distracted at the lightest brush of fingers was beyond me, but every time we made contact, I was in danger of letting my mind wander to some very distracting thoughts.

I really wanted to allow myself to be distracted.

Unfortunately, we were nowhere near where I wanted to be, and we still had a long way to go. Getting off-track in the middle of the day would not help with our journey.

I stepped back from him.

He was grinning.

I went to the leather bag on Onyx's side, pulling out the clothes I had worn before. While Ezrah was distracted by hanging the cloaks off a low-hanging tree branch, I tucked myself behind Onyx and peeled the soaked clothes away from my body.

While working on the pants, the wet clothes slid off the other side of the horse, making me jump. I peeked over Onyx's back to see Ezrah facing the other way, giving me privacy.

Once dressed, I came around Onyx, pulling my hair out of the back of my shirt.

"Thank The Light the Devoted cleaned these for us. Otherwise, I would not be wearing them," I said as I worked my fingers through my tangled, wet hair.

One side one Ezrah's mouth pulled up in a smile. "And what would you do instead? Travel naked?" As he walked behind me, pulling the shirt over his head, I found myself watching the way the muscles of his back moved intently.

"If I had to," I said, turning my attention back to where the cloaks were in the sun on the tree branch.

I heard him mutter something to himself. It sounded like *fuck me,* making me blush.

Ezrah returned to the bag and pulled out the small sack

of food that The Devoted had given us. Moving to where a few trees had kept the ground mildly dry, we sat and began to eat as the sun came out.

Warmth filled my damp skin, The Light coming just in time. I felt it tingling up my bare arms. I leaned back, closed my eyes briefly, and took a deep breath in.

Ezrah said nothing as he reclined like I was, eyes closed and facing the sun. His dark skin practically glittered, despite being out here for days. He looked clean, his complexion smooth. He did not hold his face tightly, the muscles in his jaw were relaxed, and his brow unfurled. I don't think my body would ever feel as relaxed as he seemed now. I wouldn't want it another way, I would not want him to feel the burden I do.

It was unfair how handsome Ezrah was, but more than that, he was beautiful. He held more beauty than most females. I remember as a child telling myself he and Sage ended up that way because their parents were so Devoted to The Light. Their beauty was a gift from The Light, in a way. I could see it in the way his jawbone elegantly arched upward to hug the side of his face or the way his mouth could sit relaxed or stretch into a beautiful smile. He was elegant curves with soft edges as much as he was hard lines and contrasts. I cherished it when he relaxed like this, and I could look at him and study him. I could look at him forever.

He could sense me, though. I saw the corner of his mouth pick up at the feeling of me looking at him. He waited a second before opening his eyes, likely giving me a chance to look away and save my dignity. I didn't. I did not want dignity with him anymore.

"I had been meaning to ask," I said, once he looked at

me. His smile hadn't faded. "Does Sage know about you leaving?"

His brow furrowed. "I told you that I let her know I was leaving before catching up with you."

"No, not this time. Does she know why you left that first time? Or, sorry, does she know all of the reasons?"

His eyebrow relaxed. "Does she know we were together?" He asked, his voice teasing.

I rolled my eyes as I chewed on a piece of bread. "Does she know you left, in part, because of me?"

He looked back at the horizon. "No. Well, that may be unfair. No, she doesn't know explicitly. I never explained that to her. Perhaps I should have." His voice softened for a moment. "But she has a way of… knowing. Especially with things like that."

I nodded. "I thought she knew. I figured you told her. She was pushy with me." I laughed. "To get me to talk about you. When you returned, she pushed even more. I—" I shook my head at the memory. "I never said anything explicitly, either. But she knew. I miss her."

He nodded beside me. I sat up off my elbows and picked at the food spread between us.

"I should thank you," he said, "for caring for Sage after I left. I regret many of my actions, and you know that, I hope, now. I regret doing that to her the most. She's my younger sister, I was supposed to take care of her, and I failed at that. I don't think I will ever make that up to her. I don't know how. But either way, I'm grateful she had you when she didn't have me."

I kept my eyes on the horizon so he couldn't see how the rawness in his voice brought tears to my eyes. This was all too real, too new, and he still held so much grief, not just for his parents, but for his actions. I did not necessarily feel that he shouldn't. He needed to feel this to understand that his actions hurt people. Still, it was difficult to hear. It was still so raw.

"Sage mostly took care of herself. Or we took care of each other. She was hurt, Ezrah, but she was okay. We were okay, or we will be."

I heard him sniff, and I wanted to comfort him. A small piece of me still wanted to strangle him, but mostly I wanted to hug him.

I also wanted him to feel this so he would not repeat it. However callous that might be.

Instead of comfort, I gave him a distraction. "Do you think we have made it halfway to the Sisters?"

He grimaced. "I would love to tell you yes."

"That is a definite no, then."

He nodded. "The rain slowed us down too much. We may have to take the full two days."

"A whole extra day?" I asked, not realizing how far behind we had fallen.

He shrugged. "Ruling will be there for you when you return. You have time. They do not know why you are taking so long, or about the blessing at all."

"Or the war?" I snorted.

"That, too."

I thought about that for a moment. If they did not know at home, I had time. People may worry about why my regular pilgrimage was taking so long, but they would not know why. They would assume that I was introspecting more than most people did. They might even think that it was a good thing.

That was assuming they didn't already know the truth.

"They could know," I said. "We have seen enough people since we have been out here. That first merchant on the road could have recognized me and gone straight to the palace to say something, seeking a reward."

Ezrah thought about this for a second. "He could have. But talking ill of a Ruler? He would be risking a lot to possibly get a reward. And your parents would have to believe him. I don't think that they would."

"No," I agreed. "They likely would believe none of this. Even if I was standing in front of their face, unchanged." My stomach twisted itself into something heavy. I told myself it was the cheese. I felt his eyes on me, but I looked forward. "It won't be easy to see them."

"But it has to be done," he said.

I let out a long breath. "Yeah."

I felt my hands shake, so I leaned back on my elbows again, pressing them into the ground.

"The way I see it," he said after a moment, "we have to go to the Sisters before you go home. And there is too much to worry about now, let alone later." He shook his head like he was trying to clarify his thoughts. "Sorry, I am not making sense." He leaned forward on his one hand to face me. "Let's worry about the next step and not the whole. This thing and then that one. One worry and then the next."

My heart swelled against my ribs. I felt myself nod, but it was a lie. The luxury of facing just what was immediate was not one I could afford. Not when there was a war, not when people could be in danger. Not when I was likely the cause and also the only solution. Too much would happen if I did not worry, if I did not think things through. I did not have the luxury of taking things one step at a time, but still, I nodded.

Because I understood his urge, too. I understood what Ezrah was trying to do. I just could not do the same.

This was my burden.

The food was finished, and the day was getting away from us again. I quickly checked his bandages to make sure no blood was showing through and he was healing well. We packed up the small lunch and mounted the horses again.

"Are you ready?" He asked.

I nodded.

∘   ✦   ✴   ✦   ∘

The rain held off for the rest of the day, but the clouds were threatening every time I looked behind us. Their dark gray color made the sky feel full of rage and let little light through. I tried to keep my eyes forward.

I was amazed at how easily I could ignore the pain now. My legs ached from spending so much time on horseback, and my back ached from the lack of a proper bed. I used to feel a jolt of pain every time Onyx stepped, but now my body was numb.

I wondered how my mother felt, days into her pilgrimage. She never liked riding, and when she returned from her journey, she never did again. Imagining her out here, alone, aching and cursing her horse made me smile. I missed her.

We rode quietly through the afternoon and into the evening. We did not get to see the sunset through the heavy clouds, but eventually, after passing field after field, it was dark. Ezrah trotted ahead to find somewhere to rest for the night.

By the time I joined him, he was off his horse and getting the tent ready.

"Are you excited to be in a tent again?" He laughed, his back facing me.

I was not excited to be sleeping on the ground again, but the thought of sleeping next to him gave me chills, then made me suddenly very hot.

Ezrah turned to look at me at my lack of an answer. It should have been too dark for him to see my flushed skin, but he grinned at me like he knew my secret.

"I will never take a bed for granted again," I said, coming over to help him unravel the canvas.

The sky was fully dark by the time the tent was set up. I did not know how late it had become, but by the way my mind fogged over, I knew it was past the time of sleep. Still, as Ezrah pounded in the last peg of our canvas home, I laid out my cloak in front of the doors. Then, I grabbed a small portion of the bread, cheese, and dried meat we traveled with and laid it out.

"What's this?" Ezrah asked when he turned the corner around the small tent.

"Do you remember when we used to steal food from the kitchen and bring it down to the water? And we would set up a little blanket and have a picnic?"

Ezrah smiled broadly now, and a thrill ran up my spine knowing I was the reason.

He came to me and wrapped me in his arms. I did not know my body was tense until I relaxed into his, my arms and face trapped against his chest. It was unfair that when I breathed in, he still smelled good, even after all these days. Breathing him in was like coming home. It was memories of picnics and waterfalls and libraries and joy. His hand moved up and down the length of my hair, twirling it in his fingers and making me shiver.

I did not want to leave this embrace, but my stomach ached with more urgent matters.

"We need to eat," I said, muffled against his chest. I felt the air rise and fall back out of him. Then he tilted his head down to kiss the top of mine.

That caused shivers, too.

He let go of me and lightly grabbed my hand in his. Our fingers loosely linked together as we sat on the ground by the food.

"Your cloak is going to get dirty," he said.

I laughed, "I am sure it will rain again tomorrow and wash it clean."

"Let's hope not."

The bread was stale, and the cheese was not faring well with life on the road, but it stopped the anger in my stomach. As the last of our small meal was consumed, the stars came out in the now clear sky. When he saw me looking up, Ezrah did, too. Simultaneously, like our bodies knew what the other would do, we leaned back on the cloak. Ezrah moved closer to me, and we looked up at the little pinpricks of light that pushed through the dark sky.

"Are you nervous?" He asked after a while.

"For tomorrow?"

I felt him nod beside me.

"No," I answered truthfully. "I used to worry about what the Sisters would title me. My mother always thought I would be Adenne The Fair. She told me she called me that from the first day, there was blonde hair on my head. I used to be so worried that I would not be titled that and I would let her down."

"And you're not now?"

I sighed. "There are bigger worries. They may not title me at all when they see my eyes. Or they may already know. Either way, it does not seem to matter as much anymore. I do not care what they call me."

"Are you sure? What if they call you Adenne The Foul Smelling? Or Adenne The Wide-Footed?"

I laughed. "You keep up with that, and they will call me Adenne The Kicker of Ezrah's Ass."

That made him laugh in a way that threw his head back.

When he looked back at me, his face became serious.

"No, you will be titled something very fitting." His hand came out and tucked a hair behind my ear. It stayed on the side of my face. "Adenne The Wise, Adenne The Caring, Adenne The Beautiful—"

I cut him off. "If you keep saying nice things like that, I'll never let you go."

He tilted closer to me. "I am not going anywhere."

We leaned into each other simultaneously, our lips meeting in the center.

Quickly the kiss turned from light to heavy. Too much passion had been repressed in both of us for too long. His hand came to my hips, and he pulled my body to his.

His lips moved to my neck, and I moaned his name.

I felt him pause, still hesitant to push this. He stopped moving at the crook of my neck.

"No," I breathed. I pushed at his chest to get him to lean back a few inches until I could see his eyes. "Please, don't stop."

"Adenne—"

"Ezrah."

"We shouldn't."

"I know," I agreed, and I did know, but common sense was blurry when I was on fire.

I tilted his head back to meet mine. His eyes were so close I could see them skipping back and forth between mine.

"But what if I told you that I really want this? You." My breath whispered on his lips, the finest amount of air between us.

"Adenne—"

"What do I have to do for you to give me what I want?"

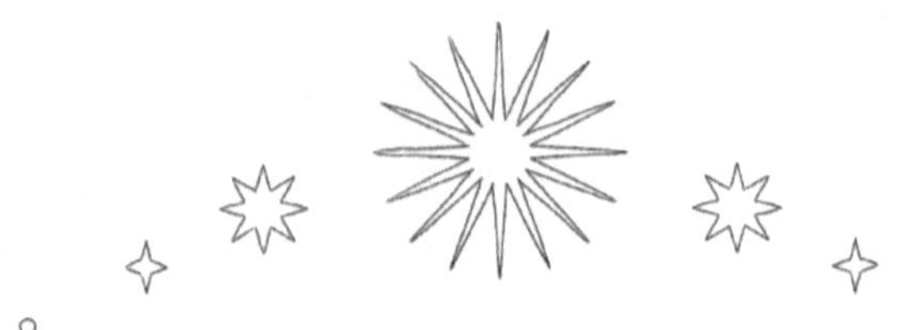

26

Together

"**F**uck," he said.

I lightly pressed my lips against his.

He did not let it stay light. Ezrah's teeth sunk into my lip, making me gasp into his mouth. As he sat up, his hand grazed my thigh. He pulled me forward until I was straddling him. I moaned at the sensation, and he pulled me tighter. I could feel his length against me.

His lips moved from mine as they followed the same trail down my throat. I tilted my head back and could see the stars above us.

Ezrah stopped at my pulse point and bit lightly. His breath coursed down my neck, and I shivered. He licked where he bit, making me shiver even more. Little gasps of air were leaving me, and every time they did, his hand on my thigh gripped me tighter. I gasped again just to feel it.

His mouth reached the hem of my shirt, just at the top of

my breasts, and he pulled back an inch from my skin. When I heaved a breath in, I felt his lips again.

This want was quickly becoming a need, and I felt it was the same for him. We both needed this.

He leaned backward. "Off," he said, his eyes meeting mine.

I would not be getting off of him.

"What?" I asked, only slightly embarrassed by the breathlessness of my voice.

"That is what you need to do, for me to give you what you want. This," his fingers moved to lightly trace their way across the neckline of my shirt, "needs to be taken off."

He smirked. Fuck me. This man would be the death of me.

But he wasn't trying to stop this from happening. Instead, he fanned the flame. He continued to meet my eyes like it was a challenge, and I did not look away. I could not let him think he won.

Even if he had. Even if I would have stripped down naked and begged if he asked me to.

I worked my shirt off, leaning back to pull it over my head, and then threw it to the side.

Ezrah was not looking me in the eye anymore. He looked at the thin silk as if he were trying to memorize it. It took only a moment for him to continue trailing his lips down my chest. I had to stop myself from pushing against his mouth harder. When he traced the edge of the fabric with his lips, my hips moved on instinct. I rolled into him, and he groaned. I did it again.

He had made his way to the center where the fabric met. He grabbed the connecting piece with his teeth and pulled. I shivered.

"And this," he said, breathier than he had been before. "This needs to come off as well."

Anything for him, anything for this.

I leaned back from him slightly and did as he requested.

If his eyes were dark before, now they had caught fire. Still a chocolate hue but touched with amber. His chest heaved up and down quickly as he took me all in.

"Beautiful," he said. "As beautiful as I had always pictured."

I flushed from my head down to my chest.

"You pictured this?" I teased.

His eyes met mine. Then, he swiftly moved, lowering me to the ground. I was under him now, and the stars circled his head. Lightly, his fingers trailed across my jawline and to across my lips.

"Every day since the last time I had you I have pictured you like this, Addie."

I wanted to ask more about that, but his lips distracted me as they continued down my body. Ezrah's mouth worshiped me, and he took his time. His hand came up and teased the breast that was being ignored with soft strokes, not quite hitting where I needed him. I arched my back into his hand, begging for more.

"Ezrah," I moaned.

His fingers swept over me. "And that. You need to continue to moan my name like that. Fuck, do you know how many times I have imagined you doing that?"

"How many?" I asked.

His mouth came down where I wanted it. I arched to meet him as his other hand worked me in a way that my body begged for.

"Fuck," I breathed.

He groaned. "And that. I want *my Ruler* to continue to curse because of what I am doing to her. I want to know how badly you want this from the sounds that you make."

His fingers found my hardened peak. I cursed again, loudly.

His breath tickled when he said, "Good girl."

Then his mouth moved over me and I relived how it felt to be connected to him in this way. I wanted to live in this moment forever. He touched me perfectly, pushing me to exactly where I needed to be. I gripped the back of his neck, holding him to me, not wanting it to end. Wanting more, to push him further, I needed all of him. Slow enough to savor yet quick enough to extinguish this fire. I wanted him tonight and tomorrow. I could never get enough of this.

"Ezrah," I breathed.

That encouraged him. His other hand was moving. I felt it come down on my thigh, running lightly up the inside, going exactly where the fire started, where I felt the most heat.

"Fuck, *Ezrah*."

He moved higher, so close to where I wanted it. Needed it.

Yet he was still dressed. That had to change.

His hand found my center through my trousers, and I moaned loudly.

His lips left my chest and returned to my mouth while his hand cupped my center. When he pushed further into me through the trousers, I gasped into his mouth.

Our lips parted slightly. "Off," I said.

Ezrah paused, only for a moment, and I used his brief hesitation to show him what I meant.

I reached for the bottom of his shirt and worked my hand under it. When I touched his bare skin, air escaped him in a hiss. I pulled the shirt up and over his head.

My hand was just below his throat. I moved it slowly down his chest, taking my time to feel the territory of his skin.

His eyes watched my hands move lower. Soft lines held powerful muscles beneath. Gentle yet hard, this was the man I knew. I wanted to explore his skin. When I brought my lips up to the base of his neck and gently peppered kisses there, he had my name on his breath. I felt completely powerful.

My hand continued downward until it met the fabric. I pulled my lips away and met his eyes.

"Off." I emphasized what I meant by tracing my finger inside the waistband of his trousers.

He did what I demanded of him without hesitation or question. Leaning away, he took off everything, leaving him gloriously naked.

I stared unapologetically. I could have had my mouth hanging open for all I knew. I didn't care.

"Addie." He had humor in his voice, pulling my gaze back to his own.

I did not answer. Instead, I propped myself up on my elbows and reached for him, needing him to be close to me again. He leaned out of my reach.

"No," he said, obviously enjoying this. Then he tugged on the bottom of my pants. "These first."

His hands ran slowly up my legs, each leaving a trail of fire. His thumbs pressed in harder than the rest of his fingers on the insides of my legs, and I wanted so badly to know what this would feel like without barriers between us. My eyes closed, and I dropped my head back in anticipation and pleasure.

"There is one more thing I need from you before I give you what you want."

I could still hear the smirk in his voice, and I knew he was about to push me past my point of control. No, he was in control. He could get me to do anything right now. I would do anything to keep his hands on me.

"I want you to tell me exactly how much you want this." I felt him shift, and I opened my eyes. He stroked himself slowly up and down. "Tell me."

Bastard.

The image of him, right now, with burning eyes just for me, almost distracted me. Coherent thoughts were nowhere to be found, and when his gaze met my eyes again, I almost lost it.

I wanted him, and I would tell him.

"I don't want you, I need you. I need you *now*." I begged, without shame. My hand had moved to my breast, trying to work myself the way he did.

He growled, his hands making quick work of my pants, stripping them off me, then his lips met my skin again, starting with one ankle. I moaned again as his breath on my thigh almost undid me. My legs parted for him instinctually, my body trying to get him closer. He was so close. I could feel his breath, exactly where my need for him started.

"Soon," he whispered, "I will have you here." He lightly bit the inside of my thigh. "I am going to take you with my mouth and hear those pretty little curses come out of you. I am going to remind myself exactly what you taste like."

"Ezrah," I breathed, parting further for him.

"Fuck." I felt his head shake against my inner thigh. "And you will love it. But not tonight."

"No?" I really wanted that tonight.

"No," he said. "You're too ready for me." He moved up slowly until our breaths danced together again. "And I think if I had my mouth between those beautiful thighs, I would lose control just as quickly as you would."

He leaned his body down so there was no air between us. I could feel all of him.

"You would?"

His forehead leaned against mine. "You completely undo me," he whispered. "I need you even more than you need me."

That could not be true.

I lifted my leg and wrapped it around his hip, pulling us together.

"You have me," I said.

And then he did.

He was slow, easing into me until I was comfortable. He stretched me in ways I had not felt in a long time. I gripped the back of his neck and held his forehead to mine. When our hips met, he lightly kissed me before whispering, "Are you okay?"

I was beyond forming words, not with the feeling of finally having him inside me again. I had fantasized about this moment as much as he had, but it was better than I imagined. My body was on fire.

I nodded, and he moved slightly. My mouth was open, gasping, as my back arched into him.

"More, Ezrah."

He hooked my leg around his waist. When he moved

again, I could feel him hit a new spot. My hips tilted to meet him with each thrust, wanting to feel his pressure, but he was being careful and gentle.

I wanted him unrestrained, like he had been waiting for this for years.

Leaning in, I whispered in his ear. "Harder, Ezrah. I want you to lose control."

He cursed and did what I asked, his movements chaotic and rough. I moaned, and he caught it in his mouth, lips as chaotic as his hips.

"Yes," I whispered.

He was hitting the perfect spot every time. Lightning moved through my body. My legs tensed.

"Ezrah, I'm," I gasped. "I—"

His lips still touched mine when he said, "Let go for me, Addie."

I did, called out so loudly I was sure it echoed across these fields. My body was shaking.

Somewhere in the back of my mind, I heard him gasp, too. His hands gripped me harder as his movements increased momentarily before slowing.

Our breaths were one, both sharing the same air as we came back down. I shuddered when he pulled away from me, rolling onto his back before pulling me into his side.

Good. I did not want any space between us.

He kissed the top of my head, and I inched impossibly closer.

"That was—"

"Everything you had imagined?"

He chuckled against me. "Am I ever going to live that

down?"

Shaking my head, I said, "no. I want to know a lot more about this imagination of yours. I want details."

"The details might scar you."

I smiled. "I can take it."

He tucked me closer to him, and I closed my eyes against the stars. For the first time in days or weeks or years, I felt calm. My mind had stilled, and I was no longer worried about what was next or what had happened. Instead, I just laid here. His chest was moving up and down steadily, and it eased me to sleep. I did not know how long he held me like that, only that I woke when he spoke.

"We should go in."

I opened my eyes to see the stars were still above us, like little pin pricks in navy fabric. The moon cast enough light that we could see each other.

As much as I wanted to ignore him it was growing cold, and we would need to rest.

"We should," I said, then waited for him to shift first.

With my head on his chest, I felt him take a big breath and slowly let it go. My head rose and fell with the action. Slowly I felt him shift, bending. Ezrah lightly kissed the crown of my head again. The sigh I let out was almost silent.

He sat us up until I was almost in his lap. He took my chin between his fingers and brought our lips lightly together.

"Thank you," he said, leaning back.

I smiled. "I think I should be thanking you."

That made him smirk. In these hard and devastating times, both of us sat here, smiling. We had made our own little pocket of joy.

"But you know," he started in a serious tone that meant our little pocket was overflowing back out into the real and cruel world. "That we probably shouldn't have done that. Not until we know how things will go."

I tried not to let my tone harden. I failed. "I thought we had this conversation. I thought we decided to try."

He nodded, not meeting my eyes. "We did. But that doesn't mean it will work. You can want things to go a certain way as much as you want, but in the end, we may not get a say."

I knew that. I knew that now more than I ever did. But I also knew that just because there were forces beyond our control doesn't mean that we don't try.

And I knew I needed him.

No, that was false. I could do this alone, but I would be stronger with him. He took who I was and gave me solid ground to stand on. I would need solid ground, coming up.

"I know that. I do. But I want to try. And you were the one who suggested worrying about one problem at a time. This is not a problem yet."

"But if it becomes one," he sighed. "I just don't want to hurt you again, Addie. That is all I'm saying. I'm worried that pushing things now will hurt you later."

His voice was gentle, soft. I understood why he was doing this. As much as I wanted to deem it unnecessary, I couldn't, and the fact that he was trying to protect me made my heart swell. But I did not need protection from him.

"Thank you, really and truly, thank you. But if a chance of hurting later is what it takes to have you now, I will risk it. I have wanted you for too long and too deeply to not risk it. I have gotten far too little of what I want not to risk it. I will have you.

I will have you as long as you let me, until you push me away or force me to let go, I will have you."

He kissed me again, lightly with that burning passion just under the surface, mildly concealed.

When he pulled back, his voice was rough. "Me too. To be clear, I want you the same way you want me. I—" He paused, then smirked just a little.

My face burned. "Oh, that was plenty clear."

His lips pressed to my forehead and he pulled us to our feet, groaning slightly at the movement. I realized I had not thought about his wound, not once. I placed my hand on his chest above the gauze.

"Is this all right? Does it hurt?"

He shook his head, but I was not convinced.

"Did I hurt you?" I asked again.

He placed his hand over mine. "No," he said. "But even if you had, I would do that over and over again. It would be worth it."

I blushed and looked down at the gauze again. There was no blood coming through. I breathed a sigh of relief.

We dressed again, mostly out of reluctance. It would be too cold to stay nude all night, and we did need some rest.

The dressing took a long time since Ezrah was insistent on slowly pulling his tunic over my head with grazing hands.

"You're getting distracted," I warned him.

"Am I?" he teased.

His hand grazed a particularly sensitive area.

"And we can't have that. We need our rest." My voice was unconvincing.

He nodded. "We do."

Then his hand moved up to graze that area again.

He leaned in and whispered in my ear. "Or, we could go into that tent, and I could have you. I could show you exactly how my imagination works."

"Ezrah," I breathed.

"Unless you need your sleep."

I kissed him deeply and pulled him back into the tent. His imagination was incredible.

We didn't get dressed until hours later. Well, I was dressed in his tunic and my pants. He had on pants, and that was all, which risked me getting sidetracked once again.

The canvas did nothing to keep out the cold. In the dark, there were only our breaths making any sound. Still, the tent kept out the rest of the world just fine. In here, it was just us.

And even though I knew that I had a next step to worry about, my eyes drifted shut. The Sisters could wait. Here and now, I could relax. I could have this moment for myself, and I took it. I would take any sort of relief in this newly cruel world. That is what Ezrah was to me: relief. Deep breaths, relaxing muscles. An escape from everything else. I did not know how I had gone so long without him.

And I wondered how I could ever live without him now.

27

I Know You

The ground shifted beneath me. When I tried to open my eyes, the light blinded me. I squeezed them shut. The ground kept moving, its warmth leaving me.

Then the ground spoke. "Addie," it said.

I took a deep breath in.

Ezrah.

Slower this time, I opened my eyes. My head was still on his chest, at an awkward angle because of how he tried to shift out from under me. "I didn't want to wake you. I am going to go get the horses ready. The sun is up."

When I groaned, I heard him chuckle deep in his chest.

Through squinting eyes, I watched Ezrah stand and stretch his arms above his head, interlacing his fingers and pushing his palms toward the sky. The muscles in his back shifted with the movement as the rising sun silhouetted his body.

The sun was making its way through our thin canvas and catching the edges of the man in front of me, giving his dark skin a golden glow around his edges. I looked at his soft features and how they blended into his sharper ones. He made me think of the sculpture I saw on the wall of the Temple. Artists' attempts to depict the ones who protect us—they had got the Deities wrong, but not because they had never seen them.

The soft lines and the hard ones. The glowing of the beings. They depicted light and life.

The artists depicted someone made by The Light to protect and care for the people.

I knew what that looked like; it stood right before me. It was not wanting to wake me until the last possible moment, or giving me the space to hold my ground in front of others while comforting me in our own quiet spaces. Knowing when to talk and when to be quiet. It was promising to give me all he had to offer. That was protection and caring.

It could even be love.

And he glowed just like the artists thought the Deities did.

"I'll be back," he said.

But before he could turn away, I said, "Ezrah." His eyes met mine. "I am going to find a way to keep you. I will find a way to give you every part of me."

He looked slightly sad when I said it, and that told me more than what I already knew, what he had already told me.

Ezrah did not think I could do it. He did not think we could have each other. It was fair. I could see why he thought that could be true. And yet, I would not let it. I would have him. I would have at least one thing that I wanted.

When he was gone, it got quiet. The quiet could be dangerous. It gave me time to think.

About the war.

There was a war.

We were about to be caught in the middle of a war.

And I knew almost nothing about it.

Justus was not forthright with his knowledge of what was happening. I did not know what that could mean, but I knew it could jeopardize me. It could do the same to my parents, who were unaware of what was happening.

Maybe I should have told them something was wrong before I left.

Maybe someone already had.

As I stood, I tried to recall what Justus had told me. He said that the Deities disagreed about how things should be done. For the life of me, I could not figure out what that could mean. As far as I could tell, and as far as my training had made me aware, things were running fine. If anything, the Deities were prospering from how my family ruled this nation. Why would there be an issue with that?

I thought of the little boy in the village we had crossed through, living without enough to eat because of his family's donation.

There are issues with it, certainly, but since when do the Deities want change? Nothing has changed in so long.

The only change in the past few decades was me; I was about to step into my rule, and that would inevitably change things. Was that what Manumit didn't want? Did he think I was going to make things worse for him?

Or was that what Justus thought?

And how would I do that, if they blessed me and told me exactly how to rule? Why was it assumed that I would be the problem?

It must be about what Justus had said, that I was foretold. I had never heard of such a thing before. I have always known that I would rule, everyone did. But this seemed like it was more than that.

Removing his tunic, I replaced it with my own before I stepped out of the tent, needing air. As I took the pegs out of the ground that held the tent in place I could hear the horses approaching.

When I turned and Ezrah saw the expression on my face, he frowned.

"What's got your face all screwed up tight like that?"

I tossed him his shirt. "Everything."

He nodded. We were back to reality now.

"What specifically?"

Specifically? "It is all just so… confusing. I have no idea why it is happening. Justus did not tell me, so if I have no idea why there is a war over our heads, how am I supposed to rule? He made that part sound so easy, but…"

When I paused, he said, "But it makes no sense."

"None," I agreed. "How am I supposed to lead through a war that I know nothing about?"

He handed me Onyx's reins. "Maybe the Sisters will know."

I laughed. "I don't think this is their department."

"No, but they seem to be knowledgeable, and they're ancient. The Light kept them around for this long for a reason. Maybe they'll help."

"Maybe," I said, but I knew I would be getting no help at all. "Before we go," I changed the subject, "I want to check and redress your wound. I don't think last night helped with your healing process."

He smirked. "I would argue that last night was exactly what I needed. And I'm fine, nothing hurts, but you're likely right, we should change the dressing and keep it clean. I'll fold the tent. Go find what you need."

I rooted through the saddlebag and found the medical pack that the Devoted had refreshed before we left. Then, I walked the horses over to a tree and tied them loosely back up. Ezrah brought the rolled tent back over and attached it to the straps on the saddle.

"Sit," I said, nodding toward the tree.

He did as instructed, pulled up his shirt, and leaned back.

My hands were still unsure and unsteady as I soaked the dressing already on him with the labeled liquid we had been provided. When it began to loosen, I gently pulled it back, and Ezrah winced.

When I looked up at him, he said, "Sorry, I'm fine. Keep going."

I waited until I thought he was breathing more steadily, then I soaked a new cloth with the other liquid. I believed this one was meant to keep the wound from getting infected, but I could not be sure of the vague labels. If that were true, though, this would not be pleasant.

"I'm guessing this one will sting," I warned.

He leaned his head back against the tree and shut his eyes. I waited until he nodded and lightly placed the dampened cloth against the wound.

Air hissed from between his teeth as he clenched his jaw shut.

"Sorry," I whispered, but I kept going. Prolonging this would only make it worse for him, and I did not want to draw it out more than necessary. He got this wound because of me, the least I could do was make sure it did not cause any more damage than it already had.

When I thought that it was clean enough, I placed the damp cloth to the side and dried it the best I could with a clean one. Ezrah was still tense with pain and it reminded me of an animal when it knew they were in trouble, ready to flee. I placed the clean dressing on and sealed it gently around the edges with the glue. I kept my hand on his chest until he relaxed. His head was still tilted back, and his eyes were shut. Softly, I leaned over and kissed just above the wound, as a mother would to their hurt child.

When I looked back up, his eyes were on me, making me blush. After everything we had done last night, I felt ridiculous that this was what heated my cheeks, but it did all the same. His hand grabbed mine, and he brought it to his mouth, pressing a light kiss to the center of my palm.

"Time to go," he said.

I nodded and helped him to his feet.

As we mounted our horses and I tried desperately to ignore the way Ezrah grunted in pain.

We tried to make as much progress as possible while it was light out. Thankfully, the sun was up, and The Light was with us. We rode quickly, so there was not much time for talking. Slowly, as the dirt pounded under the swiftly moving hooves, the clouds rolled in. I could see the lightness begin to fade. The new clouds sat heavy with a deep blue hue, like they were ready to burst with rain.

The fields here were surrounded by trees denser than some of the patches we had passed. They almost created little forests of their own in the way they were clustered.

The beam of light was tucked into those trees, completely out of place in the fading sun. I blinked, trying to see if my tired eyes were playing tricks on me, but it was still there. The beam winked at me like a reflection made by the sun off of glass at midday.

But this was no sun, and the reflection did not flash quickly before disappearing. It stayed there, beckoning to me.

Heart racing, I only hesitated for a moment before slowly trotting toward what I saw.

Before I reached the trees, I dismounted and pulled Onyx by the reins instead. That light was stronger here, and I winced away from it.

"You should stay here," I muttered. Ezrah did not listen as he followed me through the trees.

Standing in the middle of a small clearing was a man. He was tall, standing taller than even Ezrah. His skin was also darker than Ezrah's, but with that same rich tone. The man's hair was twisted into long locs that hung heavily down his back and golden wings were tucked tightly behind him. He was breathtaking.

He was glowing. Emitting this beautiful, warm light that I could feel heating my exposed skin. Despite now knowing how wrong the artists could be, I was sure of who stood before me.

Manumit.

I fell to my knees, unsure if it was out of tradition or

shock.

Or fear.

Manumit was on the other side of my problems. Of a war. And now he was here, in front of me. Standing over six feet tall. Glowing.

I heard Ezrah fall to his knees behind me. My heart pounded and I hunched over on instinct, holding my hands weakly in my lap with Onyx's reins loose between my fingers. I shrunk into myself, ready for…

I did not know. A reprimand? An explanation?

"You do not," Manumit started, his voice shaking the surrounding air, "have to do that."

I did not know what he meant. I had done nothing to him, to any of them. So far, they had not given me a chance to. I straightened my shoulders, waiting for his calm tone to escalate to anger.

"Kneel," he breathed. "You do not have to kneel. Please, stand."

Manumit's voice sounded like he was on the verge of sighing.

And while I was not entirely sure this was not some sick trick, I slowly stood on shaky legs. The sounds of shifting told me Ezrah was doing the same. I could practically feel the shock coming from him in waves as he came forward and gently took the reins from my grasp.

Focusing on my feet, I refused to meet his eyes. How Justus had described him made Manumit seem unpredictable. I supposed that all the Deities were, but Manumit was the one that wanted so badly for me not to rule that he started a war.

So, what was he doing here?

Unless he was going to ensure I would not rule.

Sweat dripped down my neck. I focused my eyes on my feet and waited to be struck, or… however Deities went about solving problems like me.

I wished Ezrah had stayed behind when I told him to. He might have had time to get away. A person who was not supposed to lay eyes on a Deity. If he hurt Ezrah, I did not know what I would do.

Tradition was such a foreign concept now.

"Look at me," his voice boomed, yet his tone was still gentle.

I would meet my fate face-on, eye to eye. Even as I sweat and my hands shook.

His eyes were the most brilliant shade of gold I had ever seen. They moved like they were molten, swirling with heat.

"I am Manumit," he introduced himself as if I would not know who he was, like the fact that he was glowing never occurred to him.

When I said nothing, he stepped forward.

I flinched.

Manumit caught the slight movement. I saw him calculate what it meant with a tilt of his head.

"So, they have already talked to you."

I swallowed deeply.

"You may speak, you know." Now he was growing irritated.

My mouth felt drier than it ever had before. My words had to fight their way off of my tongue.

"Yes."

He tilted his head further. "Which one?"

"Justus."

"Just him?"

Did it matter? I nodded slightly.

"And it seems he has told you lies that have made you fear me."

Lies? I wanted to ask him what that meant, but my mouth did not move. I wondered momentarily if that was out of fear of Manumit or loyalty to Justus.

Manumit waited for me to respond, to say anything, and when I didn't, a sigh escaped him.

"I am not here to hurt you. I don't *want* to have to hurt you. That is not a game I play intentionally. The Light would not want that. I do not want to hurt you." Relief came to me like a splash of cold water, and he continued, "We are here to tell you the truth."

"We?"

As if on cue, a thick, black smoke drifted out of the trees. It swirled forward like fingers reaching and twisting towards us. I flinched backward just as it began to dissipate.

The smoke slowly revealed a woman, the same height as Manumit. I took in her features, the long ebony hair and her almond shaped eyes. Eyes I knew.

I didn't need to wait until the last of the smoke revealed black, scaled wings to be sure. The women from my dreams.

"You—" I started.

She smiled. "We'll have to speak quickly."

"I know you," I said.

"It's nice to finally meet you. I have been waiting a long time for this moment." She stepped towards me.

"Addie," Ezrah said from behind me, worry in his voice.

I looked at him and saw his brows drawn in concern. "I-I know her. I've dreamed of her." I turned back to her and noticed her skin glowed as it had in my mind. It looked like moonlight. "You're—what—"

"There is a lot you do not know," Manumit said.

I finally found my words. "What are you?"

She smiled again. "I am a Deity, just as Manumit is. But I am not part of your texts or your history, not anymore."

"I don't understand."

"The history you know is not the truth. It was rewritten at the beginning of time," Manumit said, stepping forward to where she stood.

"At the beginning there was balance. The creator used light and dark to build this world. It made six of us, three of lightness and three of darkness. For a moment we had harmony, a perfect world."

"Then the light took over, led by my brother, Justus. He wanted all the power, so he smothered the ones made of darkness, wrote them out of history and manipulated humans into forgetting them."

I looked between the two of them for a moment, unsure why they would be joking at a time like this. I almost laughed. Then I noticed the difference of their wings, the glowing of their skin. I felt the world tilt around me, making me dizzy.

She wasn't human, that was sure. So, they must be speaking the truth.

I tried to take a deep breath, but my shallow lungs wouldn't let me. It was crazy. Someone would have known. Three Deities could not just be *erased*. My whole life I had been taught about The Light, how it created us and then the Deities.

And now one of those same Deities was standing in front of me saying that nothing I thought I knew was true.

I didn't believe it. I didn't want to. And yet, scaled wings and moonlight skin couldn't be faked.

My hands were sweating as my eyes moved between the two figures before me. I tried to take in what they said, but it felt too big for my brain to understand. Instead, I asked, "What is your name?"

"Sommanit." Her voice was melodic, soothing.

"And how did you have access to my dreams, Sommanit?"

The two Deities shared a look.

Manumit cleared his throat "We don't have time—" Thunder interrupted him.

Sommanit sounded worried when she said, "Manumit."

He nodded. "We need to speak quickly, Adenne. For all of our sakes. The world has been unbalanced for a long time. My brother and sister have kept it that way intentionally, to fuel their own powers. Your people suffer."

"Suffer how?"

Thunder rolled again and he ignored my question. "When the creator disappeared, it left behind a prophecy of a Ruler that would change everything. We have been waiting a long time for that to be true. For you."

Ezrah spoke from behind me, "You think that's her?"

I jumped, forgetting he was there. He stepped closer to me, putting the hand not holding the reins on my lower back. Somehow, he knew I needed to grounded amongst all of this chaos.

"It's her," Sommanit said.

Thunder rolled louder this time. "I don't know what I did to ask for change. I don't want change and I don't want this." My heart pounded, the heartbeat as loud as the thunder in my ears.

"It's not about what you've done. It's about what you will do." Her tone was gentle, comforting. I looked into her eyes and didn't look away. She breathed slowly, and I followed the pattern, calming myself with her presence.

"I don't know what any of this means," I whispered to myself.

"I know it's a lot," she said.

Lightning cracked in the distance. "I wish I could tell you everything, Adenne, but we are running out of time." Manumit sounded panicked. What could make a Deity panic? "I need you to listen to what we need you to do."

Tears that I could not explain filled my eyes.

"You will rule, but it needs to be different. Your people are ready for change and you will lead them to it."

"Why should I trust you?" Wind kicked up around us and I knew we were running out of time.

"When light is without darkness, there is imbalance. People suffer. You have *seen* your people suffer. Let us try to restore what harmony once was. Help us." Manumit's golden wings bristled in the wind.

"You won't have a choice," Sommanit continued. "Change is coming. Help us protect your people by doing what we say."

I nodded. Lightning struck closer.

"He's almost here," Manumit said to her. She nodded and then stepped closer to me.

She bent to look me in the eye. "I will try to tell you more. Listen to your dreams." She reached out and wiped a tear from my cheek.

"Okay," I whispered, unsure of what else to say.

"Adenne," Manumit pulled my attention away from her, "I am so sorry, about—" He shook his head. "You need to hurry home. You need to be there. I am sorry I couldn't stop it."

"Stop what?"

Lightning surrounded us now, striking across the sky. They shared a look, nodded and then bore they could tell me anything more they were gone.

28

Titled

"What just happened?" I asked.

"Are you okay?" Ezrah's eyes looked directly at where they had just stood.

"What the *fuck* just happened?" I asked again in disbelief.

The curse got Ezrah's attention. He walked to me and cupped my face between his large palms.

"Are you okay, Addie?"

He was panicking, his eyes cutting quickly around, examining my face.

I placed my hand over his and he stilled.

"I'm okay," I assured him.

His eyes were wide as they scanned mine.

"What the fuck?"

He nodded. "What the fuck," he echoed.

We stood there for a moment, staring at each other. My

mind was trying to keep itself blank because processing this new information was too difficult. Slowly, I saw Manumit's and Sommanit's faces again and started processing our conversation. As I detangled the mess, I nodded.

"Did you have any idea…" Before I could finish, Ezrah was shaking his head. "Your parents never said anything about this?"

"No. This is…"

Fake. It felt fake. I wanted to believe that this was all a dream, but it wasn't. My nightmares were becoming real. No, they weren't even nightmares. They were messages. Ones that someone invaded my mind to show me. Ezrah's features swam in front of me as I grew dizzier.

He lowered his hands from my face and looked around at the open field. Above us, the skies had cleared as if the oncoming storm had never been there.

"We're safe, at least," he said as he dropped the reins and stepped forward to examine the area. "Justus clearly sees them as the bigger threat. He doesn't want to hurt us."

My mind whirled, still stuck on the glowing skin. The wings.

"Justus?"

"The lightning. I would assume that was him. Who knows how he knew they were here, though."

That explained their panic, why they had limited time. Justus must know that this Deity, this *dark* Deity was back. That would ruin his plans.

"I'm so confused," I confessed. My hands still shook.

Ezrah turned to face me and nodded.

"Do you want to talk it through?"

I laughed. It was absurd that after all of that we would just *talk it through*. Our world just changed, history was just rewritten and we could only talk about it.

"When I spoke to Justus," I started, shifting my weight back and forth between my feet, "He told me to rule with an iron fist. He mentioned that I was foretold, like he was waiting for me. And then Manumit—"

"He said that the creator knew you would come. Or something like that."

I nodded. "The creator. Not The Light. That was weird, right?"

He nodded. "Very."

"I can't think about that. I can't."

"We don't have to. That's a problem for later on."

I began to pace.

Before my thoughts could spin out of control again Ezrah asked, "Why do you think you're the person they have been waiting for? And what did you mean about dreams?"

I faced him. "I don't know. I don't feel any different. I didn't plan to rule any differently. But…" I realized them I had never told him. With everything going on I had never thought it was important. Now, it could have been the first sign of all of this. "But, for the past few years I have felt nothing when I introspected. I haven't felt The Light in a long time. I didn't think much of it then, so it could have been that." I rambled now, playing through the possibilities out loud. "Or it could be what I have seen out here. After seeing how the people live, going a different path than the pilgrimage, I can't say I wouldn't have ruled differently. I want to help them."

Ezra's voice was gentle. "That's what they asked you to

do, to rule differently." I nodded. "And the dreams?"

"I have been having them for a few years now too. None of them have made much sense. I dreamt of burning books in the streets, the wall around Polaris going up, being stuck outside of it. I would see dark flying figures, like Sommanit. Only recently did she show me her face."

"Do you think she was sending you a message, then?"

I shrugged. "I guess so."

There was silence between us as we processed. I felt dizzy with all this new information. I wanted to sit down. At the same time, I felt full of energy, like I needed to walk it off.

"What are you thinking?" he finally asked.

"Manumit wants me to rule too, but to be this catalyst for change. To help my people by ruling them how he and this dark Deity think I should."

"So, either way, you're going to rule."

I placed my hands on my hips, looked up at the sky and laughed. "No one is going to believe this, Ezrah."

He laughed too. "I barely do and I witnessed it."

"You saw a Deity." Something that was never supposed to happen. The honor was reserved for the Rulers and the Highest Devoted.

He smiled at me, his eyes wild as he rubbed a hand down his face. "I saw *two* Deities."

"How do you feel about that?" He may not have become Devoted himself, but he was raised in the path of The Light.

"I—" He was shaking his head in disbelief. "I don't know. I was not supposed to see that. I just saw Deities, with my own eyes. That—that definitely breaks tradition, to say the least. Shit, if my parents knew what I just saw, Addie, I don't know if they would be overjoyed or scold me."

His eyes looked sad for a moment, tears pooling. It was the kind of sadness that was residual and yet always present.

"If you could tell your parents, they wouldn't believe you," I said lightly.

He laughed, and I felt relieved at the sound, "No, they would not. They wouldn't believe any of this." Ezrah looked at me with those soft features. His grief did not seem to harden him quite like it once did. His mouth used to pull itself into a hard line when he spoke of his parents. Sage told me when he first returned, he would not talk about it with her. Until one day, she broke him. She said she had never seen her brother cry that much. I wondered if that was the turning point of this new, softer Ezrah and if that was a good thing. I knew so little of grief, nothing like what either of them knew. People handled it in all different ways, of course, but was one way better than the other? Did one make the pain more tolerable?

"I didn't think they would be like that."

"No," I agreed. "Me either."

"There are more Deities," he stated the obvious, but it still felt so untrue. Like this was a bad dream or a children's story. Yet we had both seen it.

"There are." I nodded along.

"What are you thinking, Addie?"

A lot. Nothing at all. I was thinking about how none of this felt real, and yet it made sense. That after all this time, I still didn't have answers. Mostly, I thought about how it seemed like my life and my time ruling was going to be difficult no matter what I tried to do about it.

But I wouldn't say any of that.

"I am safe for now. We are safe. All the Deities need me in power, light or dark. And they all want me to align with them. I need to rule to keep them all happy. Other than that, I must figure out what *I* want to do."

He nodded along.

"So, what is the next step?"

A great question. "Proceed the way we were before, I suppose."

"To the Sisters?"

"The people still won't want to accept me as their Ruler. I am not blessed. I am *still* not fucking blessed. A title from the Sisters will help. We will go there before heading back to Polaris."

"Okay," he agreed. "But we'll have to be quick."

"Quick?"

"Manumit said something about hurrying. He was trying to rush us back home. I have a feeling that we won't want to take our time."

I nodded. "We won't, you're right. And I want to be home." My heart ached at the thought.

Ezrah went to the horses, who miraculously were still there, even after the lightning. He brought Onyx to me.

"Let's go before the clouds come back out."

I looked up at the now-blue skies, wondering how the clouds had cleared out so quickly, like nothing had happened. Shivers ran through me.

"Let's go," I agreed.

We rode the horses harder than we had before, and I felt guilty about what I had been putting Onyx through. The poor girl was trained for one adventure, a peaceful trip out and back. This journey of scrambling for answers was not what she was prepared for. I could feel her fatigue. Still, she pushed on, going the speeds I asked of her without complaint. She had a job to do.

Clouds slowly rolled back in. The temperature dropped in an instant, chilling right through my skin and down to my bones.

Slowly, the land before us changed as the fields faded away. The ground was hard packed dirt, and the further we went, the rockier it became. We were making progress.

The old Temple that the Sisters lived in was at the edge of the land, just like Polaris. It did not, however, sit on a cliff like the palace did.

My mother told me how the land got lower, and as it did, it grew damper. Trees sprouted upwards, one by one, until eventually, their leaves were so abundant they blocked out the sun. Light came through them in a bright green glow—she said it made the place feel like somewhere entirely new.

I was not likely to see this brilliant green glow as the clouds fully blocked out the sky now. I felt a drop of water land on my hand where I held the reins. I wanted so badly to pretend that I did not feel it, that I would stay dry for once on this journey, but, as if the rain was mocking me, a drop landed squarely on my nose. I watched as the drops fell and darkened the dirt. I prepared myself to again be soaked to the bone. I lifted the hood of my cloak back up. When I looked at Ezrah, he had done the same.

Each drop felt like a prick of ice hitting my skin and I wondered if the return of these other Deities was the reason Rhea felt colder. And how many more Deities were there? I still had so many questions I wished I could have asked them.

I tried to distract myself by thinking of what I would do once I returned. As much as plans rarely worked in my favor, I would like one for this.

When I got home, everyone would know I was not blessed, if they did not know already. Not only that, but they may have sensed something was very wrong. No one in Polaris would assume that meant war, not even my parents.

My parents. I had no idea what they would think about all of this. I would have to convince them that everything they knew about our history was wrong. My stomach rolled. They would believe me, I hoped. They would have to. But the thought settled in me like I ate something rotten. It was unlikely that they would have any more idea of what to do than I did.

Not that their ideas would matter any more than common advice would. I was the Ruler.

I was born to rule. Trained and taught how to do exactly one thing. I was the best person for the job. Admittedly, I was the only person trained for this life, but it was more than that. I was the one with the knowledge of this war, and I would break tradition and help the people.

Even if I was a pawn in the middle of much more powerful players, I was still the Ruler.

Nobody knew more about Rhea, how this nation functioned and what the people needed. I wanted to help them, I wanted to stop this war.

And I could.

Hopefully.

I *would*.

Because I may not be blessed, but I was ready.

On the horizon, small silhouettes of trees came into view, and my hands began to sweat. We were close.

Close to the end of a pilgrimage that I had dreamt of since I was a little girl.

These past few days I had no time to worry about what I would be titled. For a while, it did not seem like it would matter.

It still may not. The Sisters still may not title me.

I may return to Polaris with no blessing or title.

A part of me hoped I could return home to tell my mother I had gained the title she always wanted me to have: Adenne the Fair.

The title she had dreamed I would receive since I was a child. She believed it meant I would be the fairest leader of all of our family.

I believed I could be fair. I tried to be. I would continue to try to be.

In a way, the pride I would see in my mother's eyes if I could tell her that I was Adenne the Fair would make all of this worth it

And it would mean that, in some small way, I was living the life I thought I would, just in a slightly altered way.

It may be more than slightly, but even still.

I focused on those words and the title I wanted as the trees approached. One by one, we passed them, each taller and wider. The trunks twisted into themselves, crooked and bent but stretching upwards. The dark green leaves branched out widely overhead.

Below the horse's hooves, the ground grew wetter, but not from the rain. The land slowly tilted downward, sloping toward the coast. The coast and the Sisters.

The horses slowed to navigate this new land, and Ezrah came up beside me. His cloak was fully soaked through at this point, just as mine was. When his eyes met mine, they were filled with exhaustion. Dark bruises stained his skin. I looked down at his shirt instinctually, but I could see no evidence of his wound being open again. It had to hurt him, which meant I had more than one reason to rush home.

I kept moving forward, and the trees became so dense that they made a makeshift cover above our heads, blocking the rain.

I understood, even without the glow, why my mother described this place as being so green. The ground quickly changed to moss where the trees lent shade, coating the rarely walked-upon ground beneath us. It looked lush and damp. Every time the horses stepped, I was shocked at how the ground bounced back up, leaving no evidence of us being there. Vines grew up the trees, twisting themselves around the crooked bark. No sunlight came through, but this place was unlike anything I had ever seen. When I breathed in, it smelled how the earth was supposed to, before the land was tilled and the buildings came. This place was ancient and untouched.

It felt wrong that I was here.

But, at the same time, I never wanted to leave.

The further we went, the more the air changed. Something in it seemed… charged. It reminded me of how a fire or lightning burned right before it struck. It was loaded in a powerful way, but did not seem harmful. It filled me and fused with my skin, making me feel powerful, too.

I breathed deeply and took it all in. My skin did not feel cold anymore. I felt full, alive.

When I looked at Ezrah, his head swiveled, taking in every aspect of our surroundings. It was a place he never expected to be, yet here he was, at my side.

I was grateful for his presence, for his insistence on coming with me. I did not need him here, but if I were to have anyone by my side, I was glad it was him. Someone who only ever built me up, that believed in me more than I did myself. He knew when I needed help, and he knew when I did not. He was my support, my person. I was happy he was here, that I did not have to experience this alone.

"Ezrah," I called.

He looked at me, and his features softened, like my face gave him some kind of relief.

I knew so little, but my hands did not shake, and my heart did not pound. I knew what I was about to say was certain. It had likely been certain for a long time, longer than I had known. And so, I did not hesitate.

"I love you."

And then, I got the most beautiful blessing. I got to see those soft features slowly change. I got to see a slight moment of shock, where his eyebrows raised, and his full lips parted as air left him in a gasp. Then, I got to see him relax again. I watched his head shake slightly back and forth, and I watched as tears welled in his eyes.

Then, he smiled. It was the most brilliant smile I had ever seen. The world seemed lighter.

As if The Light agreed, the sun came back out. It worked its way through the leaves and created a glow.

He wiped his eyes with the back of his hand.

"Addie," his voice was raw, "you do not know how many times I have… you will never truly know. I love you. I have always loved you. There was no moment where I didn't, even if I wanted to, even when I knew I shouldn't. I have loved you despite everything working against us."

Tears welled in my eyes now, but I pushed them back.

"I don't know how you always say the perfect things."

He laughed. "How's this for perfect? It is a good thing we are on these horses and not standing face to face because I would be distracted with all the ways I can show you my love. And that would take time, which we don't have at the moment."

I blushed instantly.

"But there will be plenty of time for that later," he finished, smiling.

Later, sometime in the future, time for us.

My heart lurched like it could not believe that was true. As everything changed around me, I would still have him.

I smiled. "Lots of time later."

"For now, let's finish this. Let's go get you a title."

We rode ahead, now with the green glowing around us. I breathed deeply as I took this in. It was important to take in these moments of joy when they came, because there may be time later when I needed them. I would remember this moment for the rest of my life.

In the distance, the trees grew sparse. A clearing was ahead, and I knew exactly what that meant. We were here.

Ezrah stopped just before the edge of the trees.

"Addie." His voice seemed strained. "Whatever happens, whatever they title you, you will be a good Ruler."

Tears welled in me, and I did not know what to say.

"I will wait here," he said.

"No. I want you there. I want you to do this with me."

Silently, he agreed. We both stepped into the clearing.

Shock filled me when I saw three figures standing on the steps of a Temple waiting for me. The Temple was built of gray stone. Tall pillars sat at either edge of the open front door, though 'door' was an understatement. The front of the building was open like the jaws of a predator towering over me. It took up a vast amount of space. Many trees would have been cleared to make this place happen. Or maybe the Temple was here first. Maybe the trees came after.

Moss coated the grey stone, just as it did everything else. The forest's life in this place had overcome these tall walls, crumbling them in places.

The Sisters seemed as ancient as the Temple itself. So little was known about them, least of all their age, but they were born close to the time when The Light had walked among us. Some believed they had seen it. Some believed they were the first people The Light had made. No one could explain their age, and no one had been stupid enough to ask a Deity or a Sister for clarification.

But, for as long as it was known, they had titled my

family. Now, they will do the same for me.

I got off of my horse and Ezrah followed. He took the reins that I handed to him and nodded slightly.

One deep breath, and then I walked toward the Sisters.

The dark robes hung heavily, but they were not damp. Their hoods were up but not like the ones the Devoted wore, lacking the same crispness. These hung limply around the Sisters' faces, leaving much to the imagination. I could not see their expressions, even as my feet edged toward the bottom step of the Temple.

At the base of the stairs I stopped, unsure what to do. There was a moment of silence, and I almost spoke when the center figure's voice scraped against the quiet.

"We have been waiting for you."

"For a long time," the one to the left said.

"And now you are here."

Then the third one said, "She should not be here. She should be home."

"There is no time. She will miss her last chance."

"My last chance for what?" I squeezed in.

"No time," one of them said, though I could not tell which.

Each one of their voices sounded as ancient as their legend. They spoke as if their lungs were clouded with dust.

"I—" I began.

"Come to me," the one in the center rasped.

My legs shook as I walked up the steps. It was not lost on me that the one on the left had said I should not be here. I kept my eyes down, trying to hide the lack of blessing that I was sure they were already aware of.

I stood before the one in the center, breathing in what smelled like an abandoned place. I thought of the unused rooms at the palace, how the dust coated the white sheets laid over forgotten furniture.

A hand reached out toward me, and I saw how ancient this Sister was. The hand was just skin covering bone. Every detail could be seen. The skin was as pale white and thin as paper, but far more worn. A long fingernail scraped up my exposed arm.

"So beautiful, so young. She could have been 'The Fair.'"

"Adenne the Fair."

"It is what she wanted. She still wants that."

My stomach dropped.

"Or 'The Wise,' should have been 'The Wise.'"

"The Wise."

"The Undeterred."

"The Gracious."

"The Loved."

"But time will not allow that, either," the center one spoke. I wanted her to tilt her head so I could see her eyes.

"Yes."

"Times are changing."

"She is changing times."

"She is change," said the center one, her nail still touching my arm.

Then, she looked up, and I forced my jaw shut when I finally saw her face.

The same thin skin stretched over bone. Whiter than her hand and somehow older. Where there should be eyes, there were empty holes. The skin pulled tight around the sockets, the color darkening as it did.

I met what had once been eyes and watched the skin stretch and move, seeing every detail of what was underneath, as she spoke, "No, she will not be any of those things."

The other two Sisters came closer. I closed my eyes so I would not have to try to meet their gaze, too. I could feel their breath on my cheeks, proving they were living.

Then, all together, the Sisters whispered to me my title.

I rocked backward, almost falling down the steps.

Reality hit me.

The world swayed.

My world swayed.

I opened my eyes, and their retreating forms swam in my dizzying vision.

Air left me. It did not come back.

Panic seized me.

I was not The Fair. Not The Wise or The Gracious, The Undeterred or The Loved.

I had gotten my title.

Lightning cracked over my head, but I did not wince.

Tears rolled down my cheeks.

I knew who I was now.

How I would be known.

Who The Light had known I would be all this time:

I was Adenne the Last.

Acknowledgments

Oh, man. Writing acknowledgements? For my book? *My* book? That's something I truly never thought I would have to do. I will be typing this quickly to avoid crying, so bear with me.

I want to thank my mother and father for always loving me and encouraging my love for reading, even when it got obsessive and concerning. Thank you to my sister, who is my person at every stage of life. She may not read books, but she knows exactly how to handle my stress, of which there was a lot while publishing this book. Her constant support of me means the word to me. Thank you to the rest of my family for your support (and sorry about some scenes in this book). Thank you to my friends. I always expected the response to me saying, "I wrote a book!" to be "Are you nuts?" or "That's cute, sweetie." Instead, they always answered, "When can I read it?" and "Will you sign my copy?" Thank you to everyone who gave me the same grace and acceptance, because I was genuinely terrified to tell anyone about this novel.

For the people who got their fingers in there and helped me craft *Under The Light* into something I am proud of, I thank you from the bottom of my heart. My beta readers, Maddy, Catherine, Jessie, Jessica, Lucinda, Josie, Nina, Cassie, Sarah, Shannon, and Abigail, who encouraged me to keep going. My editors, Lily and Belle, who know where commas go much better than I do. My cover design artist, Haley, who took my vague ideas and awful sketches and made them into something beautiful.

Thank you to everyone who followed along on the journey on TikTok and Instagram. You've been so patient and supportive even though I was just a stranger on the internet. Every comment means so much to me.

I never thought I would be capable of building new worlds, and it was these people that helped me believe I could. I am thankful for them and for this life every day.

Author Bio

A typical day for Sadie, during the formative years of her youth, looked like this: Wake up, school, ignore homework to read until dinner, speed-eat her mother's cooking, return to the comfort of bed for more reading. Rinse and repeat. She has consumed novels like they were her only life source since she could remember, and so she is elated to now be writing them.

Sadie is in her final year of her undergrad where she studies English Literature (in which the novels have a surprising lack of dragons compared to her usual selection). When she is not disassociating to ink on paper, she is crafting, thrifting, shooting her bow, rewatching *Mamma Mia* for the millionth time or planning her next vacation. Sadie has a passion for seeing this world and creating new ones. *Under The Light* is her debut novel.